THE RECLAIMED SAGA BOOK II: THE COLLECTION

The Reclaimed Saga, Book II: The Collection

Copyright © 2021 by Zach Carpenter

Cover and Interior Design by Lance Buckley
www.lancebuckley.com

This is a work of fiction. Names, characters, places and incidents are the product of the author's imagination or are used fictitiously. Any resemblance to actual persons, living or dead, events or locales is entirely coincidental

All rights reserved. No part of this book may be reproduced or used in any manner without written permission of the author except for the use of quotations in a book review.

ISBN: xxx

ZACH CARPENTER

RECURRING NIGHTMARE

Screams. Fine jabs of sharp sound penetrated his eardrums with nerve splitting precision. A female's screams. She sounded like she could be in her mid-twenties. The feeling of being pressed down hard against the unforgiving solid surface of a floor was the next thing to dawn in his awareness. Broken glass shards dug into his face as more details slowly come into focus. There was pressure on the back of his head, keeping him held to the floor. He felt his ribs creak on the verge of splintering as his lungs fought against the dead weight that was keeping him pinned down.

There were other voices, from at least three other sources. The first was guttural and gravelly, like the speaker was gurgling street gravel with grease while trying to talk at the same time. Another voice, high pitched and wheezy. There was an odd clicking sound at the end of every other word it spoke. Then there was one right above him, whispering into his ear. As the voice poured into his ears, it felt like hot molasses with sharp metal filaments mixed in for emphasis. Its tone and inflection was a deep but clear baritone. It was certainly the most human sounding of the trio. The high pitched speaker sounded like it was gushing liquid between its teeth now, and as the girl on the floor only an arm's length away from him let out a raw, primal scream of naked terror, the wet, slimy sound of what could be a tongue unrolling from inside a toothy maw could be heard distinctly amid the other voices and sounds.

The girl's protests were useless as the taunts of the three voices above and around the room drowned her out, and were replaced by the sounds of tearing fabric and—what sounded like…slurping noises began to follow.

Every muscle in his body tensed the split second Mick's eyes flew open. He propelled out of his bed, his blankets swirling around his feet. The next thing he knew, he was falling. In that same instant he slapped the ground in an attempt to absorb the brunt of the fall through his hand. He rolled into the fall, kicking the tangled bedding away from his feet. In the dark, his eyes saw everything. Every shadow that moved out of his peripherals stopped when he faced them. The tingle in his eyes, as well as the fact he could see everything in perfect darkness, let him know they were glowing. He stood up, his heart threatening to explode before it could settle back down into his chest. He hardly noticed the freezing sweat that caused his t-shirt to cling to his body like a second skin.

He sank down on his messy bed and ran his quivering fingers over the damp bed of skin on his head where his hair was beginning to grow back. He tried to catch his breath. He looked over at the light switch next to the door. In the past, after a nightmare like that, his first instinct would have been to turn on the light. But there was no need when he woke up and his eyes were burning with the white hot energy of one who has been Reclaimed.

He looked over at his alarm clock. It was almost a quarter till 11:00 PM. Ten forty three to be precise, and it was the third time in two weeks that he had woken up from that same exact nightmare.

He had tried to think what could have possibly brought it on, but there was absolutely nothing his mind could latch onto that satisfied the inquiry. He knew what he was hearing was clearly a woman screaming, but he never saw her. He could hear other voices talking to one another, but he never remembered what they said when he woke up, and he always felt like he was being held down, constricted, unable to get in a full breath, and that was what usually woke him up.

The sound of scratches on the other side of his door caused him to look up. Mick quickly got up and hurried over to his door, opened it up and let Target enter his room. The boxer dog that had been tied to a file cabinet the night that thing with the knives tried to kill him, had grown into an excellent hunting companion and guard dog.

"Hey buddy, you wanna go outside?" Mick asked as he slipped into his sneakers and clumsily reached for the leash that was hanging next to the doorway, cursing as it fall to the floor. Target stood up on his hind legs, slapping at Mick's stomach with his front paws and letting out an excited *whoof.*

"Shhh! Everyone else is trying to sleep!" Mick hissed as he clipped the leash to Target's collar then walked down the hallway at a brisk pace. The other hunters' rooms past them as they hurried through the expansive armory, the meeting area, passed the security center with its humming monitors, and up through the stairs that led out of the janitor's closet in Tom's Auto. Mick punched in the combination on the keypad that disarmed the security system before stepping out into the muggy summer night. The unpleasantly warm and humid air encased his bare legs, like wearing sweaty spandex leggings. It was then he remembered he hadn't put on pants before charging up the stairs to let the dog out to do its thing. He didn't need his Higher Sight to see that his legs gleamed in the darkness. He trudged on into the parking lot of Tom's Auto with leash in hand, muttering to himself how he needed to get some more sun.

In the three years since he joined the hunters, he had lost about fifty five pounds of fat and packed on a substantial amount of muscle in its place. His skin, now free from the mind altering gray taint, was the same color as someone who had red blood warming it beneath the surface. Although he looked a lot leaner, he was still short compared to most of the other hunters. At least he could keep up with them now. His reaction times had increased exponentially. His bones had become denser and even though he still had to push his body to gain muscle, it came naturally to him. It took a lot for him to get tired now, lactic acid now taking hours and hours to build up now instead of minutes. It came in handy when he had to run across rooftops chasing a weird creature that had a human hand dangling from its mouth. He busted his butt hard for the first two years of his time with them, and every time he looked at that sparing room floor where they worked out, he smiled to himself, feeling where his teeth had regrown in—only crooked. Everything seemed to heal at much faster rates now. None of the hunters could heal nearly as fast as some comic book characters, but a broken tooth would regrow almost overnight, while a compound fracture could fully heal within a span of three to four days.

There was an odd dichotomy to the life he lived with the Reclaimed, one they all found themselves coping with nightly. While yes, physical injuries healed much quicker, it seemed the psychological tolls of keeping the creatures in the dark at bay didn't heal quite as fast. Group talks were a thing in the Reclaimed. Every time they did one, Mick felt like he was in an AA meeting of sorts. But it was in those meetings where he had seen some of the most human sides of the hunters. Having abilities that lent to one accomplishing heroic deeds comparable to the likes of a folk hero didn't stop the sudden, stomach hitching twitches one got when a door slammed or a whiff of an out of place smell drifting through the air. They were soldiers on a different front, and just like the ones fighting against terror abroad and at home, PTSD was a monster that stalked Military Personnel and Hunter alike. Probably one of the most horrifying things about their abilities was how it kept mending their bodies, just so their psyche could go through the meat grinder one more time.

After making a full circuit around Tom's Auto, and Target having marked his territory at almost every turn and bend in the perimeter, the boxer stopped and sniffed the air. Mick found himself smiling at the pooch. Their lair was surrounded by spiritual wards, most of which were illustrated with some kind of sigil either done is spray paint or holy oil, thus marking the perimeter off from any malevolent force trying to scry on the place. Now that Target was a member of the team, they were liberally reinforced with a fresh spray of dog piss.

Do not come near my humans! My pack! I maul you! Rawr! Mick imagined him thinking every time he hiked his leg up to contribute. Judah made the joke that they poured holy oil into his dog food.

"Come on boy, let's go back to bed," Mick prompted, tugging on the leash. Target stiffened against his pull, his head swiveling to the right and to the left, his wet nose surveying the night air. Mick groaned as he felt his arms go limp and his grip on the leash relax.

He sighed deeply, really wishing for his bed once more. A low rumbling growl escaped Target's belly, and he swiveled his gaze back up to Mick right before he heard the blaring of sirens off in the distance. He didn't see any flashing lights, but they were close enough that he could hear them. Target wined at the high pitched noise, and took off back toward the shop. Mick felt his grip tighten out of reflex and the dog's speed nearly took his arm off.

"I guess it's time to go to work…damn it all," Mick sighed.

FAMILIAR FACES

It was another extermination job. That's mostly what they had been occupied with during the past three years. They might as well just consider themselves glorified pest control. Mick asked Judah if they could paint that on the sides of the vans they drove. Needless to say the sides of both vans were still plane-jane black. The front lawn of St. Andrews Catholic Church had been sealed off. Police units and paramedics were standing by, and SWAT chief Dan Mendez had his teams in position.

Mick felt his entrails turn sideways when they rolled up on the church where he first accepted Father's gift. Where he was lead to believe he would be given the power to exact justice over those he now called his co-workers and family. The night he became an instrument to the eldritch horror that nearly laid waste to the town he had been trying to save. Mick closed his eyes as the van stopped. He didn't sleep very good most nights, but when he did get the chance for some shut eye, his dreams were usually molested by the quick mental movies of his memories leading up to his possession. He remembered his best friend, George Turner, his skin turning to ash as he sat there and talked with the thing inside of his friend. He recalled the way the thing that called itself Father had made him feel as if the clock was ticking for his friend, when in reality, Mick had come to terms with the idea that George was probably dead before that talk ever took place. He still had no coherent memories of what he did while possessed. All he knew was what the hunters had disclosed to him, and Valerie's scar still had not faded.

Mick had wanted to turn himself in. But there was no proof, digital or otherwise, that he was the one committing those acts. Whatever Father was, he was powerful enough to knock out any and all surveillance technology for a twelve block radius. He even had caused vehicles to die, although that part confused Mick because the hunters had said he had started a fire engine up that same night in the center of the carnage. Father was probably powerful enough he could pick and choose what he let work and what he caused to stay out of commission.

Now Mick was stuck having to deal with the current nightmare that was invading his dreams. He hoped and prayed to God that whatever was happening in that nightmare was not a recollection of something that happened while he was possessed.

The sliding door to the solid black, twelve passenger van eased open on its track. Their boots hit the ground in a fluid succession, gear passing between hands along with bandoleers of twelve gauge shotgun slugs. Sunny, Oscar, Valerie, Parish and Mick piled out of the van, while Judah, Brandon and Rufus, the bald man that had formally haunted Mick three years ago, pulled up in the silver extended cab 2014 Dodge Ram pickup that the city had purchased for them.

"So tell me why Zach gets to sit this one out again?" Mick asked.

"I dunno," Valerie said, "being in another state with Mariah might have something to do with that."

Lucky jerk, Mick thought as he fed another shell into the magazine tube of his semi-automatic shotgun.

"Hey Judah, when you gonna let us use some of our vacation time?" Mick hollered across the hood of the van to his boss. Judah smirked as Rufus tossed him a box of ammo from the bed of the truck.

"What's a vacation?" Judah asked.

"Zach got to leave," Mick said.

"Yeah but he's meeting her father for the first time so that's different," Rufus said flashing Mick his pearly whites.

"At least with the police department I had sick leave," Mick joked.

Rufus hopped down from the truck, put one arm around Mick's neck and squeezed, "You ready, gran chico?"

Mick nodded and shook his head, "I'm ready. What about you?"

"I am ready. This should be fun," Rufus said with an almost hungry excitement as he squeezed Mick's head between his bulging pectoral and bicep. After Mick tapped out on his arm, Rufus released him.

"Now I know you didn't mean to," Rufus began, "but this time, try to avoid screaming like a little girl. Can't have a repeat of that poltergeist job we did last month."

Mick felt his face flush as the voices of the other hunters chimed in. "Oh it's this story again?" Sunny asked. Mick didn't have to look at her to tell she was smiling from ear to ear. Her tone of voice said it all, *Uncle Rufus tell us the story about how Mick squealed like a little girl, pleeeeease!*

"The floorboard I was standing on was rotten and my foot went through! You would have screamed too!" Mick said, staunchly convinced of his misinterpreted outburst of emotion.

Oscar was saying something in Spanish, to which Rufus nearly exploded with laughter and began to reply in kind, pointing at Mick and shamelessly making eye contact as the two exchanged smack on him in their native tongue.

"One day," Mick began, trying to feign an indignant tone, "*Dora the Explorer* will teach me all I need to know, and then you won't be able to hide behind your Spanish to make fun of me."

Rufus had shown up at Tom's Auto, naked and weak, clothed in nothing but a dirty sheet, which he explained, had been covering his former body. His skin tone was deep tan, not ashen gray. His frame had still been rail thin, like a pathetic chain-link fence that could fall down any minute. If it weren't for the face, Mick would not have known it was the man from his childhood. His knee jerk reaction was to grab the nearest thing he could find and clobber him. But after being held back by two or more of his fellow Reclaimed, it gave him time to get clothed and fed so he could tell his story. He said Yeshua had saved his soul, brought him back in a new body, and given him directions to find the other hunters. Since then he had been working out and busting tail right alongside Mick. He stood well over six foot tall now, shoulders and back as broad as a barn door, and arms and legs about as big around as Mick's head, all muscle and only ten percent body fat. Mick hoped one day to be as jacked as Rufus, but genetics…

Dan Mendez was approaching them, clad in his SWAT attire, weapon pointed toward the ground. He had to duck under the police tape that sectioned off the front lawn of the church. His skin was likewise absent of what the hunters called "the gray taint." Since Halloween night, many people had undergone similar reclamations of their own in New Broken Edge, and likewise, many of them were eager in turn to hunt. The only reason Judah was extremely selective about accepting new members was because hunting monsters is a full time job that dramatically lowered one's life expectancy. It wasn't something he wished on anybody. Sunny and Oscar had shown the same interest as them, but their reasons for staying on were more out of safety in case Father came sniffing around again, and not because they were on a power high and wanted to shoot at the monstrosities lurking under the bed.

Dan and Judah shook hands, exchanged some pleasantries and then addressed the rest of the hunters.

"Since the call came in, all attempts at recovering the body and the civilian trapped inside have failed," Mendez said, "Around twenty-forty five, the night cleaners for the church say that the statue of St. Michael in the sanctuary…I can't believe I'm about to say this out loud…*attacked*, one of the custodians while they were shampooing the carpet. The other's quickly evacuated the building and one of them called 911. The call was originally thought to be a prank, but it was traced back here to the church." Mendez said.

"Our job is not just simple extermination this time folks," Judah said, "The civilian that placed that call did so from Father Munroe's office phone. 911 dispatchers are still on the phone with her trying to keep her calm. Her name is Lupita Gutiérrez. To make matters even worse, she is seven months pregnant according to the other cleaners who made it out."

Parish raised his hand, "She couldn't have used a cell phone and escaped the building with the others?"

Mendez stepped forward, "It's possible that under the circumstances she was not using her best judgment. She might have thought it best to use the landline so that the police could easily trace the call to the church and show up. Since making prank calls to 911 is a good way to get a visit from the police anyway, maybe that's what she was thinking. Yes we can trace calls from cell phones but under the circumstances she probably wasn't thinking about that."

"So in short, we have a dead body of the one who was killed by the statue, and a civilian trapped inside," Valerie said.

Mendez nodded. Judah stepped forward and whispered something in Valerie's ear and then embraced her. After barking some final orders, they were on the move across the parking lot and toward the front lawn of the church. Oscar and Brandon were to go in and scout out the inside of the church to get a look at that statue, and to find the office where the woman was trapped. Over the last three years, Oscar had been sharing with the team how Brandon was teaching him about astral projection. As natural born werewolves, Brandon believed that their ancestry could be traced back to beings from "higher dimensions of consciousness" as he called them. Since Mick's own experiences with venturing to the Astral Plane when he met Yeshua, he knew from personal experience that it wasn't all that hokey. Although he never encountered other beings there that resembled anything akin to a humanoid animal at all, he was learning more and more that the spirit world was a big place indeed. The long and short of it was that Brandon and Oscar would leave their bodies and scout out the inside of the church in astral form, and then return to the rest of the group outside, and one team would take out the statue, and the other would be in charge of getting the woman to safety. Sounded straightforward enough.

"Stay safe," Valerie called from behind, her voice getting further away.

Mick did a double take. He thought she was right behind him. "You're not coming for this one?" She always comes with them, charging into danger and getting dirty right alongside them.

"Nope not this time. I'm just here cause they said there was a dead body. I'm still a coroner after all Mick." She winked.

Mick shrugged, still perplexed but knowing when she meant business, "Eh, fair enough." He said. He smiled at the subtle jab she threw at him. He remembered the night he found out she was one of them and how he said she wouldn't be a medical examiner for much longer. Guess she showed him.

"If I die I'll try to fall so it looks like I was doing something cool." He called back to her, which elicited a head shake from her.

MOVING STATUES

Mick watched as Brandon and Oscar walked across the parking lot, ducked under the police tape, and then positioned themselves on the church steps. They put some earplugs in, and sat down cross-legged from one another. Within a minute, both of them looked like they had fallen asleep while sitting up. Brandon might have been swaying slightly, but he never toppled over. Mick felt a tingle in his eyes and instantly every shadow in the parking lot melted away in the radiant glow of his vision. There on the church steps, standing next to the bodies of Oscar and Brandon, he saw two large lupine forms. These forms shimmered the way a mirage would on the surface of hot asphalt. Both forms were on all fours. The two spirit wolves were larger than any wolf Mick had ever seen. Both stood about as tall as horses, and bore resemblance to the creatures known as wargs from fantasy novels. Both wolves sauntered into the double doors of the church, passing through them like mist.

"Mick, over here!" Sunny called, and as soon as he heard her voice, the tingle in his eyes stopped. He followed her voice through the crowd of EMT's, parked ambulances and a few other squad cars. He found the other hunters huddled around Mendez, who was rolling out a set of blueprints to the church over the hood of one of the police cruisers.

"There is a hallway to the east as soon as you enter the foyer, which will lead you to the church's office where the civilian is hiding," he said, gesturing with a gloved finger.

Judah addressed them all next, "There are seven of us going in there. Brandon and Oscar will report back to us when they've confirmed the condition of the civilian inside. Assuming all goes as planned, a group of you will go in, find and escort her to safety. After she is clear of the building, we all are going back in there to properly take care of whatever is in that church. Any questions?"

Sunny raised her hand, "What if while they are scoping the place out on the inside, the rest of us form a perimeter around the church and use our Higher Sight to determine if the cause of this is spiritual as opposed to an actual statue?"

Judah nodded. Mick was impressed, she was truly a sharp axe.

"That's a good idea. That seems far more likely than saying the statue of St. Michael killed someone," Judah said. Mendez nodded, "Thank you. I knew I couldn't have been the only one to think that sounded funny."

Rufus raised his hand next, "So if its spiritual, you think whatever it is could have caused the cleaners to hallucinate that they saw the statue kill? Maybe we get in there and the body doesn't have a scratch on it?"

Judah cleared his throat, "All good points. I like your idea a lot Sunny, so I want all of you to spread out around the church and search with your Higher Sight for anything that might be hiding." He said.

Higher Sight didn't turn up a single thing out of the ordinary on the church grounds. The night sky was awash in colors that couldn't be processed by the mortal eye, and the only two spirits Mick had seen were the two dire wolf spirit forms of Brandon and Oscar when they emerged out through the church doors upon finishing their initial sweep. While certainly not ordinary per say, those weren't the things they had been hoping would turn up.

The big double doors to the church opened slowly into the darkness beyond, their glowing white eyes burning a path through the dark. Their sight revealed the tile floor of the foyer, marble stands with fake plants on them decorating either side of the ornately carved wooden double doors of the sanctuary only a few yards in front of them. The doorframe encompassing the double doors was glass, which curtesy of the cleaning crew, was now spotless.

Mick shook the memories from his mind. His first time in this place had made the biggest impression on him, and now he couldn't associate this church with anything but the night his friend died and nearly half the city with it.

It was Mick, Oscar and Sunny who had been sent into retrieve Miss Gutiérrez. Before following Oscar down the east hallway, Mick couldn't help but try to get a look at the statue. Oscar, eager to get the woman to safety, almost left Mick and Sunny behind before he realized they weren't behind them.

Mick peered through the glassed in doorframe, with Sunny doing the same, only from the opposite end. His eyes locked onto the nine foot tall marble form of St. Michael, brandishing his righteous blade toward the defeated Lucifer upon which he stood. It was perfectly still, and something about its stillness this time seemed unnatural. The first time Mick had seen the impressive statue was when he came in with George for the "special service" Father had lured him into. It was exactly how Mick remembered it, in the exact same pose as if it had not moved an inch. Mick found himself wondering if the report of the statue killing anyone was beginning to get to him, fueling his apprehension when the damn thing looked perfectly normal.

He flinched when he felt Oscar's hand on his shoulder.

"Dude come on!" Oscar whispered. Sunny had already joined him.

"You both said you saw statues move before right?" Mick asked.

The two nodded.

Mick looked back over his shoulder, "You think what the cleaners said is true?"

Both teens nodded impatiently.

"I'm sorry, I'm just having a hard time with that one." Mick said.

Oscar motioned for Mick to join them and eased the east doorway open. The hallway that stretched out before them ran the length of about quarter of a football field. It too was decorated with smaller statues of various saints, mounted on small stands where potted plants also sat, creating the effect of the holy figures walking through a glade of trees. Each of these were painted, giving them a not so entirely unnerving look. It was dotted with three or four rooms on the left side of the wall. Two restrooms, a storage closet and one a breaker room. The priest's office lay in wait at the very end of the hall, the letters on the door reading "Father Ernesto, Tovilla Munroe, Parish Priest."

"We probably shouldn't have our eyes glowing when we go in. She's pretty shaken up." Oscar said. Mick and Sunny nodded as they proceeded down toward the office. Mick breathed in deep through his nose in a controlled fashion, exhaling slowly through his mouth, trying to shake the feeling that the smaller figurines on their pedestals were following him with their fixed gaze.

The office door was locked. Oscar called out to the woman in Spanish through the door, his tone reassuring. Lupita Guitierez opened the door hastily. Her long black hair was pulled back tightly in a braid behind her head. Swelled with child, her walk was more of a waddle. She appeared to be in her early to mid-thirties, firm muscled arms brandished proudly from her sleeveless t-shirt. Her eyes were rather large, reminding Mick of an anime girl, and her thin nose rested above a set of full lips.

Oscar and her exchanged a few more words in Spanish as she dried her eyes.

"She says Jorge, the other cleaner was impaled on the statue's sword." Oscar translated.

Mick noticed the door on an adjacent wall that read 'SANCTUARY,' on the plastic plaque. She had moved the desk against that door. She had covered the small glass window that was at eye level with a piece of paper from the printer in the corner, taping it to the door. The desktop computer had toppled off of the desk in her adrenaline fueled rush, cords and plugs bent and warped, now no longer any good. Mick strode over to the door and lifted the piece of paper from the viewing window.

"No!" Lupita cried, sobbing and clawing at his shoulder. Mick instantly released the piece of paper and held up his hands. He didn't know the Spanish word for 'sorry,' so he substituted English.

"She says it's been watching the door, coming up to it and scratching at the glass to try and get in." Oscar said. Mick turned his gaze back to the door as Sunny wrapped her arms around the terrified woman, trying to comfort to her the best she knew how. Freaking language barriers. From what he could see, this door lead straight out onto the stage, right in front of where the statue rested.

"Let's get her out of here," Mick said, and the two teens nodded. Mick took up lead in the front, shotgun drawn as they exited the office. Oscar was speaking into his Bluetooth earpiece, relaying to Judah that Miss Gutierrez was safe and that they were on their way out.

As soon as they hit the foyer, Miss Gutierrez tore passed all of them and out of the front doors to the church, running passed the rest of the hunters who were waiting on the church steps. Judah and the rest of the gang poured in behind her, their weapons trained on the floor.

Once they were all inside, they all took a knee.

"When we were in astral form," Brandon said, "the statue itself was exuding a strange aura."

Judah nodded. Mick knew auras were his specialty. Technically he knew they could all see auras with the Higher Sight, but Judah could tell the difference in what they meant. Only problem with that was, he had to be in fairly close proximity to its source for him to actually read anything.

"Everyone form up on me as we're going in, fan out when we get in there. Keep it in your sights. It's pretty tall so aim for the upper half of its body." He instructed.

They all affirmed and entered the sanctuary, Judah hurrying ahead at a crouch. There were other statues, other saints that were dwarfed in size by comparison to the nine foot tall statue on stage. The others stood no taller than probably five and a half feet tall, roughly the size of a short-ish person. The ceramic, indifferent gazes of the saints bore into Mick from all sides, and for a minute, he felt like he was a kid back in the pews with his parents for Mass.

Mick and Rufus ducked behind the center row of pews on the right side of the long sanctuary. Mick watched Judah as he carefully approached the statue, his guts churning into knots. He saw the veins on Judah's exposed, muscular arms light up within his flesh, practically turning him into a walking night light as he approached up the center aisle. From where they were, Mick couldn't exactly see the body, but he could smell the heavy scent of soap mixing with copper, coating the air, and he could make out the red bulk of a Rug Doctor at the front row.

Judah bent down, examining what Mick assumed to be the body of the cleaner. He saw the look on Judah's face.

Judah pressed the Bluetooth earpiece on the side of his head, "Valerie… This man's throat is missing…It looks like it was done by something's teeth."

Mick felt the bottom drop out of his stomach as those words. Miss Gutierrez had said the man had been impaled on the statue's sword! He saw Oscar and Sunny, their expressions betraying bewilderment while they poked their heads up over their pews to attempt a look for themselves.

"Got it," Judah said, turning his attention back toward the nine foot tall statue up on stage. He stayed right where he was, not moving any further. He stayed, starring at the marble masterpiece for a few moments. Mick guessed he was trying to do his aura reading thing.

One of the heads of the saint statues turned, silently and fluidly, toward where Judah was standing. Mick forced the Light back into his eyes, and immediately the tingle consumed them. With his vision illuminated, he saw its face, stiff and unmoving, was smeared with blood, the greatest concentration of it around the statue's mouth. Mick almost wasn't sure how to process the sight of the thing as it stood there gawking at Judah. He blinked, several times. Was he the only one who saw it move? It remained perfectly still. It reminded Mick of those street performers who used to paint themselves up as statues and posed in bigger cities for money. That art form had been outlawed years ago when gargoyles had been discovered as a creature type and not just rain spouts on old cathedrals. The tingle intensified, and he saw the statue's face. It was smiling.

"Boss, drop!" Parish hollered, standing from behind his pew and squeezing off a shot. Judah dropped. Apparently Mick hadn't been the only one who noticed. The thunder boom of the shotgun that violated Mick's ears left them ringing as the sound, confined and amplified by the architecture of the sanctuary, resonated deep in his ear canals. Parish's shot was true, as the statue's head shattered in a spray of ceramic chunks and a shower of black tar against the back wall. The glowing slug left a trail of white steam eeking out of the huge hole it plowed into the wall. The thing flailed its arms out and dropped to its knees, which shattered upon impact, and toppled over.

Judah was already cracking off shots himself as more of the short statues began moving off their pedestals, shuffling towards them. Chunks of plaster like substance, as well as tarry black liquid erupted all over the sanctuary. Rufus tackled Mick just as one lunged for him, emerging over the pew behind them. Mick felt the air get knocked out of him as Rufus quickly drew a magnum from his shoulder holster, put it in the thing's face, and squeezed off a round into its mouth as it opened wide. The head exploded with the ceramic crash that was drowned out by the eruption of gun fire.

Rufus quickly helped Mick to his knees, both of them staying low.

"Thanks!" Mick shouted as he huddled closely behind Rufus.

"Anytime," Rufus replied. Mick caught sight of Oscar, huddling behind one of the pews, his eyes bulging and his teeth elongating as he shook. Sunny popped up over her pew and fired at a statue of the Virgin Mary who had been positioned by the double doors they had come in through.

Judah and Brandon had dropped to an army crawl, firing at the feet of the statues that were moving through the rows of pews to get at them. Once they toppled over, the hunters quickly hopped up, and smashed the heads of the creatures in with the butts of their shotguns.

"Reloading!" Parish yelled above the noise, dropping down behind a pew.

Mick couldn't immediately identify what came over him in that instant, but the closest he could identify was an unholy union between absolute, adrenaline fueled terror and bravado all in one.

He popped up over the pew, ignoring the sharp ceramic shards that pinged and flew through the air, embedding into the sides of his face. One was walking down the center aisle, straight toward Oscar, who was still clutching the shotgun close to his chest, his face almost a wolf snout. The thing raised its staff high above its head, the stone equivalent to its robes remaining stiff as the arms themselves moved with lifelike ease.

Mick couldn't understand the words coming out of his own mouth. He just knew his throat was raw from screaming. His finger squeezed the trigger, blasting a hole the size of a fist into the back of the statue before it brought its staff down on Oscar's head. The thing quivered, stiffened, and fell forward as the limbs broke off, black blood dowsing the remains of the statue within seconds.

Mick hadn't been counting but he was pretty sure that was the last one. No one moved for what seemed like hours. The carpet was soaked black, and powdered in rubble. Sunny's voice soon broke the silence.

"You could have shot me!" She screamed as she stood up. Mick looked around, all the other hunters were standing up slowly, taking inventory. Mick's eyes drew back toward her. She was bearing down on him with her eyes, her features sharp with rage.

"Me?" Mick asked.

"Yes you!" She screamed.

"What happened?" Judah asked storming up to where they were. Mick was glad too, at least Judah could be a barrier between him and Sunny. She looked livid, and this time Mick knew he couldn't blame her.

"I saw one going for Oscar and I shot it!" Mick squeaked.

"I ducked just in time for a huge chunk of statue to nearly take my eye out!" She yelled.

"Children! Enough!" Judah yelled holding up his hands between them.

"Judah," Brandon called, holding up one of the statue's heads, "look at this," he tossed the head to Judah.

Rufus was over by Oscar in the next second, "You okay there?" He asked, bending down to offer his hand. Oscar's eyes snapped toward his hand and he reluctantly grabbed onto it. The lupine features that were pushing their way through his face faded as Oscar covered his face with his hands.

"I'm sorry. I'm really…freakin'…sorry. I thought I would be okay for this job. Guess not." He said, trying to keep his composure.

Sunny, seeming to have temporarily forgiven Mick, was by Oscar's side as well, wrapping her arms around him and patting him on the back. Mick remembered Oscar's story of how he had been nearly ripped apart by the statues in the Broken Edge Memorial courtyard. When Mick was still a detective, he had been sent out to look over that crime scene, which had been passed off as simple vandalism.

"Is that flesh?"

Mick turned his attention back to Judah and Brandon, who were using the tip of a knife to poke the broken neck under the thing's jawline.

The tip of the knife sank deep into the black exposed area of the separated neck, and withdrew with a sickening squelch. The blade trailed a thick tendril of black gunk as it left the neck.

"Looks like that is part of a spinal column, and here looks like a subglottis found in a human throat," Judah said. Upon a closer look, Mick could see that the squishy flesh of the broken off head became more solid as the inside muscles seemed to merge into the outer shell of the statue.

Suddenly, Mick remembered the dead body of the cleaner.

"Hey you said the guy up there had his throat ripped out?" Mick asked Judah, who nodded and added, "Go up and see for yourself."

Mick complied, remembering the first statue he saw move. The one with blood smeared all over its face. As he approached the still form, now covered with chunks of statue guts, Mick stiffened and felt his flesh prickle in icy waves. The man's throat was completely intact.

Immediately his detective brain began trying to fit pieces together, bits of information he may have heard through the night that might cause something to click. His glowing eyes searched the corpse for any signs of foreign energy. He looked back up at the statue of St. Michael. He could see the shimmering aura that engulfed the marble giant, just like Brandon said.

Supposedly impaled on the statue's sword, but Judah sees him with his throat ripped out. I see a statue that has blood all over its face, like it could have been the culprit, and now the body has a throat. I never saw the throat myself but...

Mick's teammates were gathering around him. "I thought you told Valerie his throat had been ripped out," Brandon asked.

Judah stood there, his face turned into a grimace of disbelief, "It was," he said, bending down to have a closer look.

"Look," Sunny pointed at the dead man's stomach. Mick followed her gaze. It was completely intact as well.

"Waita minute," Mick thought out loud. He remembered he only saw the blood on the one statue's mouth after he had caused the Light to travel to his eyes. We're all seeing different things...

"Hey guys, drop the Higher Sight for a minute," Mick said. He felt the tingle in his eyes subside, and the sanctuary was awash in darkness once again. The only light that seemed to penetrate the darkness was the meager beams of light being filtered in through the windows from the street lamps outside. Apparently everyone else did also, the lights in their eyes fading until they winked out altogether.

"Now what?" Oscar asked. Mick dug through his pants pocket and pulled out his cell phone, and turned on its flashlight. He waved it over the dead body, revealing what was left of its stomach region. The man's stomach looked like it had indeed been run through with a blunt object, only to have his insides warped and pulled out through the giant cavity left in its wake. The body still lay coated in foreign substances of the other statues, but had otherwise been lying in a pool of its own gore for a while. The stench of the man's insides mixing with the still soapy shampoo was nearly overwhelming now that they were standing directly over him. Meanwhile, his throat remained untouched.

"Oh my God," Sunny said, covering her mouth and turning her head away.

"We were all seeing different things," Mick exclaimed, "We all saw the aura around that statue right?" Mick gestured toward the carving of the arc angel. The hunters all nodded.

"Whatever is going on with that aura could be messing with out Higher Sight," Mick offered. The sound of a something crumbling startled Mick, causing everyone in the room to freeze. The sound was coming from the stage. They all turned their gaze toward the direction of the sound, the beam from Mick's phone light following. The face of St. Michael had moved to look at them, cracks forming around the neck and up the chin. Chunks of marble fell away, bounced off of Lucifer's head, and struck the stage below.

Judah was telling everyone to reload, as his eyes and veins lit back up. Brandon was undoing his Kevlar vest, and Oscar was stumbling backward, fumbling with the buckles of his vest as his jawline became like that of a bear trap.

Mick felt the tingle in his eyes return as the marble monolith lifted one sandaled foot free from its place on Lucifer's neck, taking chunks of the prince of darkness's head with it.

Brandon hurled himself toward Oscar, his large, hairy hands slicing through the buckles and tearing the boy's vest free. Oscar let out a scream that turned quickly to a deep, bone rattling howl as he fell behind a pew. The sound of his cries of pain as they mixed with the sounds of his and Brandon's flesh tearing sent Mick almost doubling over with the urge to vomit. Tears stung his eyes. As soon as Brandon and Oscar were clear, Judah gave the order to shoot. All of the remaining hunters with a shotgun in their hands let loose a torrent of blinding white slugs that smacked into the statue as it lifted one of its wings up to defend itself. The slugs smacked into the textured wing, slabs of marble bursting and raining down on them. One slug apparently made it passed the wing and nailed the thing in the face. Its head slammed backward into the wall behind it, rattling the building.

The thing actually groaned. A deep, chest vibrating groan, that rumbled the very bones in Mick's body. The thing lowered its wing, which now looked fleshy and membranous, like that of a bat. Then the face came into view. The chunk of marble that had been blown away revealed a mucus covered yellow eye with the rectangular pupil like that of a goat.

THE HORROR IN MARBLE

Mick felt a rush of air and a sudden vibration behind him. He screamed and spun around to see Brandon's enormous, clawed hand come up over the pew behind him. Oscar pushed himself up on now triple jointed legs, foam slinging off of his jaw as he shook the last bits of his human confines off of him.

"Spread out!!" Judah yelled, and the hunters scattered.

The two blood caked werewolves stood to their full height, and with muscles on the hair trigger of primordial ferocity, propelled themselves over the now broken pews toward the thing that really couldn't be called a statue anymore.

The building shook to its foundation when the two beasts collided with the thing, sending shockwaves through Mick's body. The abomination's blade swung through the air, catching Brandon on his meaty shoulder. The marble blade disintegrated upon contact with the werewolf's hide, only temporarily staggering the beast.

Oscar caught the thing across the stomach, taking with it a huge chunk of marble and more of the black blood. The other wing, still coated in its crumbling exterior, came around and slapped the werewolf off, sending him crashing through the east wall and back into the hall.

Brandon had regained his bearings and was now bounding toward the statue on all fours, his powerful legs shooting him forward like a slingshot and tearing up the gore soaked carpet as his massive arms caught the thing around the waist.

Mick slipped, busting his face on a pew. Judah and Rufus were by him in a second, helping him to his feet. Judah was yelling something to him. Probably about how clumsy he was and how they couldn't afford to be helping his clumsy butt up off the ground all the time, but he could have also just said "move!" for all Mick knew. Parish and Sunny reached the sanctuary doors first and flung them open.

The building sounded like it was coming down around their ears. Amidst the howls from Brandon and Oscar, the inhuman shrieks the thing was emanating, the sound of cracking support beams, twisting metal, and—

Mick turned his gaze back long enough to see the form that used to be a statue of St. Michael, now looking like an abomination straight out of the mouth of the abyss. The marble shell that had been its cocoon was gone. The face was riddled with bone spurs, its teeth like that of a shark. Its flesh, now stained black with blood, was also riddled with an exterior of more bone spurs that covered its chest and arms like armor.

One of the werewolves, he couldn't tell which, let out a muted yelp as the thing's serrated teeth clamped down on their throat. With a flap of its great, bat-like wings, Mick, Judah and Rufus were all flung off balance and face planted. Parish and Sunny were slammed against the wall, their grip on the door handles unable to match the hurricane like gale of wind the thing created. The windows shattered outward when the thing flapped them again, while one of the werewolves climbed onto its back and attempting to tear its throat open.

"Move your ass!" Rufus shouted as he hauled Mick up by the collar of his Kevlar vest. Mick's vision blurred. He saw the forms of his team mates running over to aid him, but he couldn't make out any defining features. His eyes were stinging and he felt air rushing into a numb spot on his forehead that was beginning to burn. His eyes stung again, and this time he couldn't open them. The scent of copper flooded his nostrils, and this time he knew that it wasn't sweat he was feeling on his brow.

He heard the sounds of heavy wooden doors being slammed into and the urgent pounding of footsteps flooded his ears, drowning out the sickening impact from the blows of the battle being waged behind him. He felt the rush of cool air hit his face. There was the thrumming of a chopper's blades cutting through the air overhead.

They were outside.

"Move back! Get these people out of here!" Judah was shouting as they emerged from the mouth of hell itself and flew down the steps.

Mick's ears were assaulted by another sudden, unwelcome cacophony. An infernal symphony of twisting metal and shattering glass erupted over his head and he felt himself tumbling down the stairs, blinded by the blood that was leaking into his eyes.

The assault on his ears was met by the panicked screams of the multitude gathered across the parking lot. A sudden rush of beating wind slammed his face into the ground as something enormous soared over their heads.

Mick felt something heavy crushing him down into the concrete. The pressure forced all air out of his lungs as the screams filled his ears, accompanied by the crashing tidal wave of gunfire. His eyes felt numb, and his brains felt like they were leaking out of his ears. His breath was gone, leaving him unable to suck in enough air to calm his growing panic. The only thing he could manage at this time was the hot, agonizing, shallow gulps for air as his chest burned. He blacked out.

Thick, calloused, sausage like fingers were curling themselves through his hair, smashing his face into the blood soaked floor. The fine slivers of glass embedded themselves into his face as the hot breath of—something was whispering to him. The breath washed over him, scalding his ear like steam from a valve. Beads of burning spittle flew off the speaker's lips and into the side of his face, jolting him back to consciousness. He couldn't make out what the speaker was saying, but he recognized the voice. The voice that sent every cell in his body screaming into shock as the vibration of the voice traveled down his ear canal and raped his ear drum with its timbre and cadence.

That woman was screaming again.

Mick's eyes flew open and he screamed, arms flailing out before him. The light that washed into his eyes caused his body to spasm as he slammed his eyes shut once more. Hands were attempting to restrain him, catching his arms and holding him back down. Blind and groping, fighting against unknown attackers, he soon heard a voice he recognized calling him back to reality.

"Mick it's okay!"

He wasn't sure how long the voice had been yelling his name, no doubt having to compete with his own terrified wails of panic.

"Mick it's me!" Valerie was saying. Mick tried to open his eyes. They were tingling, and when he did open them he had to shield his glowing eyes with his hand. He was lying on his back. Hands wearing latex gloves were firmly holding him down. The tingle in his eyes slowly began to subside and his vision was able to slowly coalesce into an image his mind could process.

He was in the back of an ambulance, two gray faced paramedics standing over him with cautious looks of unsettled hesitance etched into their faces. Mick didn't even realize he was still flinching, his muscles wound tighter than an iron coil.

"Can you hear me Mick?" Valerie was speaking again, this time her voice sounding much closer. Mick's eyes snapped toward her, the silhouette of her head blocking out the overhead light.

"T-that wasn't you screaming?" Mick stammered, trying to calm the vibrating nerves that relentlessly rattled inside of his flesh. Valerie breathed deep and touched Mick's face, "Shhh. Just lay still. You blacked out when Rufus fell on you. I saw you guys coming out of the church, saw the creature try to fly out through the stained glass window. Brandon and Oscar put it down. They are back home." She said, her voice soothing as Mick lay there shaking. He didn't realize his hands had been balled up into fists until he felt her soft hands claps around one of his.

"...It's dead?" Mick asked, after a few minutes of trying to get his breathing under control.

Valerie nodded, "Police have the scene taped off. It went down just beyond the parking lot across the street from the church."

"So where are we?" Mick asked.

"We're still on church property." She assured him.

"Where is everyone else? And did you get the body out of the church?" Mick asked.

She shook her head, "The remains of the deceased had to be carefully removed from the scene. There wasn't much of a body left to examine on sight after that thing woke up and the chaos ensued. As for everyone else, they are floating around out there talking to other officers, getting checked over by the other EMT's. Judah is having to run off the local press. A few dumb teenagers drove up on the scene with their phones out, so you can bet tonight is going to end up all over social media, along with reports of two werewolf sighted in the area."

Mick finally managed to allow the muscles in his neck to release. He closed his eyes and swallowed dryly.

"Did you get a look at that thing?" Mick asked after a while.

"Yep. Handsome fella."

Mick smirked, suddenly feeling the need to cough. After a short bout of hacking up a lung, he settled down onto his back, letting the paramedics tend to him.

"What do you think it was?" Mick asked.

"My go-to idea would be gargoyle, or something that could imitate one, but I wanna poke at it under a microscope to be sure." She said.

"That makes sense I guess. I thought they were actual living statues though. That thing was just using the statue as an outer covering," Mick said, taking a small cup of water one of the EMT's handed him. He didn't realize how dry his throat was until the first drop of the cool water touched his tongue. He greedily gulped it down and requested another.

"There is still a lot we don't know," Valerie admitted. A knock on the side of the ambulance caused Mick's head to turn. Judah was stepping up into the back of the ambulance. He kissed Valerie on the side of the head and wrapped one arm around her shoulder, hugging her close. She wrinkled her nose, turned her gaze to meet his and stated, "You need a shower."

Judah's smile reached up into his eyes, rimmed with exhaustion as he chuckled.

"Have you told him yet?" he asked her.

"No, I was waiting for you," she said and turned her eyes back to Mick, who sat patiently while an EMT fastened a blood pressure cuff around his arm.

"What's up?" Mick asked.

The couple faced him, their eyes gleaming without the actual glow of the Higher Sight.

"We've told everybody else, but we wanted to wait until you woke up to fill you in," Judah said, looking at Valerie one more time before he turned his gaze back to Mick.

"We're pregnant!" He gushed, squeezing Valerie closer to him as she did the same.

"Oh so that's why you didn't come in with us," Mick said shaking his head, "gosh you two, you know what causes that don't you?" He tried not to smile. It hurt his face too much.

"Not like you would know Mick," Judah said as he winked.

"Ouch…I felt that one," Mick said, holding his head for show, but more for the actual feeling of trying to keep his head from throbbing. He knew by tomorrow morning he would be good as new but that still didn't help the pulsating misery that was swelling through his head. Even the EMT's were chuckling at his expense.

"Congratulations guys," One of them said. Mick caught his name badge on his pocket flap—Kenny. Valerie and Judah nodded at them warmly.

"Yeah I'm happy for you both," Mick said, "How long have you known?"

"Just over a month," Valerie replied.

"Ah so it's too soon to know what the sex is then huh?" Mick asked.

Judah nodded, "Yeah, but I bet we have twins." Valerie slapped his arm and he flinched, "One is good for the time being, thank you!"

He laughed, "But what are you gonna do if the doctor says there's another one in there?"

She looked down at the floor for a second, her face feigning irritation and then looked back at him with a sly smile, "I'll make *you* carry it!" Judah's face flushed red and he burst into another explosion of laughter.

The sound of Judah's laughter engulfed Mick, causing his pounding head to throb as if inside of a pinball machine. But at the same time it also calmed him. The tension dispelling outburst of his exuberance chased away the sludge of the hunt that consumed not just Mick's life, but all of their collective vigil against the dark. The man didn't laugh often, but when he did, it was a feast for the ears in the soundless void of darkness that each of them was assigned to protect. His laugh permeated Mick's skull, brushing gently passed the throbbing headache that was the whole of Mick's existence at the moment, and settled over him like a warm blanket.

The two EMT's finished their preliminary examination on Mick, put away their equipment, and then left the ambulance to let the friends have some time, each shaking the hunters' hands and thanking them for their work that night.

UNKNOWN NUMBER

Mick felt one of his pockets vibrating. He began digging in his pocket, trying to get his phone untangled from the infinite depths that was the pockets of his tactical pants, and nearly fumbled with it once it was free. He caught it and flipped the screen so it was facing him.

He felt his brow furrow at the unrecognized number that displayed across his screen. He typically didn't answer calls that he didn't recognize, but more than that, it was almost one o clock in the morning. No one ever called him at this hour except Judah or the other hunters.

He slid the green arrow across the screen at the last second, "Hello?"

The voice that filled his ears felt like an icepick violating his ear hole. It pierced his ear drum and making him wince.

"Hello Johnson, how's your night going?" the female voice at the other end inquired.

"Agent Pallacios?" Mick asked, hoping he was about to wake up soon.

"Yours truly." She purred.

Mick bit his lip, attempting to keep a long list of expletives from flying out of his mouth.

"So," he began, "you're up late. Burning the federal candle at both ends?"

"Let me first say that I'm up to my eyes in a missing children's case, and I have an offer for you and your group to help in a federal investigation." She replied coldly.

Mick felt his eye brows rise at that. "My group huh? Former Detective Mick Johnson, the incompetent ass-monkey who apparently couldn't file paperwork to your liking, and his new group, and you're asking *us* for help? That's hilarious! Just where in the hell did you get this number? How do you even know

I'm working with any particular group?" Mick snarled. What was she going to do? Report him to Chief Scroggins or Sergeant Mills? Valerie and Judah were eyeing him curiously. He was no longer sporting a badge, so he didn't have to bite his tongue now.

Pallacios let out a long, condescending sigh, "Mick, I'm with the FBI. I could tell you your shoe size from across the country if it served national security purposes."

Mick felt himself nervously tapping the fingers of his other hand on the side of his leg. Valerie and Judah were watching him, patient and steady.

"So I'll ask you again. Does your group deal with cases concerning missing persons?"

Mick relented. The circumstances were rubbing him raw like sandpaper, but his cop senses were tingling. If children were missing, then he was obligated to look into it.

"Who's missing?" He finally asked.

"Two children by the names of Wendy Matthews and Morgan Phillips, both nabbed on their way home from school less than forty eight hours ago. A witness saw and reported it to the local authorities. There has been a steady rise in kidnappings in Denver, Colorado for the last three years. Feds have been all over this case since a pattern started developing, but none of the children were ever found, and this was the first time a witness has seen anything. As of six months ago, I'm the one heading up the investigation. It's been brought to my attention that the group you are working with has some extraordinary abilities, and you yourself have prior detective experience."

Mick looked at Judah and sighed, feeling like an internal weight was squeezing every drop of air from his body. Mick took the phone away from his ear, touched the screen and put the conversation on speaker.

"Agent, I got the leader of my group here with me right now. What you got on your plate sounds terrible, but this is a decision I have to run by him. Judah, I'd like you to meet FBI Agent Della Pallacios. Worked under her during the Tick killings. Also from the county coroner's office, miss Valerie Wellington. You remember her right?"

"Hi Agent," Judah said.

"Hello again," from Valerie.

"Greetings, and yes I remember Miss Wellington. She certainly was one of the more competent ones I worked with during that nightmare," said Pallacios. Mick found himself squeezing his phone, imagining it was that woman's neck. She began quickly recapping for Judah and Valerie everything she had told Mick.

"So you said there was a witness to the kidnaping, the kids were walking home from school," Mick began, "Usually when kids get out of school traffic picks up like crazy, and these goons were sloppy enough to do this during the rush when parents go pick their kids up? In broad daylight?"

"The street they were taken from wasn't busy at the time of the abduction," she said, "As for describing the vehicle, it was a Ford E350 van. The witness didn't get a look at the kidnapper or the driver from their vantage point but they saw enough of the vehicle to describe it and get the tag number. We ran a trace on the tags, and turns out the tags that were on the van were registered to another vehicle entirely."

"Where were they when they saw it happen?" Mick asked.

"The witness saw it happen from their kitchen window."

"And, do any of the previous children have anything in common with the two that were taken recently?" Judah asked.

"So far they have all been between the ages of seven and twelve years old. Apart from their age range, nothing else seems to tie them together. They all appear to be random, but when there is an escalation of missing children, it's a fair guess that human trafficking is happening."

"So what made you think of us?" Valerie asked.

Bingo! Million dollar question, Mick thought.

"We've seen a little taste of what your organization can do. We also know that you have two werewolves working with you. They seem to have done a decent job of keeping their identities masked from the public as to what they are. Wouldn't it be a shame for the people of New Broken Edge and the surrounding counties to find out?" She asked.

Mick's blood turned to ice as he locked eyes with Judah, who was staring at the phone. The look on his face was somewhere between amusement and pricked ire. Judah stood up, snatched the phone up from Mick and began talking.

"Yes, we have some extraordinary people working for us. You're point, Agent?" He asked, his face turning to stone.

"My point being that your group has talents that would take this investigation to the next level. Granted, what we have seen, those talents have been directed toward fighting foes of the non-human variety, and we are ever grateful. But there are two children who are missing, and you have monsters on a leash. The people of New Broken Edge have already lived through one massacre."

Mick saw the knuckles on Judah's fingers go white as he set his jaw and glanced around, his eyes catching those of Mick and Valerie.

"Also," Pallacios continued, "have Johnson check his email."

Judah looked at the phone screen and handed the phone back to Mick.

"What's in my email?" Mick asked, his tone snippy. Just then the phone vibrated as a notification appeared in the bar at the top of the screen.

"Just open the attached file I sent you. I'm sure it will persuade you," She said. Mick rolled his eyes and pressed the email notification. The attachment was a video file. The file didn't have a title—only a date. One that caused Mick to feel like his stomach was about to drop out from him. His skin flared to life with electric adrenaline that made him want to bolt out of the back of this ambulance.

The date on the video file read 10/31/2012. Mick felt his lungs beginning to shrink. A blanket of icy panic surrounded him as he felt the ambulance beginning to shrink all around him.

Mick's thumb hovered over the file, barely touching it.

"Facial recognition is such a bitch, isn't it Johnson? It's a good thing we captured your face before the whole city lost power that night. You are a dangerous man. As far as the Bureau is concerned, you're a mass murderer. The fact you haven't been put on death row is more of a testament to your usefulness to society in regards to your abilities than it is to our competence."

Mick felt his throat go dry as he tried to form words, but nothing came out. He was floating on a crumbling platform in an ocean of bubbling magma, blinded and choked with thick clouds of sulfur.

Judah cut in, thankfully, "Give us twelve hours and I will personally get back to you. We're in the middle of cleaning up a mess on our end. My team needs at least five hours to get some rest but I can have a few of my people on their way to Denver by tomorrow evening."

"That sounds wonderful sir. I appreciate your time." Della said, her tone becoming exceedingly pleasant. Mick hung up, laid back down and closed his eyes, with Judah and Valerie's conversation about the details being drowned out by the sound of the blood flowing through his ears.

"If she wanted our help finding the kids all she had to do was ask," Mick breathed out after settling his nerves a bit. Judah leaned against the doorframe of the ambulance and let out a long slow breath as Valerie stood up and put her arm around him.

"Obviously she didn't think that was enough." Judah said.

BLIND IN THE DARK

11:52pm, Mountain Time,

The darkness that had become the new constant in her life had made it impossible for her to know how much time had passed. All feeling in her hands, feet, lower body and back had left her, although she could not tell when, because she had woken up like that. All she knew was that wherever she was had to be huge, because her voice echoed whenever she called out. The sound of creaking metal hinges could be heard at random times, followed by sloshing, wet footsteps of something off in the distance. It was usually after she cried out she would hear them, and the closer they sounded, she regretted ever calling out. Sometimes, what sounded like a metal grate opening off in the distance somewhere would wake her up just as she felt herself drifting out of consciousness, and she would hear the sloshing again, getting closer each time.

Wendy Matthews sat with her arms and legs bound to what she guessed could have been a wheelchair. It rocked smoothly whenever she attempted to struggle against her restraints, scooting forward little by little with her body weight. She was soaked and dirty from head to toe. The smell of her own urine and sweat, mixed with the musty place she was in was ever present in her nostrils, in her clothes, and on her skin. The only thing she could remember was that she was nine years old, and that she had been walking home from school, on a Thursday afternoon with her friend Morgan. Everything else afterwards was just pitch black.

She could hear water dripping off in the distance somewhere too. The steady sound of what she imagined to be cool, fat water droplets plummeting down toward a pool was torturous. Her throat felt like cured leather, the inside of her mouth coated from top to bottom with dust. Her tongue felt like a deflated slug that had been rolled in salt and stuffed into her mouth. The sound of that water made her want to scream and cry out for a drink. She imagined in her mind it was the leaky sink downstairs in the kitchen of her house. She felt hot moisture spring to her eyes, but it was instantly sapped by the rag, or whatever type of fabric that had been secured around her eyes.

"Let's take this off shall we?" A voice said behind her, and she nearly sky-rocketed out of her skin, taking the wheelchair with her. She hadn't even heard any footsteps, nothing to signal there was something behind her. It was the first actual words she had heard spoken since she woke up here.

She felt the tight rag that had been bound around her eyes, which had been the source of the throbbing in her head, being loosened and suddenly an overwhelmingly blinding light was shining in her eyes.

She snapped them shut and turned her head the other direction as the sounds of three different cackles exploded all around her.

"That light at the end of the tunnel's not Heaven baby girl." One of them said. Suddenly she felt the wheelchair scooting forward as the howling laughter continued.

"Where are you taking me?" She finally managed to squeak, her mouth hot and dry, her vocal chords cracking from disuse. They didn't answer.

"What d-do you want with me?" She asked again, asking the only question she had dared not to ask for fear of finding out the answer. But no matter how much she feared the answer, if one came at all, she couldn't stand not knowing any longer.

"It's not what we want with you, it's what *he* wants with you," One of the three said. She hadn't expected such a quick and vague reply, and she flinched at the sound of the voice. All she could tell was that each voice sounded male.

"W-what does that mean?!" She pleaded, each word an exhausting effort to speak. Even though the blindfold had been taken off, the watering in her eyes was making it impossible for her to see anything, and one of them kept clicking that flashlight on and off in her eyes.

"You better pray for your sake that he likes you. You wanna know what we do to the ones he doesn't like?" One of them hissed, the voice slippery as an eel.

She screamed at the touch of the speaker's wet tongue, the mucus covered organ tickling the side of her ear when it finished its question. The three around her gave mock sympathy cries, and then amped up their mocking tones with a scowl. She heard another door being opened in front of her, and then felt the wheelchair being lifted from the ground.

"What are you doing?!" She cried. They gave no answer, but just kept laughing. She wobbled back and forth as the chair rocked this way and that in midair, feeling like she was on a cheap carnival ride that was on a rickety downward slope. With each downward jerk of the chair she could hear the sounds of the three captors' footsteps. The smell that was wafting its way up to her face smelled like rotten meat that had been left in a sewer. The jerky motions of the wheelchair in midair as she descended, along with the strong odor caused her to dry heave what little bile she had left in her stomach down the front of her shirt.

"The pretty little thing's getting pukey on us boys," one of them sneered.

The teetering motion continued for at least another minute until she felt the wheelchair touch down on even ground again.

"Get that door open," the one wheeling her from behind ordered.

"W-were are you taking me!?" She asked as she heard the door in front of her open. She was pushed along, feeling the bump rattle her in the chair as they crossed the threshold. She suddenly felt the wheelchair stop, and heard the voice of the one behind her say, "Here ya go doc. Ya think he'll like this one?"

The Doc, the one being addressed, was silent for a couple seconds. The answer came in the form of a coarse, gloved hand, fingers wrapping around her face, covering her mouth as the hand jerked her head from side to side, as if sizing her up for a display. She found herself zeroing in on the pounding of her heart against the inside of her chest. A new surge of panic had been pumping through her since the voices first began to speak, and she could subtly feel her fingers again as she twitched at the end of the arm rests of her wheelchair. But making a fist was still impossible.

The hands were traveling all over her now, behind her ears, down her neck, on her abdomen and over her arms, squeezing lightly as if feeling her muscles. She shivered as the cry she was trying to stifle came eking out of her like smoke from under a cauldron lid.

The Doc took his hands off of her and she allowed her tensed muscles to ease slightly. She heard footsteps walking away from her.

"Well?" another voice behind her asked impatiently.

The Doc's answer came in a series of sharp, suppressed metallic pops that made her jump, her nerves screaming at her. The next sound she heard came when she felt a gust of wind against her feet, as the one standing behind her fell backward and hit the ground so hard it rattled her insides. The others that had accompanied her down also fell, and from the sounds their bodies made as they hit the ground, she guessed they must have been big, weighing about as much as the wrestlers her daddy watched on TV. However, none of that mattered when she felt the spray of warm moisture against the back of her head and the left side of her face.

The residual echoes from the bodies hitting the ground subsided, fading into the soft footsteps of the Doc as he stepped closer.

Through all this, since the blinding light had flooded her vision, Wendy's eyes had remained closed up tight, and so they remained even now. Even though her mind was screaming for a look at the Doc, screaming to be cut loose, to be taken back to her parents and rocked until she was sure all of this was just a bad dream she could wake up from and forget about. She trembled there in her soiled wheelchair, her breaths sharp and shallow as her chest continued to constrict against the labored expansion of her lungs. If she passed out that would almost be a mercy.

She couldn't see, even though she attempted to ease her eyes open. There was a light source from somewhere, and even though she guessed she wasn't facing it directly, its illuminating rays still were too much for her retinal nerves to process.

But she could feel him standing in front of her, tall, silent, and unmoving. She pictured him wearing a white doctor's coat. The others had called him Doc after all.

"Where do you live?"

The voice that invaded her ears caused her to flinch. It was harsh and sounded like metal scraps being drug across a gravel parking lot. Her body shivered against her own control. She allowed the shivering to take her, no longer having the strength to fight the violent spasms.

"Where do you live?!" The Doc snapped and she jumped, the sharpness of his voice echoing all around her.

With no restraint or forethought whatsoever, she answered, spilling her address to him in a torrent of pathetic, choked sobs. Only after she spewed out her address did the dread settle over her of what the Doc might do to her family.

She heard his footsteps circling around her, and then the click of what she thought could be a knife.

"No! Please no, no, no!"

She instinctively began thrashing her limbs about—and her arm came loose. What feeling had returned to her limbs allowed her to feel the restraints sloughing off. One arm was free.

"Hold…still," The Doc hissed in her ear, quickly repeating the process on her other arm, and both legs.

She tried to wiggle her toes, flex her fingers. The movement of each joint took some painful effort as the blood began to circulate unhindered again. She tried to stand, and when she faltered she nearly toppled over. But she managed to stand, even if it meant holding onto the side of the wheelchair for support. She tried to ease her eyes open yet again, this time with a small margin of success. The bodies that lay behind the wheelchair looked the size of a regular grown up, not big and muscly like she had thought. Each one wore jeans that had been shredded in various places, dirty, nasty looking shirts and hoodies. She didn't see their faces. But she could make out that each body was soaked in the collective pools of their own blood. There were three of them.

She heard a small plastic pop, like the sound of a small lid being popped off of a large plastic jug, and then she heard a steady trickling of liquid, followed by the Doc's footsteps. The sounds were instantly accompanied by a new hellish smell that soon invaded her nostrils and clogged her airways. The smell was so thick she could taste it on her tongue as she choked and gagged.

"What are you…doing?!" She pitifully managed between violent coughing and gasps for air that wasn't saturated with whatever that smell was. Through the coughing she thought she could almost hear a liquid hissing.

"I'm melting the bodies," came the Doc's voice.

"You're what?!"

It was quite some time before he spoke again, but when he did, he ignored her inquiry, and asked a question of his own.

"Can you walk?" The Doc asked.

“I think so,” She replied, hoping that she would indeed have the strength just to take a single step.

“Take my hand. I’ll lead you out of here and get you back home.” The Doc’s voice softened. She reluctantly reached out, feeling his large gloved hand take hold of hers.

“Can you open your eyes?” he asked. She felt her lip tremble again, her face flushed as heat rose up from her chest. It was lucky she was holding his hand, because just trying to open her eyes around a strong source of light, after having her vision snuffed out for who knew how long, was painful.

“No,” She said, trying not to let her voice crack, trying to keep herself from shivering.

“Good,” the Doc said, and with that, he slowly began leading her up the way she had come.

ROAD TRIP

We left New Broken Edge about an hour ago, and here I am, crammed into the back seat of a van with three other people who admittedly tried to kill me three years ago—Two former demon worshipers and a friggin werewolf. What are the odds?

So I got about five and a half hours of sleep last night. Some people can thrive on that, but I'm still trying to learn how they do it. My eyes feel like they are burning and my muscles are still sour as hell. At least I can walk.

Pallacios…she sent me footage from that Halloween night three years ago. I sent it to Zach so he could watch it for me. He says given how shaky the footage is, he thinks it was taken from a cell phone camera. He watched enough of it to tell me at least that much, but he couldn't finish watching it himself. I can't blame him. I shouldn't have sent it to him, not while he's away with Mariah. I guess sending it to him was easier since he's out of state, and I wouldn't have to see his face after the fact.

There is a part of me that is relieved. I don't know how to explain it. Knowing that there is now proof is better than lying awake at night wondering what that thing did while it was inside of me. Ultimately I know it was me though. I let that thing in. I gave it what it wanted, because I bought its lie that to save George and protect my city, I had to let it in. That's what it boiled down to. By the time I had broken, justice was no longer a factor in my motivation. The potential to save George was, and I thought letting that thing take control was the only way. So while the thing inside of me did most of the damage, it was me who'd opened the door.

I guess the cop part of me can sleep well now. But knowing that the proof is there on my phone…Maybe I should have had Zach delete it when he offered to.

Mick felt his pocket buzzing again. He folded his pen into the flaps of his notebook and dug his phone out, and felt what little energy he had leave him at once.

"Yes Agent?" he asked.

Not wasting any time for introductions, Palacios jumped right to the matters at hand. "Johnson, Wendy Matthews has been found. Her parents rushed her to the hospital early this morning around o'three hundred our time. She said—"

Mick squeezed his eyes shut. He hadn't had enough coffee to keep up with her this early in the morning. But then Mick had to remind himself it was literally one in the afternoon.

"That's great but could you slow down a pinch. All I understood was that the girl has been found."

That evoked several whispered questions from those in the back seat, erupting all around him with, "Is she okay?"

"Shhh, let him talk,"

"Guys chill."

Pallacios cleared her throat again, "This morning around three o clock, Wendy Matthews and her parents came down to police headquarters. She said she had been rescued by a strange man with a scary voice, who she kept calling the Doc. When asked who Doc was, she couldn't give an answer. She's still so shaken up she couldn't give us any more than that."

Mick let those words seep into his being, let them permeate him. He plugged his phone into the AUX cord, letting Pallacios's voice come through the car speakers.

After briefly filling everyone else in on the details, she continued, "she had been sprayed with what appeared to be blood. She was swabbed and the clothes she was wearing were collected at the hospital so forensics are analyzing those now."

Mick leaned his head back into the headrest and closed his eyes, "Okay so did the parents see this Doc character?" he asked.

"No. She said he placed her own finger on the doorbell and pressed it, and then he was gone. No one else in the area reported seeing anyone suspicious fleeing her residence in the early morning hours, and that's understandable given what time it was." Pallacios said.

Silence settled over each of them like a sticky film. Mick looked around at each of them. Rufus, still driving, had his eyes hidden behind a pair of shades, but his jaw was set, his knuckles white as he gripped the wheel. Oscar was looking down at the floorboards, running his hands through his hair nervously. Sunny had her hands clasped in front of her mouth, her eyes closed. She opened them briefly to wipe moisture out of them and looked at Mick.

"What about the other kid, Morgan Harris?" Mick asked.

"He has yet to be found, and Wendy's too shook up at the moment to disclose any more." Pallacios confirmed.

"Poor thing," Sunny said, her voice dropping to a whisper.

"Do you think we could have the opportunity to speak with her ourselves?" Mick asked.

Pallacios was quiet for a second, as if thinking, "That can be arranged, but until she is stable, her parents don't want anyone talking to her. She was dehydrated and apparently her captors didn't feed her while she was with them. And you won't be permitted to speak with her unless an officer is present."

"Well," Mick started, "when the results on her clothes come back will you let us know what you got?"

"I most definitely will," Pallacios said. The conversation soon wound down to a close, and then Mick hung up. Mick was kind of surprised. She managed to go most of the conversation without sounding like a condescending old hag. Of course, good things never lasted.

We're not stupid, we know we wouldn't be able to talk to her unless another officer is present.

"What do you guys think about this Doc person?" Mick asked.

"That's hard to say right now," Rufus said, "could be anybody."

"Could be another hunter," Oscar offered.

Mick shrugged at that one, "I guess. But at this time we don't know what the evidence will reveal. I think that's kind of a stretch given how little we have to go on."

INTRODUCTIONS AND UPDATES

Mick groggily lifted the foam cup of coffee up to his lips, and slowly sipped on the steamy, caffeinated goodness that was bound to give him a good boost for about an hour.

"Find anything interesting?" Mick muttered to Rufus, who sat next to him on his left. His comrade sat with his eyes fervently scanning the Denver post website for potential jobs they could pick up while in the area.

"Nada," Rufus said, looking up from his phone long enough to cut off a bite of his steak and pop it in his mouth. "Most jobs I see posted are listed as 'completed', so the hunters up here must be on top of their game."

"That's good, but disappointing," Mick drawled. Rufus nodded and kept scrolling. Mick squeezed the burning sensation out of his dry eyes and opened them to the sight of the tall, slender Hispanic/Italian woman walking toward their table. Her dark hair that Mick remembered being longer, was now a long pixie cut with her hair parted down the left side of her head that actually helped make her look younger, if not more interesting.

Huh, that's different, Mick thought. She wore a dark gray pant suite with a white blouse. He chased the coffee down with a huge bite of scrambled eggs as the woman drew closer, and suddenly the food, which had been very flavorful and savory to begin with, now tasted like mulch chips.

"She's here," Mick said without looking up. He felt everyone else's head turn upwards as their space was now invaded by the presence of another.

"Good morning Johnson" the familiar voice said, beckoning Mick to look up. Della Pallacios stood right next to him, hand extended and with that same high and mighty, disinterested look in her eyes. Mick set his fork down and extended his hand, his movements rigid as if wearing wet clothes.

"Good morning Agent," Mick said taking her hand firmly, and for a brief moment the temptation to squeeze just a little tighter than he normally would crossed his mind, but then he thought better of it. Her grip was actually strong enough for the both of them. Everyone else stood to greet her as well.

"This is my crew, Rufus, Oscar and Sunny," Mick said, as hands reached across the table to be shaken.

"Pleasure to meet you miss," Rufus said.

"The pleasure is mine," she insisted, "You all are doing us a huge favor by showing up."

"Pull up a chair I guess," Mick said, and Pallacios obliged, stealing a chair from one of the other tables nearby, and then going to the breakfast bar to load up a plate. She came back with a plate covered in modest portions of scrambled eggs, toast and a waffle topped with an assortment of berries.

Mick proceeded to stuff his face, trying to drown out the fact that she was even there as the others made small talk with her. She was actually quit pleasant to the rest of them.

She probably has a thing for Rufus, Mick thought. *I wonder if she ever managed to brown-nose her way to the top like she was trying to all those years ago?* Finally the conversation turned toward something worth his attention.

"The sample from the girl's shirt has been processed," Pallacios said after taking a swig of juice.

"What did they find?" Mick asked.

"It was blood, but these samples had a much higher white blood cell and hemoglobin count than blood from a normal human or even an animal. The white blood cell count was similar to a patient with leukemia. Also noted were much, much higher levels of iron and notable amount of bile from an unknown source. But the sample is human. Just with much higher levels of those other properties. It also had a more brownish or black color to it."

"So what is our role in this investigation going to entail?" Rufus asked as he set his glass down on the table and began to cut off a piece of his steak. Pallacios straightened in her seat and met his eyes.

"Well," She began by clearing her throat, "I dropped by the hospital around eight this morning, visited with Wendy's parents. She's been on double IV's since she was admitted. She is feeling much better now. Her parents are still kind of leery about anyone speaking to her at the moment, but she was sitting up and eating when I came in. She said she is ready to talk about what she remembers. I was going to arrange for one or two of you to speak with her later today." Mick saw her eyes drift over towards Sunny.

"Would you be willing to speak with her later this afternoon perhaps?" Pallacios asked.

"Oh definitely." Sunny replied, "Have you told her parents and her what we are?"

Pallacios nodded, "I informed them of your specialties, and how certain factors may necessitate the involvement of hunters like yourselves."

"So," Mick began, his voice exuding the same amount of enthusiasm as a dead fish, "based on what little she has said, if she was saved by this Doc character you mentioned, then is it reasonable to assume he is someone who may possibly be out looking for Morgan as well?"

Pallacios nodded at Mick as she picked up her glass for another dainty swig of juice, "Quit likely. She didn't tell us much but what we gathered was that the men who brought her to him spoke to him like they knew him."

Mick nodded, pushed his plate away. "So they know the guy, he turns on them, and returns the girl to her parents. Kind of strange, but not uncommon."

"How do you mean?" Sunny asked.

Mick leaned forward, "Sometimes it might seem more advantageous to one party to turn against their colleagues if it means they alone have a better chance of getting away with the crime. We won't know much else until we talk to the girl, but if she confirms what Pallacios just relayed, that they spoke as if they knew each other, then it's worth looking into."

"Why return the girl though?" Rufus asked. "That's what is bothering me about this whole Doc character."

Mick shrugged, and Pallacios shook her head. "Guess we won't have anything else to go on until we talk to her," Mick said.

"Should I write down notes or any other questions we might want to ask her?" Sunny asked.

"Smart girl," the Agent remarked, "That's a wonderful idea."

Sunny then pulled out her phone, and started taking down the questions Pallacios said she would need to ask. Questions ranging from, "Do you know where they kept you," and "what can you remember about—fill in the blank."

Mick rubbed his eyes, "while Sunny is out doing the interview, mind if we try and get in touch with the local hunters in the area? Find out if they know anything?"

"You're welcome to try. Our communication with them hasn't turned up any useful information as of yet, but that may have changed overnight, the way these things develop." Pallacios said as she stood from the table, and began digging out her wallet for her card to go pay for the meal she had just eaten.

When she came back, she handed Mick a card with the CNHC Foundation's address and number. It appeared they were sharing some office space with the police department down at the Denver Crime Lab.

"Got a phone call to make," Mick said, holding up the card as he got up. The others nodded, shrugged and got up for seconds.

The line rang once. Twice. Three times, and then a fourth before he heard an automated voice playing in his ear, giving him a prompt to press one for English, two for Spanish. For obvious reasons, he pressed one.

"You have reached the Counter Non-Human Coalition, Denver, Colorado, division fourteen. Please leave a message with your name, date and time of incident, location of the incident, and a brief description of the incident itself. Thank you."

There was a beep, and Mick began leaving his message, "Hi this is Mick Johnson, I'm with an independent group of hunters located in New Broken Edge, Kansas. I and my team are up here investigating with the local authorities and the FBI concerning a missing children's case with—" There was a click. Mick looked back at his phone screen. It said the call was still going.

"Counter Non-Human Coalition, this is Tiffani Mettlen, how may I help you?" A pleasant female voice asked. Mick put the phone back to his ear, "Yes, hi! My name is Mick Johnson," he rattled off almost word for word what he meant to say in his message, asking to set up an appointment to speak to any of the local hunters concerning a possible non-human link to the kidnappings and to discuss the strange blood sample.

"I'm sorry Mr. Johnson, but our director is out of the office until next Thursday. All of our available hunters are out on their own assignments and as you know, scheduling an appointment with any of our hunters has to be cleared through him first." Mettlen said, her voice still maintaining that same sweet tone.

Mick scratched his head and thought for a minute, "I understand that ma'am but I and my team are aiding in a federal investigation, and it's imperative that we be able to speak with someone about—"

"Our policies are clear Mr. Johnson. I can refer you to our website if you would like to read over them in full." She said. Her voice was starting to sound automated. No person Mick had ever known could truly maintain that exact level of sweet, sincere intonation in their voice when being challenged. She was talking again.

"If you would like I would be more than happy to forward you through to his voicemail where you can leave him a detailed message about your inquiry."

Mick caught sight of Pallacios as she walked out of the restaurant area of the hotel, shot him an indifferent glance, and walked out of the door.

Mick ignored her option, "The agent who gave me your organization's information is Della Pallacios. She said she spoke to one of your field workers prior to us coming up here. We have a lead now with some DNA evidence and we—"

There was another click. Mick looked down at his phone. The time the call had lasted displayed on the screen before it flashed away and back to the home screen. Mick cursed and shoved his phone in his pocket.

"Fuckin' hunters…" Mick grumbled as he rested his back against the wall, rubbed his eyes and then proceeded up the hallway to their room.

MAGIC TRICK

"Hi sweetheart, remember me?" Pallacios asked the girl as she sat up in her hospital bed. The girl nodded her head as she struggled to get a brush through her thick, wavy hair.

Sunny and Rufus stood in the doorway next to a police officer with short, cropped hair, and standing with his hands tucked onto his belt. She looked passed the door frame, made awkward eye contact with a woman she assumed was Wendy's mother, and smiled out of reflex. Short blond hair, with a slender build, she wore a sleeveless white button up blouse. The man who was her dad wore glasses, was a little chubby in the face but otherwise was pretty stoutly built, wore a green t-shirt with the logo of some university on it, and of all things, plaid cargo shorts.

Sunny tried not to stare but those shorts were difficult to unsee. She looked up at Rufus, who stood leaning against the doorframe, the light from the hallway glistening on his bald head. It was so different seeing him in a flesh and blood body. She remembered him clearly as the shriveled husk that stubbornly clung to life as a backup vessel for the being she had called Father. She had seen his astral form, hovering behind his old body beneath that sheet. The way his coat billowed out beneath him as he floated in the air, the fierce, hungry look he carried in his yellow eyes at the time. Hungry for the life he wanted so strongly to sap from others. Sunny had recalled doing the ritual that had bound Mick to Father, who subsequently sent out Rufus to spy on him. Even though three years had passed, when she looked down at her fair skin, or caught a glimpse of herself in the mirror, or saw Rufus standing and interacting with physical objects in the real world, it felt like waking up from a nightmare. One in which all her closest friends and family had tried to kill someone very dear to them while each served some eldritch, dark presence. Her life as a hunter had replaced her former identity. She was no longer Skylah. Skylah existed only in the nightmare. A nightmare that her brother never got to wake up from. A nightmare that she remembered whenever she looked in the mirror, remembered when she was bound to Father. It was the same face, just without the gray taint. She caught herself when she was in a room full of those still living their lives with that taint, wondering, *can he still find me?*

"You okay prima?" Rufus asked, causing her to look up at him. He was smiling but his eyes said without words that he had noticed something was on her mind. She waved him closer and leaned in to whisper in his ear, "Just caught myself remembering how crazy things were between all of us three years ago. Me, Oscar, you, all of us tasked with trying to make Mick's sanity break so Father could claim him. Now we are all on the same team, trying to help this little girl and find her friend."

Rufus snickered, "What sanity did Mick ever have?"

She smiled and punched his shoulder, "You're terrible."

Rufus nodded, "This is new?" he asked as he put his hand on her shoulder and the two walked a couple paces off to the side, close enough still so they could hear when they were called.

"Something else on your mind though?" He asked, and with that question she knew she had been caught. She nodded and ran her hands through her long blond hair.

"I hate myself for feeling like this. But sometimes when I'm around other people, and I see that they are still tainted…I know they are the people I'm fighting to protect, but I wonder if…If Father ever wanted to find me again, could he sense me through one of them?"

Rufus nodded as he listened, "Why do you hate yourself for feeling like that?"

Sunny thought for a second, "Because I don't ever want to have a mentality that is 'Us' and 'Them.' The people with the gray taint don't even know they have it. I don't ever want to treat someone different because they haven't had the taint removed."

Rufus nodded, "Prima," He said as he began. He always called her that. "I can't say I know the answer to that. I was bound to him for alotta years, and trying to understand him and how his mind worked literally caused my astral form pain. I didn't know you could feel pain in the astral realm. But apparently there, all your senses are turned up to eleven. So if he ever had the ability to do anything like that, I never knew about it. Because he shut me out most of the time. I was nothing more than another pair of eyes for him. So…does he have things in the astral realm that can see us? I know he does. Because I used to be one of them. But what helps me be more confident, is that if they can see me, I can see them too," he said, temporarily letting a flash of Light illuminate his pupils and then died down.

"But I don't think he can sense you through other human beings," he finished.

"…I hope not."

Finally they were motioned into the hospital room by the officer. The lighting in the room was very sparse with the blinds drawn. A small lamp off to the right side of the girl's bed offered some light by which to see her, though dimmed heavily by a dark lampshade.

Wendy Matthews looked up at them as they entered the room, her green eyes sizing them up. She sat with a stuffed puppy that she had pulled out of a toy bucket filled with candy from the hospital's gift shop, lovingly stroking the stuffed animal's fur. The first thing Sunny noticed about the girl was how big her eyes were. Sunny said hello to the parents when she and Rufus were introduced, and when she shook dad's hand, she knew immediately where Wendy got her eyes from. Wendy's cheeks, full and fleshy, also sat on either side of a small, delicate looking mouth. Her fingers as she stroked the stuffed dog weren't fat or pudgy, but definitely weren't slender like her mother's. She looked at Rufus apprehensively. He was the tallest one in the room after all, so Sunny guessed she would be a little intimidated by him.

"Wendy," Pallacios began, "these are two of my friends. They came all the way from New Broken Edge, Kansas to talk to you and help us find your friend Morgan." Wendy shook her head.

"Hi there," Rufus said, smiling great big. That was something else Sunny had grown to respect about the man. His smile had a way of drawing a person in. Rufus could look like he was about to knock a person's head through a brick wall, but when he smiled, it was disarming in a way she envied. It worked with Wendy though. The little girl returned his smile warmly and even extended her hand to him, which he shook gently in return. It opened her up enough for Sunny to receive the same warm smile and greeting herself.

"We've heard about what a strong little fighter you've been lately," Rufus said.

"I didn't do much fighting sir, I was just tied up the whole time," Wendy piped off, smiling wide and showing a gap in her teeth. Everyone in the room chuckled, or at least smiled at that.

"Well sweetie it sounds like you were in a really scary situation, and you held on and came out of it like a fighter. I bet you'd make a great hunter someday." Rufus said. Wendy shook her head, "Thanks."

"Are you excited to go back to school and tell all your friends?" Sunny asked.

Wendy's face fell and she shook her head, "Not without Morgan. It won't be the same if we both can't tell our friends together."

Sunny felt the floor falling out from under her so to speak. She should have thought that one through. Sunny scolded herself mentally for not thinking, trying to ignore the feeling of the eyes of girl's parent's drilling into her.

"Well I can assure you," Rufus said, "we want you to both tell your friends how you survived together. Has Agent Pallacios told you that we hunt monsters?"

Wendy nodded her head, "Oh yeah she has, and I think that's really cool! Morgan says he wants to be a hunter when he grows up! He draws pictures at lunchtime of him shooting monsters and stuff! He's really good too! But one of the teachers found it and reported him to the principle so he doesn't draw anymore." Wendy said. Rufus shook his head.

"Ah. Yes well, drawing pictures in school of monsters and shooting them might scare the other kids so I'm sure your teacher was just trying to make sure that didn't happen," Rufus said.

Wendy nodded her head, trying to show that her eyes weren't watering at the mention of her friend.

"Wendy," Rufus began, "we were wondering if…you feel comfortable trying to remember anything about the night you were rescued, would you be able to tell us?"

The little girl sat there for a little bit. Her father came and sat down in the chair next to her, stroked her hair and nodded his head, whispering to her that it was alright. Sunny watched the man comforting his daughter, and was instantly reminded of what a far cry "Father" had actually been from a true father figure.

"Do you think it was monsters who took us?" Wendy asked. Rufus shrugged, "We don't know yet. Certainly anyone who would kidnap children is a monster in their own right, but we are here in case it turns out that those who kidnapped you turn out to be monsters that aren't human."

The little girl nodded, and then closed her eyes as if trying to remember. She sat there for a while, her small mouth trembling slightly. When she opened her eyes she said, "We got taken on our way home from school. We were supposed to ride the bus that day, but Morgan said he wanted to show me the drawings he had at his house. So we both lied and told our teacher that we weren't riding the bus, and that our parents were going to pick us up. We slipped through the crowds when parents actually started showing up, cut through the playground and began walking to Morgan's house."

Rufus shook his head slowly, "Mmm. I understand," he said, "tell us what happened next."

Wendy looked around the room, her eyes landing on Sunny for a second.

"There was a van that started following us when we were half way to Morgan's house. We only had I think…seven more blocks to go. It was a big white van. The windows on the sides looked really dark. Two men got out of the van and ran toward us from down the street…" She trailed off then, as if lost in the recollection.

"Did you see their faces?" Sunny asked, chancing another go at conversation.

Wendy looked up at her and blinked, "No…I can't remember. I don't know…When they ran at us…it didn't look like running…They got out of the van…and then they had us and were loading us into the back."

"Were there any other cars around? Anyone outside their houses that tried to help you?" Sunny asked. Wendy shook her head, "I don't remember. We screamed but…" Her voice trailed off again.

"It's alright honey," her mother said, walking to the other side of the hospital bed and took her hand.

It didn't look like running…they got out of the van and then they loaded them up…but she said they ran from down the street, Sunny thought.

"They were down the street. I'm not lying. I blinked and then they were as close to us as you are now," she said, looking at Sunny with shining green eyes, moist with impending tears.

Sunny shook her head, listening carefully.

"I don't know how long they kept us. I was so thirsty. No one ever talked to me. They tied me up and left me. And my eyes were tied shut so I couldn't see a thing. I would call out for Morgan and I would hear something walking through water or something."

Rufus stepped into the conversation here, "You were in a place with water?"

She nodded, "I could hear water dripping somewhere. Whatever was there with me was walking through the water on the floor."

"Did it make any noise like a growl or something?" Rufus asked. She shook her head, "No. It was quiet except for its footsteps."

"But it sounded like normal walking?" Sunny asked.

"Yeah it did."

"What about the person who rescued you?" Rufus asked.

"Oh Doc?"

"Yeah tell us about him. What was he like?" Rufus asked.

Wendy sat there, her lips drawn in a tight line as she looked like she was trying to remember.

"I can't remember." She said, her eyes falling down to her stomach as if getting ready to be scolded.

"That's okay!" Rufus beamed, to which the little girl looked up confused. Rufus looked around at the rest of the adults in the room.

"If it's alright with all of you, I have a magic trick I would like to do. It could help us learn what she can't remember. Would you like me to try?" he asked.

Wendy vigorously shook her head yes, her eyes looking to her parents, pleading for them to agree as well.

"What all will this *magic trick* entail, exactly?" Pallacios asked.

"I'm going to read her mind," Rufus said bluntly.

"But," Wendy started, "If I can't remember, how will that help?"

Rufus smiled, "Our brains store all kinds of information. When we can't remember something, it's not that those memories are gone, it just means they got misplaced and we can't find them. Nothing is ever truly gone. Have you ever walked into a room and forgot why you went in there?" He asked.

"Oh all the time," she admitted.

"That means your thought you had about why you went in there got misplaced. What did you do to help you find it?"

She sat there for a second or two, thinking as she picked at a hangnail on her thumb.

"I leave the room and go to the room I was in before so I can remember what I was doing when I wanted to go into the other room." She said. Rufus shook his head.

"When I read your mind, I'll be looking at the memories you had before you met Doc. Maybe that will help you remember. It will be just like going into the other room to try and remember," Rufus said. Wendy shook her head, showing she understood.

To block out distractions, Rufus had Pallacios close the door to the room, extinguishing the light that poured in from out in the hallway. For good measure, he had the mother turn off the lamp that rested next to Wendy's bed. If she had been kept in the dark for the time she was missing, then making the room as dark as possible seemed fitting to help in recreating the memories. Rufus pulled up a chair next to her bed, as close as he could.

"Alright, now that the stage has been set, I want you to close your eyes, and lay back as if you were going back to sleep." He said, to which she replied with a reluctant look in her eyes.

"I don't get to see how you will do the trick?" She asked, her hopeful tone balancing on the edge of disappointment. Rufus shook his head, "For me to do the trick you have to close your eyes. That's how the magic can work. But you have to believe it will work without seeing it first. Understand?" He asked. She nodded.

"I guess I understand," she said and then leaned back into the bed, letting her head be enveloped by the large pillow. After confirming that she was comfortable, Rufus asked her to hold out her hand. She did as instructed, and he gently took her small hand into his. A thought flashed through his mind as his fingers made contact.

Have I ever held a child's hand before? He caught himself wondering. His memories of his former life seemed void of any recollection he had of ever holding a small hand like this. Most of his memories involved the last three years of his new life, along with the hellish landscape of the astral realm he had dwelt in for the years prior to his body withering to a husk.

He remembered feeding off of the lesser beings that populated the small corner of the astral realm he inhabited all those years. The things his former master had once called "Little Outsiders." Lesser spirits that fed off of the energies of hate, despair, lust and greed, to name a few. The imps made for a quick snack but never compared to the life force drawn from an unsuspecting human. His time spent on the astral plane was also filled with learning how to, on occasion, push a random individual out of their body and take control. Full on possession. At times he caught himself wondering why Father hadn't just made him do that with Mick. But he supposed the eldritch being's plans involved Mick riding shotgun after Father had grabbed the wheel. He shook the recollection from his mind, returning to the here and now.

"Now," Rufus said, his voice gentle, "do you feel like your body is getting heavy? Feel it in your arms, your chest, in your stomach?"

"Yeah," She said.

He nodded, "Great. Now, from here on out, you don't have to do anything. I just need you to keep relaxing, and remember that day. Anytime it starts to get too scary, just squeeze my hand." He said.

With those words, Rufus sank deeper into his own chair, closed his eyes, and as time passed, he allowed a tingling to ripple across his skin. It didn't take him long to reach that state.

"Wendy?" He asked.

"Hmm?" She responded.

"No matter what happens, I'm right here." He said.

WENDY'S STORY

He felt a drip of freezing water splash down onto his bald head. His eyes protested against the tightly bound cloth he felt pressed against his own eyes. Rufus went to move his hands and feet, only to realize they had been bound to something cold and metallic, with a little padding but nothing more.

There was a constant dripping off in the distance that was beginning to drive him mad as an overwhelming realization started to dawn on him—he was thirsty. The insides of his mouth felt like the cracked and parched ground of a land without rain. An image of a dessert floor, deprived of any moisture arose in his mind as he opened his mouth to try and speak.

"Is anybody there?!" He squeaked in a little girl's voice. It was Wendy's. He heard nothing in reply, save for the feint sounds of footsteps sloshing through ankle deep water somewhere off in the distance. Several long moments passed in perpetual stillness, with the only break in the monotony of silence being the trickle and dripping of water onto whatever the floor was made of.

His skin was alive with the sensation of a stale, unmoving icy chill as he shivered there in what he assumed was a chair. It seemed to rock back and forth with his weight when he tried in vain to break through his restraints. Might have been a wheelchair.

"Let's take this off shall we?" A voice said behind him, causing him to jump. It had been so long since he had heard those sloshing footsteps. He hadn't even heard anyone come up behind him. He could feel hands working vigorously behind his head to untie the knot in the cloth that bound his eyes shut. Once it was off, he tried to blink away the colors that kept pressing themselves up against his retinas. But his eyes snapped shut when he heard a sharp click of a flashlight, and felt a hot beam of bright light flood into his eyes, overwhelming them with its radiance. There was laughter exploding all around him, echoing off of the surfaces of whatever this place was. Three separate voices. He instinctively wanted to reach his hands up to shield his ears from the barrage of sounds that assaulted his ear drums, but his hands were stopped short by the restraints.

"That light at the end of the tunnel's not Heaven baby girl," a voice hissed from somewhere. He could feel the chair he was in gliding forward smoothly as one of the laughing voices slipped behind him and started to push. So his idea about the wheelchair was correct at least. They were mocking him. He protested, asked them questions that were only answered by more mocking laughter and the continuous molestation of his eyes by that damned flashlight beam. Suddenly a question he felt himself asking was answered.

"It's not what we want with you. It's what he wants with you," one of the three voices said.

What he wants with you, Rufus thought in his mind. He jumped on that one.

"W-what does t-that mean?" He pleaded, and each word he said drained him of any strength he might have had. He felt like his vocal chords had been soaked in salt when he tried to speak.

"You better pray for your sake that he likes you. You wanna know what we do to the ones he doesn't like?" Another voice replied harshly next to his ear. He felt something slick and wet slide up the contour of one of his ears and he flinched, every muscle in his body convulsing at the touch of whatever had just violated his ear.

He suddenly felt the wheelchair he was in being lifted from the ground. He fought to control his breathing, fought to filter out the smell of whatever was coming up the stairs to choke him. It was a smell he recognized, had smelled often when the hunt took him to the gore ridden lair of whatever monstrosity that plagued the people of the world. The smell was suffocating him as it insisted on being breathed in. Through all of this, the urge to keep his eyes closed was fueled by the beam from that damn flashlight. How satisfying it would have been to rip free from his restraints, relieve the person from their flashlight and pummel their faces with it until their skulls caved inward. The tingle of energy on his skin reminded him of where he really was. The way reality operated on the astral plane was fluid and oftentimes, nonsensical. If he wanted to alter the girl's memories by tearing out of the restraints and doing just what he had thought previously, he could easily do it. But that would defeat the purpose of trying to learn what had truly happened. He played along, keeping his eyes shut as the bastard with the flashlight continued to taunt him with it. Eventually they had reached the bottom of whatever staircase they had gone down, and there was the sound of a door opening. He felt himself being wheeled along the ground and the glow of some other source of light from somewhere else.

"Here ya go Doc. Ya think he'll like this one?"

Bingo!

There was no response for a while, although he did hear the sound of footsteps turning as the one being addressed acknowledged those who had brought him in. He felt a gloved hand touching him, inspecting him, turning his face from side to side. From the second the hand touched his skin, something inside of Rufus reeled against his guts like a viper coiled up to strike defensively. Something instinctual, primal, something that warned him to flee. He fought against the urge to tear his restraints off, blast his way out of here by whatever means he could manifest, and return to his body.

But the only problem with doing his magic "trick" with Wendy, was that if he left her here, she would be trapped, unable to return to her own body, and left to suffer whatever altered course of events his meddling would have caused to happen here in this place. Put simply, her body would slip into a coma. They were both reliving this night, the two of them as one entity, she being the vehicle and driver to Rufus's passenger. And Rufus knew that an unstable passenger could still pose a fatal threat to the driver. He hadn't pushed her out of her body, but was sharing it with her. He steadied his frantically beating heart, the one he was sharing with Wendy, and just as the gloved hand left his face for the last time, the primal instinct to tear loose and flee left him.

"Well?" Came one of the voices from behind him, the speaker's tone annoyed. Rufus felt Wendy flinch as he heard three distinct metal pops, followed by what sounded like shell casings hitting the ground. He felt something wet and warm spray him in the back of the head, the side of his face, and the back of his shirt. The three behind him fell hard, the impact of each body hitting the ground sending a shockwave of vibration that he could feel up through the floor.

Time seemed to stand still. There was dust mingling with the stench of the blood, which smelled fresh, and it made Rufus nauseous to try and breathe too deep.

"Where do you live?" A gravelly voice asked, breaking the silence like a hammer through a glass table.

Rufus could feel himself beginning to shake uncontrollably again as the primordial fingers of hysteria tried to wrap themselves around his throat, like the tentacles of some dark beast from the depths of the earth. He felt them dragging him under, and he felt his muscles tighten against his restraints as he began to yank against them.

"Where do you live?!" the voice snapped, jarring Rufus back to rationality. He stopped tugging on the restraints, mortified at what he almost tried to do. He swore he almost felt the restraints nearly give with the force of his muscles as he pulled against them.

He had nearly done what he couldn't afford to do. He felt words springing to his mouth, leaping off his tongue. An address. Wendy's address. The click of a knife. After another brief moment of panic, they were free. He tried to open his eyes against the light that was streaming into his eyes from somewhere.

He saw as he clung to the sides of the wheelchair, three male figures, each laying in a pool of their own blood. He snapped them shut against the light that was hanging above his head. He guessed from the humming it was a florescent that was about to quite. Still, he strained against the unpleasant glow, to try and see more. That smell was coming from somewhere, and it had been present before the people who had brought him down here were shot.

The room they were in was a wide open area with walls that had rusted dark shades of red and brown. If Rufus had to make a rough guess, the room looked to be about twenty by forty feet. He could see the stairs they had come down. The upper ceiling was bordered by a catwalk, from which many chains and pulley systems were attached via crane arms, all operated by control panels on various places on the rusted walls. But it was what hung from those chains that caused Rufus's stomach to turn, and his blood to boil.

Hanging upside down, bound by their feet, were the bodies of six different children, three boys and three girls, their wrists splayed open and their throats cut, with their blood being collected in new, sterilized fifty gallon drums. Each of them, bled dry and left to hang like discarded scraps of meat, their faces sagging in dull expressionless masks that looked like they were nothing more than plastic store mannequins. Their eyes, though sunken and lifeless, still demanded his attention. He imagined for a moment how vibrantly bright their eyes might have been when they were alive. He tore his gaze away, snapped his eyes shut once more as he tried to calm their breathing, to try and get control of his thoughts. Any strong feelings he had here, could potentially alter the surroundings. It was bad enough he had almost tried to fight his way out of here and scramble Wendy's memories. Not only that, but however Wendy felt about the Doc in her subconscious would cause this memory version of him to be that much stronger than Rufus was ready for. He was experiencing all of this behind the eyes of a terrified little girl, who no doubt viewed the Doc as holding the power over her life or her death. Rufus could not take him on here. Plus, he couldn't handle it if one of those hanging children decided to smile at him in response to his rising dread.

A feint popping sound was heard, followed by a steady trickling noise as Rufus looked over in the direction of the noise. A figure he presumed to be the Doc stood over the three bodies, pouring something over each of them from a clear, industrial grade gallon jug. The gloves he wore looked like those worn by roofers and construction workers. He looked to be about five feet, eleven inches tall. He was built like an athlete, like an Olympic swimmer or track runner. His jacket was smeared and stained with God only knew what, and a hood pulled up and obscured the back of his head from being able to make out anything further. The acrid stench that wafted off of the three bodies reached up Rufus's nose, down his throat, and caused his chest to react in a violent coughing fit.

"What…are you doing?" He felt himself asking, as Wendy's voice came out of his mouth between coughs.

"I'm melting the bodies." The figure replied without looking back.

"You're what?!"

He watched in fascination as the Doc did his work, emptying out the rest of the container's contents on the remains, stepping around them to thoroughly coat them in the concoction but never stepping around them in a way that revealed his face.

"Can you walk?" the figure asked, still not turning.

"I think so," he said, feeling his eyes close against his will just as the figure was starting to turn.

"Take my hand. I'll lead you out of here and get you back home." After grasping the gloved hand once more, and steeling himself against the urge to tear his own hand off and flee from this figure who was evoking such feelings of primal terror, he took one labored step forward. Then another. More slow and tedious steps ensued, each one demanding strength that he didn't have.

"Can you open your eyes?" The Doc asked.

"No," he lied.

"Good."

RUDE AWAKENING

Rufus caught himself sneaking glances here and there at their surroundings as they ascended the metal labyrinth Wendy had been kept in. Graffiti and rust marred nearly every inch of the metal walls. Pieces of trash of all different shapes, size and faded color littered every path they took. Rufus had lost count of how many sets of metal, double doors they had passed through, and the many sets of tightly winding metal staircases leading up and up. Some mesh catwalks that nearly caused his heart to drop into his stomach loomed up ahead, and he knew for a fact they were going to have to walk across them.

Once they were finally outside, Rufus felt he could fully open his eyes. The night sky above was a dark blue, filled with stars and minor cloud cover. He looked back and around at his new, outdoor surroundings. Steep hills rose up on either side and behind where they had just exited. They had walked through a gate, built into the side of the steep hill behind them, and again covered with graffiti. Other than that, from what he could ascertain, they were out in the country. They walked passed a circular concrete platform, which finally told Rufus the clue he was needing. He remembered reading about places like these.

There was a vehicle parked close to a path which he could see from here, leading off to the main road. A very nondescript clunker of a car, other than a baby blue hood to stick out like a sore thumb from the rest of the car's flaking, sun bleached, used-to-be-dark-brown-or-maroon exterior. Looked like an old Buick from the late nineties or early two thousands.

"Where are we?" He heard himself ask in the little girl's voice.

"You can't see. It doesn't matter." The Doc answered. Suddenly Rufus felt dizzy, and one of his steps, which weren't that stable to begin with, faltered. If it hadn't been for the Doc's firm grasp on his arm, he would have went face first into the dirt and stickers. But the Doc's grip was like an iron vice. He was yanked back up onto his feet, and heard a deep voice in his head.

Go to sleep now little one. I will carry you.

The sharp, piercing howl of a child's vocal chords threw him back into his body. The jarring transition from the astral plane which mimicked the countryside outside of Denver, back into his body that rested in his chair caused him to almost flail in his seat. He sat up, eyes wide as the hysterical faces of Wendy's parents and Agent Pallacios drilled him with contempt.

"What the hell did you do to her?!" The dad roared as he stood up, sliding his chair across the floor with his motion. Rufus, still fighting off the disorienting feeling of the transition, stood up on unsteady legs. He still felt like they were jelly, and almost dropped to one knee, but Sunny braced herself up against him in time.

"Sir, just remain calm," Pallacios was saying, trying to calm the father down as two nurses and a security guard exploded into the already cramped room. The officer with the red face walked over to Rufus and Sunny, and with a nod and a very stern voice told them in no uncertain terms it was time to leave. Rufus looked back at the wailing girl in the hospital bed, and suddenly it hit him. He knew they were sharing a mind during the experience. And so, consequently, whatever he saw, she saw too. She could have very well recognized some of those kids that were chained upside down, their blood being collected in the drums beneath them.

"One of t-them…smiled at me!" She shrieked. The mother was holding Wendy's shaking body to her chest, rocking her back and forth, reassuring her.

As they were both escorted down the hallway to the elevator, he turned and looked at the officer, "They were keeping her in the Titan Missile Silo. There are other kids there," Rufus breathed out, and the strength it took to say those words left him feeling just as withered as he was when he lived in a rotten recliner, draped beneath a sheet.

NOT A MONSTER

The boy's eyes snapped open with a start, his limbs feeling electrified as he sprang up off of the cold, thinly carpeted floor. He looked around, his frantic eyes scanning his surroundings that had again changed for the third time since the day he and his friend Wendy had been taken. Ice cold sweat and dust clung to his skin. Morgan's trembling hands shook with tension as he eyed the paintings of happy cartoon animals that were painted across the top of each wall in what appeared to be an abandoned classroom, devoid of any desks or chairs. A cartoon baby deer that looked like Bambi was among them. Others were present, an antelope, a bear, a clumsily dancing elephant, to name a few. On one of the old, green chalkboards, he saw words written, which at once made him feel nostalgic. The words on the chalkboard read, *Line Leaders—Rose, & Bruce. Messengers—David, & Richard. Bathroom M—* and the rest had been smudged away. He had been a messenger at school the day they had been taken, running notes down to the office for his teacher, Mrs. Weatherwax. Yet the words reignited a creeping dread. The stillness of the room felt uncanny, as if he had awoken into the start of a nightmare. It felt so untouched, as if this place had been abandoned and left in its natural state to decay in its rawest form. Still and silent. The setting his nightmares usually happened in.

The dread that kept gnawing at the base of his brain only released him from its suffocating grip whenever his captors caused him to fall asleep. He wasn't sure what it was they did that caused him to go down, only that there was some kind of smell involved that he had never smelled before.

The gray brick walls were dimly illuminated by the rays from the sun that shown through the windows above him to his left, some with the blinds drawn, while still others allowed for him to see the clear blue of the sky. His eyes landed on the analog wall clock that was lying on the floor over in a corner, and he went over to inspect it. The clock read twelve forty one, but Morgan quickly realized that was the time it had stopped. The wall behind him showed a different kind of dancing animal. The Cat in the Hat was painted on that wall, next to the numbers 0–9, along with a mural of the Hungry Little Caterpillar.

He went over to one of the doors and tried the knob. It jiggled a little in his grasp, but otherwise was stuck firm. He ran a hand over the top of his head, feeling the dust as it made his short, dark hair feel coarse and rough. His hand came away slightly damp, covered in dust and flacks of what looked like drywall.

"What would those hunters in the video we watched at school do?" He wondered aloud to himself, suddenly remembering the folded up piece of paper he had in his pocket the day they were taken. He felt the ferocious pounding in his heart slow down to a manageable, quick paced throb when his fingers pulled out the folded up drawing. He had shown Wendy this one, and had another at his house he had meant to bring but had forgotten. He felt his hand close around the drawing in a fist as an overwhelming swell of rage began to bubble up through him, threatening to spill out of his eyes.

It's my fault...If I hadn't forgotten that drawing...If I had just waited to show her the next day at school, then we could have just rode the bus, and we wouldn't have got taken, and she— He stopped himself short as he doubled over and hugged his knees close to his chest. He had called out to her once already. He didn't dare call out to her now. The fact she never responded sent stabbing waves of guilt through him, thoughts of what they might have done to her, and all because of his eagerness to show her a stupid drawing he had made the night before school.

He wasn't sure how long he sat there, hugging his knees closer to himself as the minutes ticked on by. All he knew was that right now, sitting here in this abandoned classroom, he was beginning to fall apart. When they were nabbed off the street, he remembered punching one of the men in the jaw. He had been in fight mode every time when he was conscious, up until now. While trying to stay calm, he occupied himself with trying to remember his captors' faces, but his pursuits were unfruitful. But he remembered that they weren't wearing masks!

He finally unclenched his fist around the lined notebook page he had drawn on, and loosened his grip on his legs. He unfolded the paper, to see the drawing he had shown to his friend that day—was now altered.

He threw back the piece of paper, starring at it in horror as he tried to comprehend the new additions that had been made to his work. It had been a drawing of him, wielding a chainsaw, its blade chewing through a demonic looking form with large bat wings and the face of a spider, but with an otherwise humanoid body. He had redrawn it three times, to get the gore just the way he wanted it. But now…His face in the drawing now had a mouth full of jagged fangs, dripping with red ink. The eyes of the drawn portrayal of his likeness were now blacked out entirely with black ink.

"You don't like it?" A voice asked from behind, causing him to reflexively make a fist, as he shot up onto his feet and turned to face the source of the voice. A man was standing in the shadows of the doorway he had tried to open earlier. A thick, distinct stench followed in the wake of the voice, which smelled of sweat, blood and rotten eggs. Morgan could barely make out any features on the man's face, but his silhouette nearly rooted him to the floor, his blood pumping through him like frozen tar.

He was so tall Morgan could only see his chin, the rest of his head and face obscured as the doorframe revealed nothing except the bottom half of his face. The man's skin on his longer than usual arms looked pallid and leathery. The fingers on one hand curled in all different directions, making his hand look more like a deformed animal paw with wild, unruly claws that twisted and bent at angles none were meant to go. His rail thin build, clothed in nothing but a greasy sleeveless t-shirt and overalls, was as thin as a fence post in Morgan's mind to an almost cartoonish extent. He watched the figure as it stood there in the doorway, watching its bottom lip twitch.

"Why don't you like?" It asked again. Morgan looked down at the picture, his eyes boiling over with tears.

"Who are you?" Morgan asked, gritting his teeth. The figure just stood there, the bottom half of that face as solid as steel. The man didn't answer the question, but just stood there, silent as a statue while his bottom lip kept twitching.

"I thought you would like it," the man's voice seeped out into his ears as he stretched out his deformed hand toward the drawing on the ground.

"I'm not a monster!" Morgan yelled, his voice squeaking as his voice rose in volume on the word monster.

"The Collector thinks so."

Before Morgan could even think to ask who the Collector was, a small noise off to his left caused him to briefly break his eyes away from the man. There was another door he hadn't seen before. Off to his right. In that moment he couldn't think if he actually had seen it or if he had just assumed it was a closet if he had. But something had made a noise over by that door. He found his strength and tore his feet free from the spot on the ground he had been frozen to. His legs throbbed with the surge of energy as he pushed his way toward the door, cutting through the air with his feet faster than he remembered ever being able to. He heard movement from behind him just as his fingers touched the brass knob of the door, and in that split second, he felt the knob turning full circle.

Click.

He flung the door wide open and burst forward out into a dimly lit linoleum tiled hallway. He could feel the heavy, rhythmic thud of each footstep from the man, or thing as it pounded its way toward him. There were other rooms across the hall from the door he had just burst out of. Instead he bolted to his left, into the dark and nearly tripped when his foot smashed into a short set of stairs. He cried out more out of instinct than pain as he hurled himself up the stairs, ignoring the burning throb in the toes of his right foot. He could see a tall, gangly outline of something out of the corner of his eye as he pushed forward, now beginning to truly feel the near-crippling sting in his toes.

"The Collector will choose you!" The man's voice rode the walls to catch up with him as he ran blindly into another immensely long hallway. There were lockers and coat hooks hanging on either side. He could see some light coming from up ahead to his right. He hurled himself forward. As if running through a nightmare, his legs stiff with taut nerves as his bones and joints felt the impact of his steps. The piercing hot jabs of agony from his toes that were consuming his foot and shooting up his ankle. He rounded the corner and willed his foot to cooperate with him. There not ten yards away from him was a set of double doors, light pouring in through the window panes in either of them. He forced himself to move toward it. The ground shattering thumps of his pursuer were less rhythmic now, as if he had actually managed to shake him loose, if only for a precious few seconds.

His hands gripped the brass bars of the door handles, feeling his imminent freedom at hand—until they wouldn't budge. He cried out, his voice cracking as he shook with hot anger and primal, paralyzing hysteria. He shook the bars on those double doors, and looked out of one of the window panes. His heart leapt within his chest. A small dog, maybe a cocker spaniel, was barking at the double doors from the sidewalk. It was on a leash, and at the other end of the leash, was a woman dressed in workout clothes, cursing at the dog and trying to get it to rejoin her in her run.

Morgan slapped his hand flat against the glass, screaming for the woman's attention. He slapped the glass harder, not feeling any pain now, pure adrenaline pulsing through his limbs. The woman from the sidewalk was startled by the commotion as Morgan threw himself against the doors, shrieked, yelled and beat on the glass. It was working. She had her phone out and was dialing a number, running up onto the lawn of the school, up the concrete porch and to the window, her other hand wrapping around the door handles from her side.

The woman's voice was muffled as it tried to penetrate the glass. He couldn't make out what she was trying to say. The only thing Morgan could even begin to try and decipher as he frantically tried to read her lips were something like, "going to be okay." He then saw the woman's eyes widen as she broke eye contact, and she yelled something Morgan couldn't make out. She was looking *behind* him.

Rosedale Elementary—built in the early nineteen twenties, and had closed down in 2005 due to budget cuts. Today, it had also been the place where a witness claimed to have briefly interacted with a boy that matched the description of the one who went missing recently on the news—Around nine years of age, of African descent, brown eyes, slender build. The boy was pulled back into the shadows by an inhuman looking clawed hand that covered his face. Mick and the rest of the hunters had responded to threats in abandoned buildings before, interviewing witnesses about what they saw on the property, going over blueprints, dealing with property managers and so on. Tonight as the sun began to dip below the horizon and the sky was bathed liberally in purple orange light in the distance, none of those procedures mattered. Morgan had been spotted in that building, and the witness said she had tried to comfort him through a pane of glass as she dialed 911. There was no time to ascertain what the NHT (Non-Human-Threat) was, especially only going by the witness's description of a single body part. A huge, inhuman, clawed hand really didn't narrow it down that much.

As the hunters sped toward the school building in the caravan of law enforcement vehicles flashing their lights, Mick's hand's gripped his seat belt tightly. When he wasn't doing that, he found himself checking the magazine of his side arm, making sure he was at a full clip. He patted the pockets on his vest and belt, taking stock of the first aid supplies, twine, salt, holy oil, lock picks, batteries, matches and extra ammo housed within each pocket. He sometimes wondered why they even needed batteries and matches when they could see in the dark, but he knew there was always a use for such things. Spending a few years in Boy Scouts growing up had served him well, especially as a hunter. One could never afford to not be prepared when dealing with something that could potentially dismantle your rib cage with its jaws, or burrow into your spleen, or possess you and make you run in front of a bus. Not knowing what they would be dealing with was eating at him, but that paled in comparison to the blood that was boiling with hot adrenaline in his veins. He was glad that Morgan had turned up so soon after they arrived. Getting them returned safely to their parents was the reason why they were here.

Stop lying to yourself. You're here because Pallacios has you by the nut hairs! He reminded himself. He closed his eyes and rested his head against the headrest. After Morgan was returned home safely, then what would happen? His mind drifted back to the knowledge that he had video proof of that night, which would have nearly gone down in history as the second massacre of his city, on his phone. He felt his insides shudder as an anxious wave trembled up from his belly, into his lungs, and settled at the base of his skull. That was her leverage against him. He tightened his fist to the point he felt his knuckles crack. The audacity of that bitch. Blackmailing him into helping was unnecessary. She had their involvement the second she said it was a missing children's case, regardless of any paranormal involvement or not.

Ultimately, he had been the one to take the saw to the city's throat that night. He couldn't rely on the fact that his intentions at the time were to save his friend, who had probably already been dead before Mick had any choice presented to him. The whole thing made Mick wish she would just slap the cuffs on him and call it done, and leave everyone else out of it.

"How's everybody feelin'?" Rufus barked as he looked up from the road into his rearview mirror at Sunny and Oscar.

"Feelin' good!" Oscar said, his eyes shining in the dim light of the back seat. Sunny smiled and flashed a peace sign, and then returned her gaze out of the window, resuming her nervous ritual of rubbing her arms, something Mick noticed she did every time they went out.

"Anxious," Mick said, absent mindedly, "I don't like going into these kinds of situations without having an idea of what it is we're supposed to detain or kill."

Rufus shook his head, "No one does. But those are the ones that test what you're made of and make you grow."

Mick looked over at Rufus, "Nope. Still short." He said, picking his heels off the floor boards and pretending to swing them back and forth.

Rufus chuckled as he brought the van around the corner of the school, parked it alongside the police truck Pallacios was riding in, and everyone piled out, boots hitting the ground in rapid succession.

The school loomed up ahead, a two story Victorian style building roughly the size of a city block. The brick face of the school, beaten and ravaged by the elements, was an amalgamation of earthen brown, and on rare occasion, a dingy yellow. The Victorian style archways caused the various sets of double doors around the building to seem out of place, their modern dullness at contrast with the vintage designs they were set in.

"Johnson!" Pallacios barked, causing him to grimace. She was striding up toward him, the bold reflective FBI letters on her vest reflecting light from the police cruisers.

"Chop chop!" She shouted, clapping her hands together, like he was a dog. Mick felt the acidic torrent of profanity that was about to rage out of him, saw her face make impact with the backside of his hand—but the fantasies were soon cut off by a hurried pat on the shoulder.

"Come on. Don't let her get to you." Rufus said as Mick felt his strong hand guiding him away and toward the school.

"Did she really just stop me to…tell me to do something I was already doing?" Mick seethed. Rufus zipped up his black leather biker jacket with the red strips that ran across the shoulders and down the sleeves, checked his gear, and nodded, "Sounds like she did." He slapped Mick across the shoulders, "Time to work!"

SEARCH AND RESCUE

A pair of bolt cutters made quick work of the padlock on the back door, decorated with the usual 'ATTENTION: NO TRESPASSING' sign that was peeling off. The hunters took point upon entering the building, with the police taking up the rear behind them.

Under more customary circumstances, they would be scouting around the building from the sidewalk or from across the street, using their Higher Sight to see any foul energies, or something that would give them a clue as to what was making the building its lair. Time didn't grant for any such preparation this time. Not when a kid's life was at stake.

The cops would look for Morgan while the hunters looked for whatever possible non-human threat was still holed up in the building, with both teams splitting off to cover more ground. If one team ran into the other's target objective, then they would contact each other through the wireless communicators each of them had planted in their right ear.

Mick went in behind Rufus, his pistol out and held up by his ear, and when he stepped across the threshold, he immediately felt the constricting, invisible fingers of his old friend, Claustrophobia, squeezing around his lungs.

The stairs descended into a confining boiler room, which stretched into a narrow basement hallway of gray brick, the only source of expansion on either side of the route being various storage rooms. Mick felt his heart thrashing in his chest like a rabid animal. He brought one hand up and slapped at his face a couple times, and began to count down under his breath from one hundred. A little part of his brain was starting to act up, the one that constantly begged to know why he had joined up with these people. Nearly every job they took ended up with them delving into some kind of crowded, cluttered, narrow space to exterminate something that could easily snuff his lights out. Every time he faced down the abundantly toothy maw of some other worldly horror, he was counting on it to rip him to shreds quickly. In Mick's mind it was much more merciful than suffocating, or gradually being crushed by walls that got narrower by the centimeter with no way to escape. Getting his neck snapped or his head bit off would be a far more desirable way to go.

"Ninety three, ninety two, ninety one," he breathed out softly, feeling his nerves begin to steady once more. He didn't care that the others might hear him. They had been on enough missions together for them to know why he needed such a mechanism. Something he always had to remind himself mentally of, was that every room, no matter how cramped it felt, was always bigger than it looked.

The police split off from the hunters, hurrying up the stairs to the first floor in single file with their weapons out and trained on the ground off to the side.

Mick steadied himself, listening to the ghost-quiet basement as his team moved through the tarry darkness. He forced the Light out into his extremities, feeling the energy burble and lap at the inside of his body, tingling up his throat and pricking his retinal nerves like needles. Mick watched the Light burn the darkness away at its edges, chasing it down the hallway. But with the darkness blotted out, Mick could now see with more defining clarity the tight corners, the low ceiling where rusted piping ran over head. The doorways that seemed just large enough for one to step through while having to duck. His legs became noodles and his tongue felt like a bristly sponge while his stomach did a backflip. Rufus was turning to have a look in the first room up ahead to his left. Sunny went in after him, followed by Oscar. Mick pressed his hand against the doorframe, forcing himself through the cramped doorway. This room looked much bigger than Mick originally thought. Isles of steel wracks ran down the length of the room, each shelf holding some container with a non-flammable label of some kind. They each took an isle, inspecting the length of the steel wracks and looking in corners for any sign of—

"What was that?" Oscar whispered as everyone froze. Immediately Mick felt exposed. He was standing in the middle of the isle that was right in line with the door way. He ducted behind the isle close to Oscar and trained his pistol on the door, waiting.

"I heard it too," Sunny whispered. Mick inclined his ear toward the doorway, trying to listen for what his werewolf companion had picked up. The same chilling silence that had brushed through his ears upon entering greeted him.

"What did you hear?" Rufus whispered.

"Breathing." Oscar replied.

"You smell anything?" Mick asked. Oscar nodded, his face looking queasy, "smells like rotten meat."

"Oscar, take point," Rufus instructed, nodding his head up toward the door. Oscar nodded, his pistol at the ready. Mick watched as he sniffed the air again, and then he saw Oscar nod over his shoulder for them to follow. With each step, Mick's muscles grew tighter, the tendons stretched taut like twine.

As they emerged from the mouth of the basement and out into the first floor, Mick could breathe a little easier. His nose filled with the stale scent of settled dust. The archways of the doors were curved, with a small staircase off to their left. The linoleum tiles in the wall, made to look like bricks, were dull, their features as blunt as a wooden spoon. A circular mural of children's faces adorned the wall to their right, the point of view shown from above as if each child were lying in the grass, looking up at the painter and arranged in a circle. The words, "Flowers of one garden," were painted next to the mural in English, Spanish and another language Mick couldn't recognize. A hanging white domed glass light fixture with chipped gold plated trim was over the door directly ahead of them.

Then as if he had walked through a wall of fog and into another realm devoid of all senses but smell, the stench of spoiled meat, drowning in blood raped his nostrils and lungs, stinging his eyes as he fought the urge to cough. The smell was so overpowering now that Mick's eyes were watering. He saw Oscar raise a hand to signal stop and they all listened. Mick heard the sounds of a quiet thud playing through his ears, growing more distant down the corridor to their right. He heard the feint sound of commands being issued, code talk and the occasional static reply over a radio.

Mick saw the back of Oscar's head twitch and a low growl bubbled up from within him. "It's on the second floor," his voice dropping nearly an entire octave. Oscar turned toward the short staircase, leading them at a hurried pace as his ears began to prick up. Up the small staircase they went, leaving behind the residual sounds of police officers clearing the administration office behind them. It was not the true second floor of the building, just enough to elevate them another four feet or so. Mick inhaled a sharp breath in through his mouth, fortifying himself against the mortifying smell, and followed his fellow hunters deeper into the darkness.

THE SIRE'S SONG

A sprawling hall stretched before them. Between the doors that lined the walls on either side, were shelves to stash books, and hooks mounted into the wall to hang coats. Mick steadied his breathing as best he could, his electrified nerves coiling tighter and tighter as his hand gripped his pistol. He noticed this was happening and resumed counting down from where he had left off.

53, 52, 51, 50, and soon, once he reached the number thirty nine, he felt his hands beginning to relax. They were reaching the end of the hallway, approaching the staircase that would take them upstairs to the second floor. Suddenly Oscar turned around, his eyes not channeling the radiant white of the Reclaimed, but shining a deep reflective gold.

"What's wrong boy?" Mick joked, relying on their chemistry as hunting buddies and more or less family to save him if Oscar found the joke distasteful. He didn't seem to notice though.

"In case we get boxed in, shouldn't we switch to our machetes?" Oscar asked. Mick looked back at Rufus, who was nodding his head, "That's not a bad idea. Can't risk shooting each other," he said as he slid his sidearm into his shoulder holster and withdrew the twenty four inch blade out of the sheath on his back.

"Sunny," Rufus began, "Since you're the one with the bow, and we all trust your aim, stay behind a little ways. If the thing flees, you can bring it down, or at least wound it. But if we get caught in a melee fight I would rather you have some distance between it and you."

Sunny nodded.

Mick holstered his sidearm and withdrew his machete from its place on his belt, feeling the heat from the Light pulse through his gloved hands and into the handle. He watched as the energy traveled up the length of the blade with a sizzling hiss, transmuting it into the same stuff he had flowing through his veins. The process was repeated with the blades the others carried, a choir of hissing, illuminous blades that lit up the darkness of the staircase.

The stone silence of the hallway they emerged into was near absolute had it not been for the creaking of their boots, the rustle of their protective gear as it brushed up against their bodies and on occasion each other. Really Oscar was the only one not making a single noise, his face set in the direction of the thing's scent. Mick thought he caught the yellowed glint of claws at the tips of his fingers, but he kept his eyes forward as they went on, not stopping to check the rooms they snuck passed. Oscar knew where the source of this choking stench was hiding. As they neared a room on their left with the door slightly ajar, Mick began to hear a sound that made his stomach reel. Wet, slapping sounds, caused his face to twist up in disgust. The incessant slurping and gulping of a greedy mouth, lips and tongue guzzling large quantities of something thick and wet.

There was a voice mingling with the sounds also, between gulps, the words crafting themselves into a melody Mick recognized from his childhood.

"Sire loves me…this I know," the voice sang between draughts, "for his blood tells me so…from his veins I drink in life. He sustains me…at his side."

The incessant melody kept up as they drew closer, "Yes, Sire loves me. Yes, Sire loves me. Yes, Sire loves me…" Mick swallowed as his mouth went dry when the gulping resumed.

"His blood tells me so…"

The voice sounded more or less human. Oscar held up a hand and crept forward, his face set hard against the direction of the noise. Mick watched him as he drew nearer towards that door, his movements deliberate and full of intent.

His eyes flashed in their direction and he waved them over. Mick and Rufus, with Sunny staying behind them a ways to give them room, all approached. There inside of the room, on their knees, was what looked like a man. A tall, undernourished, nearly skeletal man, wearing overalls and a sleeveless t-shirt. The man was on his knees, looking like he was drinking from…Mick couldn't see from this vantage point. He couldn't tell what it was, only that it was a fairly cylindrical object.

Oh my God! Mick thought as he shifted his weight to try and see around the top of Oscar's head. The cylindrical object was connected to something that moved independently on its own at a joint. Mick could now clearly see, with the addition of fingers that balled up to make a fist, this man was slurping blood from someone's forearm. He watched transfixed as the man gripped the arm even tighter with an object that resembled a mess of tangled digits there in the dark. When one of them flexed, that's when Mick realized it was the man's own hand. With the man's good hand, he laced his fingers through those of the one he was drinking from and moaned.

"Go!" He heard Rufus whisper. The sudden crash that Oscar made as his foot kicked the door all the way open startled him. Mick's eyes adjusted as the Higher Sight, revealing the blood covered, rail thin face of the man that had been drinking blood from someone's arm. The gaunt face stretched unnaturally as the man let out a shrill scream that reverberated deep down Mick's ears. Oscar reached him first, swiping at him with his machete, glowing blade whizzing through the air to make contact. The man bent himself completely over backward, crab-crawl style, and scurried away through a door to an adjoining classroom on all fours like a blur.

Oscar growled, and this time Mick saw the muscles bulging in his arms, as he dashed off after the thing Mick thought was a man. Rufus dashed passed Mick, his blade cutting a swath through the darkness, as Mick took a second glance back over his shoulder.

Where was the arm?! There was someone else in here! Mick thought as he took one final look over his shoulder, seeing that indeed, he was the only other one in the room.

"Sunny it's heading into an adjacent classroom further up the hall," Mick relayed as he charged through the room, following the sounds of doors crashing in on themselves, shrieking and growling.

"I see them!" Her voice came back into his ear piece. Mick crashed through the main doorway to the classroom he was currently in, out into the hallway and came out next to Sunny as she had an arrow knocked as Rufus and Oscar wrestled with the awkward, gangly form of the thing.

The fleshy mass of clawed fingers caught Oscar across the face, sending a shower of blood spewing toward Mick as he charged into the fray. Rufus circled around the thing, slicing it across the nap of its neck, and dropping it to one knee. Mick closed in to block off its only opening—only to have the thing bat him away with its good hand into the wall. His vision exploded into a blinding flash of white, and then swirled to black as he dropped to his knees. His machete had fallen somewhere. He heard the telling *thwang* of Sunny's bow, heard the piercing shriek of pain as it made contact. His vision blurred back slowly as he staggered up to his feet. The hallway was a dance of darkness, attempting to overpower the radiant glow of his teams' blades. The thing was still up! Sunny fell backward, tucking her chin in as she rolled back, dropped her bow and came up with her own blade. The freak lunged and ducted nimbly as the hunters closed in.

Mick cussed as he ran forward, trying to channel the light into his vision again. Nothing. His vision only blurred over. But he finally saw the glow from his machete on the floor, still carrying the altered blade. He snatched it up just in time to see a dark, gangly shape flailing its way down the hall toward him.

Every hair on Mick's body stood erect as a breath of icy wind blew through him at the sight. He sliced in an upward vertical strike, stepping into the attack and hurling his free hand—now a fist—into the thing's collar bone. His blade connected, and so did his fist. The thing doubled over. Sunny jumped onto the thing's back, wrapping her legs around the torso and locked her feet together when they crossed. Before she could plunge her blade into the crooked thing's neck, the deformed claw caught her up by her left eye, slicing a deep gash at the top of her cheek bone, knocking her blade free from her grasp. She only shrieked in fury as she grabbed onto the thinning strings of greasy hair on top of its head, threading her arms around the creature's slender neck in a choke hold.

Mick went for one of its legs and slashed at one of its knobby knees. The wet crunch of his machete getting stuck in the thing's leg sent a jarring shockwave through the blade, up the handle and into his hand as the thing dropped to its knees again. This time, the man, this slender parody of a normal human figure was holding his disproportionate, deformed hands up over his head. Rufus and Oscar closed in, pistols now trained on the thing. Mick drew his and aimed it at the thing as Sunny released it and did the same.

"Where's the kid?" Rufus asked as his glowing stare met with the grossly stretched face of the man, who's smile was as jagged as a scrap metal cleaver.

His teeth, stained crimson from his drink of choice, looked like the planks of a wooden fence if they were each a different length.

"The Collector knows." The man's face beamed, almost bright enough to rival the glow from their weapons.

"Who is the Collector?" Rufus asked again.

The man spit out a crimson glob that landed on Rufus's chest. Rufus looked down at the slimy red sludge that clung to the surface of his jacket, and then turned his burning eyes back to the grinning face.

"The Collector will choose him," the man giggled.

Mick saw the dancing beams of flashlights approaching from the other end of the darkened hallway. The sound of combat boots crushing the ground as the police approached.

"What did ya'll catch?" asked the leading officer at the head of the armor clad group.

"He's more or less human," Rufus said as he stepped away for the police to close in on the man. Mick saw the color drain from the faces of the cops when their lights shined over the man's face. The freak's eyes didn't even react when the beams of their lights shown in them.

NEW ROLES

The steady eyes of a predator watched from across the street as the flashing lights of police vehicles and ambulances washed the school's surface in alternating hues of red and blue. The awkward, gangly, inhuman rail of a man wearing bloody coveralls and sporting a deformed hand was being escorted by police and crammed into the back of a squad car while the officer read him his Miranda rights. His frame bent forward at an uncomfortable angle as the door he entered through slammed shut.

The Doc's eyes observed, unblinking. Standing just on the other side of the street, obscured from the awareness of the authorities. If their eyes did land on him, their minds would process the scenery around him. A trick he had learned from his Sire.

The smell of an oncoming storm was lingering in his nostrils as his eyes traveled upwards to the rolling black sky. He pulled his hood up over his bald head and stepped away, further back into the shadows as thunder shook the heavens above. A small park lay before him, beyond a chain linked fence, which he scaled over, parkour style, and landed in muddy gravel behind a bench. He stood there, listening as the first beads of falling moisture began to pelt him. He proceeded through the park, passed under the spaceship themed jungle gym, out into the now freely falling rain, looking no more suspicious than a typical grungy wonderer who frequents such places at night on the way to where they are going.

A pair of footsteps fell in line beside him as a rough and animalistic voice breathed out, "How are things?"

The Doc kept his gaze straight ahead, as he knew the fellow next to him, "There are hunters in the Collector's city," he answered. An owl let out a soft hoot in the trees overhead as they approached the gate to the fence that surrounded the park.

The one walking next to him was silent for a moment, and then spoke, "This could play to our advantage," he mused. His voice sounded slightly optimistic.

Doc knew that for his friend to sound optimistic at all was a rare thing indeed. The Doc nodded his head in wary agreement, but then added, "Or it could complicate things further."

Doc turned his eyes to meet the gaze of his companion, who's black, reddish eyes returned an annoyed look, "Hunters can be played if ya know how to move them around the board."

"Denver is a big board. It's too risky." The Doc said.

His walking companion was silent for a minute before answering, "Whatever. I'll keep an eye out for the kid at Whitehaven. I bet that's where they will take him first."

The Doc shook his head, hopping over the fence once he reached it. His friend, a man an impressive five inches taller than he was, undid the latch and stepped through instead.

"Keep me informed." Doc said.

"Always," the strange eyed man said, and with that, the two parted ways, as if they didn't know one another at all.

DNA tests had identified the tall, thin man with the deformed hand as Ronald Tregorr. The police, as well as Mick and Rufus had their chances to question him, and both times he was unusually cooperative and freely chose to answer all of their questions without a lawyer present.

The swab taken from his mouth, along with Rufus's jacket that he had spit on, were turned over to forensics, and had the same exact similarities to the blood found on Wendy's shirt. Human, but with the same disturbing additions. Both samples had disturbingly higher levels of hemoglobin and white blood cells, and much higher iron levels, with a measure of bile from an unknown source that, upon further analysis, contained mutagenic properties.

Tregorr, when asked about Morgan, disclosed that he had been taken to a place called "Whitehaven." He didn't fail to disappoint with the information he provided. An address to a warehouse located on Zuni Street. After reviewing blue prints of the building, which took up half a city block, plans for a stake-out ensued.

The building itself wasn't officially called Whitehaven on any documentation. Tregorr said it was what his people liked to call it. It was a hulking, three story white brick building, with bars on all the first floor windows. The windows to the other two floors, though, appeared to have been boarded up and had the faded and chipping portraits of children's faces painted on them. On the west side of the building, the one with the faces of the children on it, was a message painted in English and Spanish about lead poisoning and a number to call to have one's home inspected. The occasional homeless sat in the shadows, keeping to themselves.

Of course that's what it looked like through a mundane lens. There were times Mick shuddered at what the Higher Sight could reveal. At times it was enough to make him wish he could curl up into a ball and become invisible. When he saw things that lurked beneath the skin of the world, it made him wonder if raving drug addicts really were hallucinating. Perhaps those hallucinations were really just things that had been there all along, waiting to be noticed by someone attuned to just the right frequency.

The gargantuan thing he saw wrapped around the structure was translucent and pulsated with blue veins. The vision of an impossibly large, yet very distinct human hand clutched the building from above, the wrist fading upwards into the reeling sky that boiled with brownish black clouds that belched and formed various humanoid forms as they shot out and descended upon the hand clutching the building. The claws on each finger dug into the ground. The homeless that milled about in alleyways and shambled along the building's perimeter were still present, though when seen through the Higher Sight, were unrecognizable. Some of them were missing entire limbs, others impaled with crude, metal instruments of various kinds or hypodermic needles, their astral limbs that remained bound with tourniquets. Yet all of the shambling forms had one commonality between them.

Each of the spectral shamblers from time to time would cease their shuffling patrol, turn towards one of the colossal fingers that shielded the structure, and would sink their teeth into the flesh, coating themselves in a brownish black ichor as it gushed forth from the bite marks. Feeding until their spirit forms became engorged like a tick. Sometimes the spectral forms would attempt to burrow themselves inside of the flesh of the fingers that twitched and bent in response to their presence.

Many times Mick had to shut off the Higher Sight. He could only stand looking behind that curtain in short bursts. Those colossal fingers twitched anxiously, as if there was an awareness housed within those bony digits.

Mick suspected that whatever entity the hand was connected to could feel the presence of prying eyes. The way the joints cracked and shifted reminded Mick of the way an animal gets fidgety when it senses danger.

None of their stakeout efforts revealed Morgan's location. For all that the Higher Sight revealed, it was not x-ray vision.

Upon further questioning, Tregorr told police that the vagrants and squatters that loitered on the building's premises were there as guards, and that he himself had been among their ranks. When pressed further as to what they were there to guard, he stopped speaking.

Now as Mick, Rufus, Sunny and Oscar sat in the briefing room with a slew of Denver's finest, listening to Pallacios give out directions, it was becoming clear to Mick what was going to have to happen.

"Okay, each of you will be going undercover," Pallacios said. "Rufus, your new alias will be Juan Valdez; you are an illegal immigrant who crossed the border four months ago and hitchhiked all the way up to this state. You are"—she double-checked the papers—"thirty-seven years old and are divorced from your wife of ten years, just in case anybody asks." Pallacios ran through each of their fabricated backgrounds. Oscar was a hard-drinking young adult named Arturo Juan-Carlos Enriquez who had a bright future ahead of him, but ran away from home before his first semester at the community college he had enrolled in. Sunny's role would be a more support based one. She would not take part in the undercover operations of this extraction, but would help out more by relaying whatever information the boys uncovered to Pallacious. A role she vocally protested against but ultimately lost due to Mick overriding her objections.

"So what am I?" Mick asked. She handed Mick his folder with his fake information in it and smiled.

Mick quickly scanned through the information, taking note of his fake name, Devin Saint; marital status, divorced; and former job description—washed up comedian.

"You wrote this crap didn't you?" Mick asked, looking up. He caught Pallacios smiling as she sat back down at her desk.

Bitch, Mick thought to himself as he closed his eyes.

Now that Mick thought about it as he stood in the dimly lit parking garage with his friends and Ronald Tregorr, the whole washed up comic scenario was kind of funny. He made the mistake of telling Rufus not to say anything to the guys back home.

"Not a word, Rufus! Or I'll take all the firing pins out of your guns!" he threatened while trying to keep a straight face.

Tregorr was talking. Mick hadn't been listening to a thing he was saying this whole time. He was more concerned with hoping the clothes Pallacios had bought from Goodwill were enough to make him look the part of someone down on their luck. The frayed, cotton, fingerless gloves were a nice touch. They had stained the jeans with motor oil, and poked holes into the navy blue Budweiser t-shirt he was wearing. It definitely made him feel homeless. The gray, pullover hoody he wore was just enough to cut the chill on the air tonight.

"Our ride," Tregorr said. Mick saw the headlights of a large van creeping into his line of vision. He looked up, trying to get a good look at the drivers through the dark windshields.

"No turning back now," Oscar said.

"Don't be nervous, guys; we got this," Rufus said.

The sliding doors on both sides opened up, and three men came out. The bright headlights kept their faces darkened as they were backlit from behind.

"New recruits, Tregorr?" one asked. The deformed figure nodded emphatically, holding his clawed hand with his normal one. The three men stood there, looking them up and down like pieces of meat.

I just hope I can remember everybody's fake names, Mick thought. One was walking over to Oscar, sniffing his neck.

"You smell funny," one of them said.

Oscar stepped closer and replied with, "You try sleeping in a refrigerator box for a month and only having one change of underwear!"

Rufus grabbed Oscar by the hood on his filthy jacket, said something in Spanish, and forcefully shoved him back. The three men from the van were chuckling and getting a kick out of the display.

When one of them got close to him, only then could Mick make out a few details about the guy's face. The man's skin looked like a dehydrated melon rind, stretched snuggly over his bald head. He had the odd appearance of looking like he had been put through a meat grinder, yet the quality of his skin from what Mick could tell, paradoxically was not because of heavy scarring. Mick thought it could have been just the way the guy aged, but yet in his own way, he didn't look old. Sure he looked older than Mick, about mid-thirties, but yet for all the unnaturalness about the man's visage, it seemed as if it was normal. A walking paradox of a person. His eyes were dark and beady, almost shark-like, and as they bore into Mick's eyes, he could feel a palpable hungry energy drawing him in. Only after Mick felt himself blinking like something was in his eye did he notice that the man's eyes had a more normal quality to them now. Still hard and dark, but yet the animalistic hunger he sensed from the man a moment ago was gone.

"Come on! Let's move!" one of them said, grabbing Mick and Rufus by the shirt collars and pushing them toward the van.

He climbed in with Rufus and Oscar right behind him. Immediately they had gunnysacks placed over their heads, and then Mick heard the sliding doors close with a heart jarring impact as the door slide home on its track, sealing them in.

WHITEHAVEN

Twenty one, twenty, nineteen, shit, eighteen, seventeen…shit, Mick counted down in his head, stilling himself as his heart rate bounced back and forth. In truth, since having the bag shoved over his head and being herded into the large van, this was the third time he had counted down from one hundred in his head. At least his hands weren't bound, and in the fleeting moments of semi-calm when his heart wasn't about to explode, he knew that he could breathe. He hadn't passed out yet. At least they hadn't bound his limbs. He didn't know if he would be able to remain calm in any way if that happened. He also kept reminding himself in a separate part of his brain that the burlap bag over his face was extremely thin, that air was passing through and he wasn't about to suffocate.

What caused his heart rate to spike though was when the driver and the other two guys began sniffing. He could tell they were trying to be subtle about it but that only made it worse.

Mick felt the van ease to a stop, and then the engine was shut off. The gunnysacks were removed from their sweaty heads and the rush of cool air that splashed over his wet hair and skin felt like being dowsed with a gallon of ice water. The shocking change in temperature was instant and Mick let out a loud breath of relief. He caught Rufus's eye, who was nodding calmly to Mick and subtly motioning with his hand for him to try and reign it in.

"Let's move," one of the men growled as the sliding door was opened, and they all stepped out. Mick, Rufus, Oscar and Tregorr followed the men into the alley, being led to an old metal door with flaking paint and a dim light shining above the entrance. Mick looked up, seeing the side of the building they had all observed through the Higher Sight earlier. He felt the hairs on his body stand erect as he recalled that one of the fingers on the giant hand could be just within arm's reach of where he stood.

The door had a padlock on it with a combination. Mick thought he could try and watch the man to get the combination, but they were standing at an angle that if he had tried to look, he would have looked too obvious. The lock released, and the door opened, scrapping the concrete with its bottom edge. Mick saw a faint glow coming from inside. Soon they felt many hands pushing them into the dark doorway. A strobe light was going off somewhere in this narrow hall way. The smell was the first thing to hit him as he stepped across the threshold. Something he only smelled at crime scenes, and the choking thickness of the stench physically hurt his head as he tried to breath, each shallow attempt at air only stabbing needles into his brain. He swore that the smell was starting to congeal in his mouth, tasting like rotten, blood soaked meat.

They finally came into a room that wasn't lit any better than the hallway, except for a lava lamp that was on a table in the corner. A man sat shirtless at a messy desk, with various kinds of sharp objects, bloody paperwork, and a plate full of something Mick dared not look at, though he thought he saw it move. He was scrawny, but not sickly. His lanky frame was covered in various tattoos and intricate geometrical patterns that crisscrossed in certain areas. As Mick looked a little closer, he noticed that the patterns had tiny letters running parallel to the designs. He couldn't read any of them but he was certain some of the designs looked a little familiar. He had seen something like them in one of Zach's occult tomes he did research out of. His reddish hair was shaved on one side of his head, with the rest of his stringy, greasy locks flipped over on the right side of his head. His face sported a rather unusual looking nose that didn't look like it fit the rest of his thin face. It looked upturned and flat, giving the impression of a pig snout.

Upon seeing the newcomers, he rose to his feet, his lower half clad in camouflage cargo pants and wearing muddy hiking boots with the leather on the toes worn away, revealing steel toes. The jingling of a keyring was heard with his footsteps as he advanced. He spread his arms out in greeting to Tregorr and the other three creeps.

"Ah, I see you come bearing gifts!" He said, his voice betraying either Australian or British accent.

"Tregorr said he found 'em wondering about over in Ruby Hill Park."

The tattooed man clapped his hands together and rubbed his palms as he nodded and looked past the men towards the new blood, "Well boys, name's Ralph. You and I are gonna be good mates. Anything happens out there, I had better know of it." He said with a glint in his eyes as he stepped forward.

That smell was starting to envelope Mick's head in a bubble. It wasn't really coming from Ralph, and not even really the thing on his plate. It was coming out of the walls, up through the floor. He thought he felt finger tips brushing up against his leg from the floor. He dared not look down for fear of being right.

Mick made the mistake of looking past Ralph though, and he gulped involuntarily. Chains, belts, saw blades, flails, cattle prods, and an assortment of BDSM gimp masks, ball gags and handcuffs were hung on the wall behind his desk.

Shitshitshitshit! Mick screamed in his head as Ralph's eyes swept from Oscar, Rufus, and then to him.

"Do tell me, what are your names?" Ralph asked excitedly as he slapped a hand down on Mick's shoulder. The impact of the scrawny man's hand was jarring and put him off balance. It felt like a concrete slab with fingers fell on his shoulder.

"Juan Valdez," Rufus said, squaring his shoulders and looking down at Ralph who was about four inches shorter than him, which made Mick feel slightly more comfortable. Oscar straightened his posture and said his fake name, "Arturo Enriquez."

Ralph's eyes glinted unnaturally as he looked each of them over, and then they landed on Mick again. Mick nervously jerked his eyes to the side, trying to appear casual and look at something hanging on the wall, failing miserably.

He felt every skin cell on his body tingle with an icy chill as Ralph stepped closer to him, "And what's your name wee one?" He asked, singling Mick out as the shortest one in the group. He shot a nervous glance over at Oscar, who he just noticed was a couple inches taller than him, but not by much.

"Uh…Devin, Saint…Used to be a standup comic, was great at birthday parties" Mick said, spewing out his fake background info. Rufus shot him a glance and twitched his head, subtly trying to convey the additional information about his false profession hadn't been asked for.

Ralph's eyes lit up and he snickered, "Oh did ya now? Is that why you're homeless?" The others in the room laughed heartily with him. Mick's eyes shot toward them as they cackled, and the one who was looking him over before they loaded up in the van, the walking paradox, was laughing wide with his mouth open. A fence of yellowed, jagged fangs rimed the top and bottom gums in the man's mouth, with the canines on top and bottom being slightly more pronounced than the others. He blinked. The man's teeth were normal again.

"Tell us a joke then!" Ralph beamed, going back to his desk and sitting on its cluttered surface, folding his lean muscled arms over his tattooed chest.

Shitshitshitshitshit!!! Mick thought, looking over at Rufus and Oscar.

"O-okay. Um…" He stood staring at the leering faces of their captors. Usually Mick could come up with stupid one liners, puns and bad jokes on the fly. They were practically his second language. Now, staring at the faces of people that kept changing when he looked at them, in the heart of what looked like a bondage dungeon with a desk, and a nauseating odor clogging his pores, he felt he was only a hair's inch away from bursting into tears as he laughed manically at his incoming demise. His current predicament seemed like a pretty bad joke.

Three monster hunters walk into a bondage dungeon. They're dead now!

Tell the Monopoly joke. Another voice said inside of his head. Mick blinked.

"What?" He said out loud, and then realized it. The face of Ralph, once bordering on gleeful anticipation, fell to a confused scowl. The faces of the other three men were like a stone wall, looking unamused. Tregorr stared wide eyed, still waiting to hear something funny.

Mick didn't dare look over at his companions. He imagined Oscar shaking his head and Rufus face palming.

Mick! The Monopoly joke, now! He felt his right arm twitch and suddenly realized who was speaking.

You can't be serious! Mick thought, suddenly remembering the joke Yeshua was talking about.

Open your mouth and start talking. Your cover is on the line here, Yeshua insisted.

"Do I have to gore it out of you?" Ralph asked standing, and that's when Mick noticed something hanging off of his belt by leather thongs. Ralph was reaching for them, untying the leather straps that held them. Two unnaturally long bones that looked like they could have been the tusks of a massive animal of some sort each carved with the same type of symbols and runes that Ralph had tattooed all over his upper body.

Mick saw Rufus and Oscar tensing up, their postures not visibly altered to the untrained eye, but he saw their bodies become taught like drawn bowstrings, ready to step in and take him if he stepped closer.

Do it Mick!

Alright fine I'll tell the stupid joke!

"Why do people throw Monopoly money at strippers?" Mick asked, his voice rising like a frightened child about to get beat. Ralph stopped, a fist wrapped around each tusk he held, his arms shaking and eyes wild. He stopped for a second, and Mick could see the gears in his mind trying to think of the punch line on his own.

Ralph turned toward Tregorr and the other three and shooed them out of the office, through the door on the east wall. They shut the door behind them, sealing them all inside with Ralph. Mick liked the odds a lot better now. Three to one. They could all take him if it came down to that.

"Why do they?" Ralph asked, the tone in his voice wary, as if he was questioning if this joke would even be worth it or not.

"Because they have *fake* boobs!" Mick declared, cupping his pectorals and pushing them up.

Ralph's eyes flashed with an appeased amusement and he turned his head to the side to chuckle, and then turned back to look at Mick.

"Well fuck me! With those kinds of jokes what kind of birthday parties did you do?" He asked between chuckles.

"Quinceaneras," Mick said, to which even Oscar and Rufus began to laugh. Mick stared in stunned silence. Not only had that worked, but his teammates were actually laughing at something he said. He savored it, realizing that was probably going to be the only time it ever happened.

"No wonder he's homeless eh boys?" Ralph howled as he turned away toward his desk laughing, laying his tusks down on the desk and grabbed something off of his plate. Mick winced as he made a slurping sound. He looked over at Oscar and Rufus again.

Thanks, Mick thought.

Stay sharp in here. Not everything you meet in this place will prove to be an enemy, Yeshua said. Mick felt a shudder pass through his body along with electric tingles creeping over his skin.

Ralph was rummaging around in one of his desk drawers, and soon came up to them and handed each of them a walky-talky.

"There ya are mates. Channel three for all of those is what you'll need to be set on. If you need to charge the batteries there are charging stations in here," he said motioning with a finger toward one of the other walls where a row of charging stations and boxes of batteries were sitting. He took a key from off his keyring and motioned for them to follow him through the same hallway he had dismissed the goons out of earlier.

The narrow hallway lined with boxes, crates and wooden pallets and lit by a single flickering fluorescent opened up into a room about the same size as Ralph's office, lined with cages full of various types of firearms.

"What goes on here requires a high level of protection at all times. You will be assigned different positions based on your skills, which I will interview you on in about"—Ralph looked at the clock hanging above the door—"three, two, one, now. You, baldy," he said to Rufus, "how good are your eyes?"

"Good enough," Rufus said.

Ralph grabbed a pair of heavy night vision goggles up off the rack and handed them to Rufus. "You'll be on the roof mostly, lookin' out for pigs and such. In case of any other types of wonderers, let the boys on the ground take care of them. Bums tend to unnerve those we don't want milling around the premises. If you see the fuzz drivin' by, stay low and don't do anything to draw attention but report it on your radio."

“What actually goes on here?” Mick asked, before he could take it back. It sounded like a logical question at the time, but he felt eyes on him again, drilling into him with an icy stare.

Ralph was smirking at him as he reached into one of the gun cages and handed him a Beretta 92F and Oscar a Glock, “If you keep your nose clean and don’t fuck up, you might find out. All that is required of you gents, is to simply patrol the block, and report any prying eyes to me or my friend Hank.”

“Who’s Hank?” Oscar asked.

Ralph smiled, “Oh you’ll have to meet him. He’s simply a treat!”

BAD JOKES

It had been almost two hours since the meeting in Ralph's office. Mick looked at his beat up watch—11:02pm. He sat down behind a dumpster in the dimly lit alleyway, watching the residual light from the street lamp across the street fighting to eat up the shadows. He had crossed paths with Oscar while milling about the block, pretending to be looking for a dry place to curl up and lay down. So far it was just Oscar and him that could be seen on their "patrol." Rufus lucked out, being up on the roof. But as soon as a chill swept over Mick, cutting through his meager attire, he remembered that being up on the roof without any wind blocks was probably not as fun as he thought. To pass the time he imaged Rufus with icicles forming under his nose, but that got old after a good thirty seconds.

Just patrol and look for any suspicious lookers, and in exchange they give the homeless a place to sleep and food to eat. Sounds simple enough. Mick thought. Though the prospect of staying in this building, essentially cut off from any communications with his team, was sending nervous chills through his stomach and back, he understood full well it was going to be a necessary evil if they were to even stand a chance of finding Morgan. His thoughts drifted back to Tregorr and how easily he spilled the beans about this place. He had let his tongue wag freely in the interrogation room, knowing full well that everything he was saying would be used against him in court. He didn't seem to care.

But none of this information answered the one single question that Mick and the other hunters had been asking themselves since he gave them the address to this place: Can he be trusted? What if Morgan was already dead, and this guy had led them here just to expose their identities to whoever ran this place? All things Mick pondered as he sat there shivering.

He almost hadn't heard footsteps in the alley approaching from the other side of the dumpster. They sounded too…heavy to be Oscar's. He chanced a glance around the dumpster's rusted metal corner to see the imposing outline of a figure nearly as wide as Mick was tall. He towered over him, looking like he stood well over six feet. The shadowy figure wore a hoodie, drawn up over his head, obscuring his features. All Mick could see was the outline of this hulking meat house as it drew closer, and instantly felt himself shrinking back behind the dumpster, praying to Yeshua that the man hadn't seen or heard him. Was it another guard? He was dressed in ratty attire similar to Mick, so it was entirely possible. How long had this guy been out and about? Was he one of Ralph's boys? Of all the things Mick knew for certain, he was too big to miss.

"I see you," The man's voice breathed out, a true baritone mixed with the sound of gravel being crushed into powder by the massive jaws of a titan.

Mick's blood froze as he sat there, remaining perfectly still, hoping that the man was talking to someone else, never mind the fact Mick was the only other one in the alley on this side of the building.

"Fresh meat! I'm talking to you!" The voice bellowed, sending Mick's spine shooting up into his brain. He trembled as he slowly inched out from behind his cover, feeling utterly naked to the predator that circled the sky above him. His trembling hand gripped the handle of the Beretta that he tucked into his belt.

"You one of Ralph's?" the man asked when Mick stood to his full, unimpressive height, all of five foot, eight inches. He nodded frantically, more to dislodge actual words from his throat than anything else.

"Yes," he choked out as he attempted to stand up straight and square his shoulders back.

The dark figure, its face obscured by the shadows of their hood, stood there, appraising him without speaking. Mick looked down at the enormous hands the man held down at his sides, and in the darkness, as a passing car briefly illuminated the alleyway for a second, he noticed the sharpened edges of exaggerated clawed fingers.

Immediately he began running through all the options in his mind. If he channeled the Light into his gun, the bullets could do some damage to whatever this man was. But he risked exposing himself as no ordinary bum, and would endanger not only his life, but Oscar and Rufus. Besides, claws didn't automatically equal monster, and even though he had to constantly remind himself of that fact, Mick was aware of it.

Being in the best physical shape of his life up to this point, he wagered he could possibly outrun the man. But all it would take is two steps and the man could cross to him and grab him by the hair easily. Even though Mick had found himself grappling with horrors of the night on a couple occasions, it didn't mean he could take this man if he had to. The Light would give him an edge no doubt, but he knew a weapon was only as good as the one wielding it.

He continued to let his eyes adjust to the man's form, trying to pierce the veil of darkness his face hide behind.

"Name's Hank." The man said, extending his hand to Mick. He eyed the appendage warily, and slowly extended his hand.

Okay, so this is the guy Ralph was talking about. Be cool. Don't get killed.

Mick braced himself as he wrapped his fingers around the man's massive hand, expecting a crushing grip that would render this one hand useless. The man's skin felt like touching a block of ice. Yet the grip, though firm, didn't crush his hand. Mick felt the breath he had been holding suddenly escape in a relieved sigh.

"He said you're the comedian," The stranger said. Mick shook his head, suddenly put off by how this meeting was going.

"I'm not that funny," Mick said, trying to back away nonchalantly and hoping the big lug wouldn't notice.

"He didn't think so."

Just don't ask to hear a joke. Mick thought.

"Tell me a joke," Hank said, spitting on the ground. Mick's face went slack.

Oh for God's sake!

He began wrestling for something that could potentially placate the beast of a man before him.

"How do you get a blonde on the roof?" Mick began. Hank stood there, his arms crossed, his general countenance one of disinterest.

Shit, okay…crap, what was that other one?

"A little Japanese dog bit a man. Guess what happened to the owner?" Mick said, regaining his footing.

Hank lifted his head back all the way, the vertebrae in his neck popping like crunchy granola, but not enough to reveal his face.

"What?" He asked.

"He got the shih tzued out of him!" Mick said, and then took a cautious step back in case the punchline earned him a backhand across the face.

Hank just stood there, silent and unreadable in the shadows.

"So," Mick continued, "I haven't seen anything weird. Not since I've been out here."

Hank nodded, a grunt escaping his throat, "No police cars?"

Mick shook his head, "Only one but it drove on like normal. It didn't look suspicious."

"Police are always suspicious. You're sure they didn't notice you?" Hank asked.

"Yeah, positive," Mick lied.

Hank stood there for a moment, and Mick thought he might be weighing the answer he gave him. Suddenly Mick heard a buzzing coming from overhead, and illumination flickered all over the alleyway above the old dumpster. The meager rays of light that attempted to wash the darkness from the alleyway only partially illuminated the stranger's face—and it was a gut wrenching, heinous thing to behold. Mick caught the startled yell in his throat before it could breach his mouth. At first Mick thought the man's face had been eaten by some creature, spit out and glued back onto his head. But upon noticing Mick's discomfort, Hank lifted his hood off his head and let it fall back, his face twisted hideously into what might have been a smile. Might have been a snarl. Mick couldn't tell. All he could tell was he was staring into the face of something no longer of the human variety.

The man's visage, the gnarled, pointy ears that flexed on the side of his head, the long, greasy white locks of thinning hair that crept down the sides of his head and down his broad chest, imprinted itself onto Mick's mind. The black, shark like eyes that now had a strange reddish hue to them. And the teeth were like jagged rows of splintered bone.

"You seem skittish," Hank observed as he stepped closer.

"W-what? No…not skittish at all," Mick stuttered, trying to catch the breath that had escaped his lungs the moment that light came on.

"Is it because you're impressed by my handsome mug?" Hank smiled.

Mick wasn't sure how long he stood there aghast, trying not to run. The strange man, or whatever it was that stood before him cocked his head to one side.

"Ralph tell you what goes on in there?" Hank asked. Mick shook his head, trying to get the words to come out, "N-no," he gulped out. Hank nodded as a sinister look crossed his ghastly face.

"You're about to learn. You got a meeting with the boss," he said, putting his clawed fingers on Mick's shoulder and squeezing as he turned him around and began walking with him down the alleyway.

HEINOUS VISIONS

Mick could vividly recall the sensation of his stomach lurching whenever he missed a step on the stairs in the dark as a kid. But this time, the feeling didn't stop. He felt his stomach trying to free itself form his body, while his lungs fought for every precious breath he could take in as Hank's hand remained steady on his shoulder, the tips of his claws now puncturing the fabric of his hoody. He felt like his insides were being wrung out all over the floor as he was marched through the ever narrowing hallways, only dimly illuminated by purple and red rope lights every twenty feet or so. His entire body screamed to get out, begged for him to muster up the nerve to wrench himself free of Hank's iron grip and run, but all he could do was obey the prodding of the thing he met in the alley. His skin felt like a livewire, feeling everything, and nothing all at the same time. He nearly blacked out, but he managed to stay upright. He tried to form words, but nothing escaped the confines of his throat. The sound of his own heartbeat slamming into his ears over and over again was beginning to give way to an unimaginably high pitched ringing.

And that's when he realized that it wasn't ringing. It was screaming! His vision went black again. He felt like he was falling, his stomach shooting up through his throat until his face connected with the concrete floor. He was only vaguely aware of the fact that the surface he was now splayed out on had a grainy feel to it. That screaming intensified as he suddenly heard the sounds of slurping. A smack. Thick fingers lacing themselves through his hair and pulling upward. A voice breathing hot air into the side of his face.

He thrashed, opened his eyes, but all he saw was darkness. He had nearly forgotten this nightmare in the heat of everything that had transpired over the last few days. Or had it been weeks? His sense of time had become fractured as he thrashed under the weight of whatever was crushing him down into the floor. Despite his eyes being open, he saw nothing. It was then that he realized that was the only mercy he was getting from this experience.

"I love it when they squeal!" A voice came from out of the darkness, ever blending with the screams of that woman, until suddenly, a loud snap was heard that sent a shockwave of ice through Mick's body. He felt moisture on his face. A warm, coppery moist spray. The fingers released themselves from his hair, and then the mercy he was getting from his darkened vision started to fade.

The torn and revolting mess of a woman lay before him, only identifiable as female because of her face, just barley. At first he thought she was a red head, but then soon realized that her scalp had been torn from her skull and was just barely hanging on. The eyes stared out into the distance, unblinking, and dilated. The woman's mouth was a gaping pit, her mouth stretched to the point of dislocating, her jaw frozen in a silent scream.

Mick found his strength, and with no reason he understood at all, felt a compulsion to rush to her side, to hold her in his arms and demand God, or whoever was cruel enough to let this happen, to restore her body and her life. The surge of energy he felt evaporated as soon as he moved and he face planted back into the floor as he tried to move on an arm that would not support him. The floor, no longer concrete, was hard wood. He looked over at his arm that he had tried to brace himself on. His ulna had breached the flesh on his arm, the fractured bone, bloody and jagged as he observed it. He looked up. The remains of a full bodied mirror stood behind the dead heap of his lover on the floor.

My lover? Mick thought. That couldn't be right. He didn't recognize her. But that didn't stop the compulsion he felt to crawl over to her on a broken arm. He willed himself to inch forward, each centimeter wracked with ever growing agony as he discovered that it wasn't only his right arm that was broken. The jagged, teeth like edges of his shattered and fractured ribs were tearing holes through his lungs, causing a fountain of deep crimson to erupt from his mouth when he tried to breath.

After crawling on his belly for what seemed like an eternity, he finally managed to reach the still, mangled form, and upon getting closer, wished he hadn't. The woman's throat was a bloody canyon. Her bloodied clothes were nothing but ribbons and both of her legs were bent at the wrong angles.

Mick tore his eyes away from the heinous sight, the very act itself sending new jolts of electrified agony through his body. But as he did, he caught sight of his reflection in the cracked mirror. It was distorted by the spider web cracks that ran through the glass. The bloody, battered face of the one staring back through swollen eyes was frozen in hysteria as blood continued to pour from the mouth. Hair that had once been blond and neatly groomed was now matted and caked with blood from the lacerations that ran over his forehead and through the scalp. He tore his eyes away when he felt one of his hands touch something on the floor that gave way to a glassy crunch. He looked down. A pair of thick rimmed glasses lay crushed beneath his hand. He looked up at the mirror yet again, this time seeing the backwards reflection of what appeared to be a calendar hanging on the opposite wall. It was turned to January, 1968.

This isn't right! It's April, and its 2015! Mick thought.

His heart raced faster than the rest of him could keep up with, only speeding up as he heard the creaking of a door off somewhere. His breath caught in his throat as he tried to remain quiet. Shuffling, limping footfalls crept into his hearing. Mick froze, shaking there on an arm with a compound fracture as the sound of the footsteps approached across the blood soaked floor towards him.

THE COLLECTOR

All he heard was the shuffling footsteps. He felt his lungs shrinking in his chest, attempting to take in air they had not the capacity to hold. Every nerve in his body screamed with even the slightest inch of movement as he attempted to right himself, to move his legs, to dig his nails into the blood soaked wooden floor for purchase. He collapsed, hearing the fractured bone jutting out of his arm tear even further through the flesh, sending his mind freefalling into a fiery abyss of ravenous, apocalyptic pain.

Two floating points of reflective red hovered there in the darkness, high above the floor, staring straight down at him. Mick could not tear his eyes away. He saw a general outline of a tall shadow, with a gaunt, pale face that barely revealed any feature beyond that of a long, black beard that disappeared into the rest of the shadowy mass as it cascaded down toward the floor.

Cold, concrete floors, the walls of which were lined with crates, garbage bags and an enormous looming figure, were the sight that greeted him. Hank stood over him, his face no longer hooded but hideously unnerving to behold as the red rope lights cast their crimson glow on his visage. His eyes had changed. Either that or they just reflected the color of whatever lighting he was in. Two blood red orbs were drilling Mick deeply as he lay there on the floor, shaking, but relieved, once he saw his arm was intact. He flinched when Hank stuck out his hand, but quickly took hold of it. He wondered how wise that decision was, given that he nearly flew upwards off of the ground the very next second. He hadn't been prepared for the sudden lift-off, but he was now on his feet again.

"What the hell happened to you?" Hank growled. Mick was still shaking but he tried his best to answer.

"I…I blacked out."

"You were thrashing on the fuckin' ground like a goddamn fish out of water." Hank hissed. Mick felt himself shrinking into himself as Hank scolded him. It didn't matter though.

Stay in character, he told himself. Here on the first floor Mick could see a loading and receiving bay for semi's to back up to when they unloaded. Since this building hadn't been used for a couple decades however, no fresh cargo was in sight. Instead, various figures milled about, some of them being the same vagrants Mick had seen the previous day. Rickety bed frames with prison style bed roll mattresses lined the walls.

There was a commotion by a crudely erected cage, constructed of scraps of chain link fence and sheet metal that had been bolted into the ground. Inside, two shirtless men who appeared in their forties were grappling, slamming each other against the clanging walls of the ramshackle construct designed to house their fury. The other homeless guards gathered around the cage, fists pumping in the air as their champions' fists bashed into each other's faces. Limbs were contorted, someone screamed, and the crowd continued its chorus of carnage.

They were approaching a set of stairs that connected to an overhanging balcony of sorts. As they climbed the stairs, Mick took a better look. He could now see that the cage had been constructed around a blue mat, like the kind used for karate dojos or MMA. It was smeared with blood in some places. He watched as the one who seemed to be winning, hauled his opponent up onto his feet, his head swaying to the side as blood painted the entire left side of his face. The man slammed the broken foe up against the inside of the cage wall, rattling the structure. At the encouragement of the wild crowd, he licked the blood off of his opponent's drooping face. Mick turned his eyes away at the sight, just in time again for another scream of terrified agony to reach his ears from inside of that cage. He dared not look.

The balcony had turned into the second floor. Mick couldn't be sure, but as they went on he could hear what sounded like…A cello, and a violin, coming from somewhere on this floor. That was something no one reported during the stakeout. But with this being a warehouse, Mick guessed that the insulation in the walls kept a lot of noise from breaching the outside.

He listened to the stringed instruments, suddenly trying to decipher if what he was hearing was an actual instrument, or a recording. It sounded vaguely like a Tchaikovsky piece. All he knew for sure was that it seemed to be in a minor key. The melancholic melody seemed in a way to be almost soothing. Almost. It would have completely had that effect on him had the setting not been rife with tormenting visions of mutilation and nightmarish death matches.

"Go on in," Hank said when they got to an unassuming, rather plain door, "I'll wait here in the hallway. And uh, don't speak unless spoken directly to, okay?" Hank instructed.

Mick nodded and turned toward the door, feeling his heart dropping down into his shoes as he struggled forward. He flexed his fingers, struggling to breathe deeply.

One hundred…ninety nine…ninety eight… He began counting in his head as he stepped forward, reaching out to grab the doorknob. His fingertips touched the cold stainless steel of the knob, which by comparison looked fairly new compared to the rest of the door. His skin tingled and he flinched backward as the knob quickly turned from the other side, unlatching the door and opening enough for a thin, misshapen face to poke through.

Tregorr popped his head out, smiling through rotten teeth at Mick, whose heart was in his throat.

"He's here," Tregorr giggled as he pushed the door open wider, enough for Mick to enter. Tregorr didn't move however. He simply stood there, the anticipation of Mick's entry beaming out of his face. Mick looked passed him into the large room. Old throw rugs were used for carpet. Two men sat off to one corner on the far left of the room, one with a cello and the other with a violin. One bald and emaciated looking, the one with the cello, was sporting the same, misshapen pointy ears that Hank had, his complexion equally sickly and pale. The other with the violin, a rather shorter but equally gaunt fellow, had a massive jawline, one in which the serrated teeth in his head gave him the appearance of a perpetual growl. They glared as he approached, but continued to play just as fervently as if he was nothing more than a late straggler into their performance.

He stepped through cautiously. It was somewhat L shaped in its layout. Where the stringed duet were sitting was the part of the room with the bend in the L. When he turned the corner, he saw that he had not been the only one summoned to this meeting. His heart leapt with a sudden optimism that he attempted to quell quickly before it could jinx anything. Rufus and Oscar stood before a desk, blocking the view of the one who sat behind it. They both turned to look at him as he approached, their faces unreadable. They were better at this gig than he was.

"Closer" A monotone voice boomed from behind the desk as he approached, thick with a Russian accent. The strings in the corner stopped their song, picked up their instruments and exited the room in a deliberate but calm fashion, as if the spoken words of the boss was their cue to exit stage left.

Mick stood next to Oscar, his eyes meeting that of the speaker as he sat behind his desk. Cold, lupine eyes that fixated him still, boring into the center of his soul with their frozen gaze, and he couldn't look away. The man's eyes seemed like a violent storm. Two swirling abysses of infinite, frozen wastes. His first instinct was to run out of that room, to pump his legs faster than he had ever done so before, and never look back. But against every survival instinct, he stood firm, clutching his fists so tightly he felt the skin on his palms tear open as his nails dug through.

The man behind the desk noticed too, and his eyes looked toward Mick's shaking hands. His thin face, framed with long flowing black hair and a thick beard that ended at his collarbone, looked on fascinatingly at Mick's trembling hands.

"Gentlemen," his voice spread out, like clumpy butter, "My honor to make acquaintances," he said, finally taking his eyes off of Mick's shaking hands, and again meeting their gazes.

"Your names," he said. With every word he spoke, more of his features were coming into focus. His skin looked papery thin, with traces of blue blood vessels running beneath the surface, all snaking towards his eyes, which gave the impression they were darker than they really were.

"Juan Valdez," Rufus said.

"Arturo," Oscar said.

Mick froze. Only for a moment though, but it was enough to warrant a curious head tilt from the man, "Devin Saint," he said, successfully without sputtering. The man smiled, his teeth thankfully obscured behind his black beard.

"I am called, Collector." He said standing up to his full height, an imposing six foot four inches. He wore a long, dark gray tweed coat that looked like it was from the early nineteen-twenties, over a faded black button up shirt that looked like it was bought at a second hand store, and dark slacks held up firmly by an interlacing leather belt. Tregorr shuffled over to the man.

"My associate tells me interesting things about you," The Collector said, his eyes searching each of them.

Mick caught a glimpse at Tregorr, that hideous smirk as he eagerly looked them up and down too, his deformed mess of a hand twitching. Mick looked at Rufus, whose poker face was like a stone wall. Oscar on the other hand was starting to look nervous. He could see his nostrils flaring and the flesh on the back of his neck beginning to prickle. Rufus held his posture perfectly, looking straight ahead and standing almost at attention like a soldier in line for inspection. But Mick couldn't help but keep shifting his eyes back and forth from the Collector, to Tregorr, to Oscar, as now they were both eyeing him.

Tregorr you son of a bitch! Mick almost yelled as he tried not to move. The Collector's mad stare darted toward Mick, looking amused.

Surely he didn't hear that, Mick thought as the Collector stepped out from behind his desk, the deformed beanpole following closely at his heals like a loyal dog. The Collector walked closer, the sound of his footfalls strangely nonexistent. Not muffled, but not audible whatsoever. Mick looked down at the ground to make sure he was actually stepping on the floor. Old lace up boots from another era covered his feet, not making a sound as he casually walked closer.

The Collector looked down at Oscar and smiled, standing less than a foot from him. Mick's blood ran cold once more and his stomach fell. A soft rumble, not terribly loud but distinct enough it could be heard, was emanating from Oscar. Rufus and Mick both stared at Oscar as they realized the rumble they were hearing was a growl. Oscar's eyes, now watering as he rapidly began to blink, were changing color.

Rufus was shaking his head and mouthing 'no!' Mick blinked. A gunshot went off somewhere in the room. He didn't see any of it happen. The only thing that registered in his head now, was that Oscar's head was drawn back as a white, veiny hand threaded through his dark hair. The Collector's head was turned sideways, his teeth clamped firmly around Oscar's larynx, blood shooting out over the Collector's face as Oscar struggled to change forms. His mouth was stretched open in a silent howl, his teeth rapidly pushing his human teeth out of the gums and wolf fangs descending as the Collector easily manhandled him to the ground.

Rufus's eyes were glowing, the hand that held his pistol constricted by Tregorr's good hand, and his deformed hand pinning Rufus to a wall as Tregorr's mouth dropped open, and his rotten teeth bit down on the side of Rufus's neck as the two struggled.

In the half a second this all registering, Mick pulled his pistol free from his belt, felt the rush of celestial fire course through his veins and flood his eyes with burning power as he pulled the trigger and fired into the Collector three times. The Collector's face sprang up, taking chunks of Oscar's neck with him, stretching sinews until they snapped. His mouth hung open in a bloody drooling maw, the eyes now sunken and black with a red dot in their center. The Collector slammed Oscar's head into the floor as he stood up swiftly and glided toward Mick.

Mick backed up, and squeezed the trigger again, hitting the man this time in the chest, seeing the holes of appear in his shirt—but no Light was shining out of the holes. It was the last thing Mick noticed before the Collector slammed his palm into Mick's sternum and sent him flying backward into a bookshelf.

"I've been shot before little hunter!" he scoffed, backhanding Mick, sending him to the floor.

"Poisoned!" He shrieked, slamming his fist into Mick's face. Mick's vision exploded with color as his head shot to the side with the impact.

"Bludgeoned!" He said, racking his talons across Mick's face.

"Fed through hole in icy river! Your tricks won't work here! Not on me!"

The Collector grabbed Mick and hauled him up off the floor by his hoody like a limp scarecrow. The slashes in his face, at first numb, were now filling with warmth that soon exploded into hellfire as his cheek gushed red. His body was numb, and as he was jostled about, he felt like he was floating. His Higher Sight was gone. It had only lasted as long as it took him to squeeze the trigger. He caught a brief glimpse of his fingers through the fingerless gloves he was wearing. The veins were glowing, but the bullets in his gun had not been altered.

He felt fingers threading themselves through his hair yet again, drawing him back to the present moment, and he felt an explosion of adrenaline as his skin tingled with the energy of the Light. He screamed in fury and kicked. It felt like kicking the side of a building as the Collector smiled and threw him to the floor.

Mick sprang up, driving strikes quickly and straight with his fists, stepping into the punches and following through. Each blow connected, but had no effect. Finally, as if fed up with Mick's pathetic attempts at valiance, the Collector caught Mick's last punch. His mad gaze drilled into him, his mouth and beard stained with blood and bits of flesh as his mouth hung open in a serrated, bloody cavern. It was then that he realized the hand that was holding the battering ram of his arm at bay, was the same hand he had seen resting upon the building earlier that day through the eyes of his Higher Sight.

"Welcome to Collection."

Вампир (Vampire)

He could feel the pain even before he started waking up. Mick's face felt like it had been smashed with blocks of concrete, and his shoulder blades felt like they were on the verge of slipping out of their intended places. It wasn't till he tried to move his head up that he felt the burn of deep gashes in his flesh, all over his chest, arms and even his neck. He gasped from the burning sensation that engulfed his body as he struggled to find footing, but to no avail. The crushing disappointment of feeling his feet flail in midair only served to make the jackhammer in his skull more forceful, chipping away at the interior of his skull. It was then that he became aware of the dull ache in each of his fingers. The dull ache quickly roared to an inferno of blazing agony as he reflexively tried to clench his fingers, only to have them burn with excruciating pain all over again. He remembered driving his fists into the Collector's face and body, and recalled how it was like punching a brick wall.

He could hear a door open and close off in the distance as his mind fought to try and remember what had happened earlier. His left eye felt swollen shut, but when he was finally able to open his right eye, his vision adjusted to make out the details of the room he was in. Whatever this place was, it was lit only by an old flashing sixty-four-watt bulb that hung from the ceiling a few feet from where he was hanging. It looked like it was a 16x24 square foot room with concrete block walls, the ceiling made of metal rafters that were covered in metal grates, and a hallway to his left, where he heard the door.

He could also make out that his wrists were now suddenly burning as the skin around them was pulled against the links of some rusty chain. His shoulders felt like they had been stretched out of their sockets, but moving them as he tried to pull himself up proved that they were merely strained to the max, and had not been dislocated. He was also shirtless. He strained through his good eye to observe the room more closely. When his shadow wasn't blocking it out, he could see dark brown stains dotting the floor beneath him. His jeans were stained with drying blood from the gashes in his flesh.

"You awake mijo?" a familiar voice asked.

Mick twisted, trying to see if he could rotate himself on the chain as he tried to spin toward the sound of the voice, wincing and cussing as he did.

"I want my lawyer," Mick grumbled as he spun around, catching a quick glimpse of Rufus's bloodied, also shirtless form. He looked to be in much the same shape Mick was in as his head hung down, blood dripping out of a split and swollen bottom lip. His muscular frame looked like it had a barbed whip taken to it. But when Mick looked closer he could see the perfectly parallel gashes weren't from a whip, but from something's claws.

Oscar hung next to him, blood staining his shirtless chest all the way down from where the Collector had bitten him. His chest was rising and falling silently as he looked up, revealing that his throat was whole and healed. Sweat and flecks of dust were mixed with caked blood on one side of his face as he looked over at Mick and nodded.

"What's up?" Oscar breathed out.

"I told Pallacios using Tregorr as an inside man was a bad idea," Rufus said, spitting a glob of blood out on the floor.

"Well she was never interested in listening to sound reason from anyone below her," Mick breathed out.

In his mind's eye, quick, flash-like images were splatting all across the canvas as Mick recalled seeing the Collector wrestle Oscar to the ground effortlessly, his teeth buried deep into his throat. Mick had seen Oscar shrug off mortal injuries before, so that fact he was alive and conscious was no great surprise. Then it clicked. He wasn't sure what he had ever thought he would feel if they were proven real. Certainly in his new line of work, he had wondered if such creatures could be real, and if they were, why had they not been discovered. The layer of ice that suddenly encased his body caused him to feel like his head was detaching from the rest of him.

Okay…you know monsters are real. You've seen werewolves, you've seen ghosts, demons, mutant, flesh warping creatures in the sewers. You've even seen a freakin slasher scarecrow. Why couldn't vampires be a thing too? Seriously, why are you surprised?

His inner thoughts only served to feed the growing nauseous pain churning in his stomach. Remembering the images of Tregorr from Rosedale Elementary, down on his knees, holding what looked like a person's arm up to his mouth, slurping blood from the wrist.

"Rufus," Mick breathed out, "Tregorr bit you didn't he?"

"Si…He only managed to break the skin though."

"He didn't suck your blood though?"

"The Collector sucked mine," Oscar said.

"No Mick, Tregorr is dead. I shot him in the face before I was backhanded and brought down here." Rufus said. He leaned his head back and tried to reveal the side of his neck. A puffy bruised ring in the shape of human teeth was on the right side of his neck.

"I'm fine, thanks for asking," Oscar sighed as his body dangled next to Rufus.

"You're a werewolf! I figured you'd be okay," Mick said, his chain slowly turning his body away from them.

"I can still die bro, it's hard to heal with a guy's fangs stuck in your throat." Oscar growled.

"So…we are dealing with…vampires…Oh my God," Mick said, feeling his mouth going dryer with each word he spoke.

"You gonna be okay?" Rufus asked. Mick shook his head, feeling his guts turning to mush as he hung there. A high pitched ringing, which began so quietly he barely noticed as it snuck up on him, was beginning to drown out the voices of his friends. The only other noise it was competing with was the sound of his own blood pumping through his ears. The thunderous hammering of his heart as it sped up, causing the edges of his vision to darken as he hung there like a worm on a hook.

Can they hear my blood pumping through my body? Can they smell it?

He felt like an ethereal, icy hand was holding onto his airways, holding them tight like the reins on a wild horse about to be broken. He looked down at his bloody chest, and nearly began thrashing right there, seeing the slick, wet crimson gloss on his skin. His head felt like it was being squeezed by a vice, his vision alternating between bursts of darkness and pixelated rainbow sparkles that obscured his vision of his friends in the room.

The chain slowly eased him back around to Rufus, who was looking behind Mick, his face torn in a fit of rage as his lips peeled away from his teeth in a snarl. Oscar's eyes had changed to their wild, lupine color again as his teeth were shaped into glistening white spikes in his gums. His veins bulged and his muscles popped. Mick spun around, all sensations of floating and suffocation continuing to clash as his eyes landed on a shadowy shrouded figure there in the dark, marked by their distinct red eyes that hovered high off the ground.

The one called the Collector stood there in the dark, his hands stuffed into the pockets on his tweed long coat. His long black hair, blending seamlessly into the shadows, was pulled back into that same ponytail he was wearing when they first met. His face was deeply serene, almost comparable to a stained glass window portrayal of a Saint. The contrast only served to accentuate the menacing glow of his blood red eyes as he stepped forward.

Mick involuntarily began thrashing, kicking his boots into the chest and face of the thing that was looming before him. His efforts were repaid with an outstretched hand that froze his limbs in place. Other sounds were starting to emerge. Oscar was howling, pulling against the links of the chains that held him. Rufus was spewing what Mick only assumed could be curses in Spanish. Or it might have been Latin.

The Collector's hand shot up toward Mick's chest with the same impact of a SWAT team's battering ram. But instead of knocking the air out of him, he felt—heat. Pulsating, soothing heat that originated from his sternum and spread outward. It was then he remembered earlier. The fight in the office. The Collector's hand sending him flying backward into a bookcase with an open palm strike to the same area he felt the radiating heat. The pain engulfed his ribcage, wrapping around each rib like a horde of snakes, entangling themselves into his organs—and then, nothing. The sounds of the room came back at full volume, no longer competing with the sounds of his panic attack. His vision came back fully and he watched in horror as the Collector repeated the same process on Rufus, and on Oscar. Upon being touched on the right side of his neck, Rufus's body straightened like a plank of wood, like he had just endured a lightning bolt passing through his body. Oscar went limp, and his bestial features receded back into his flesh when the Collector grabbed him by the throat, in the same area he bit him.

Mick's mind kept flying back to the fight in the office, watching the Collector touch them in the places they had sustained damage. He didn't feel any pain when he got hit in the chest, but then again he was in a berserker rage to defend his life and that of his friends. Pain wasn't something that immediately registered to his brain in the heat of that moment. Sure Oscar's throat had healed enough for him to regain consciousness. Was he trying to heal them?

"Vampire, you call me?" The Collector's voice slithered out as he turned to Mick. He stepped closer, close enough Mick could spit on him, but he dared not.

"You call your healer…vampire." A disingenuous smirk crossed his face, "I call you…murderer." He hissed, pulling an object from one of his pockets.

Mick felt like the floor had opened up beneath him to a raging pit of lava, waiting for that chain to snap as he plummeted headlong into the incendiary depths. The object's flat, rectangular surface lit up in the creature's clawed hand, and Mick recognized his phone's wallpaper.

How did he get my phone?!

The Collector's eyes beamed as he held the phone upright in his hand for Mick to see what he had pulled up. A video file with a single date for its file name—10/31/2012.

Mick felt his muscles in his neck become taught with fiery wrath, the heat descending down his spine and turning to an arctic chill in the next breath. The Collector's clawed thumb hovered just over the file.

"Please…don't," Mick struggled to say as his eyes began to burn. His plea was blatantly disregarded as the Collector's finger pressed the 'play' icon. The screen showed nothing for half a second before the first signs of panicked movement were present. Agonizing screams, each indistinguishable from man, woman or child, spewed from his phone's speaker, distorted by their volume. The footage that came up on the phone's screen was that of a bloody sidewalk, littered with debris from dismantled parade floats. Mick saw the hurried, shoed feet of the one filming in the shaky frame just as a metallic creaking of a car's chassis groaned and shrieked. The phone came up to a sea of swarming, hysterical, costumed citizens, running to and fro in a frenzied attempt at escape. He saw the grotesque bodies of the things that lived in the sewers, each hideous form spontaneously sprouting extra limbs, tendrils, and wielding various weapons. Each one grabbing a fleeing citizen at random, hacking their bodies to pieces, or impaling them on their newly sprouted limbs to use as wrecking balls as vehicles and storefront windows were obliterated with the flailing, still living victims.

The metallic scrapping screeched out of the phone again, and this time the camera stayed focused on a distinctly human form, its arms wrapped around the front end of a Toyota Camry, picking it completely off the ground and hurling it off to the side with an effortless twist of its body. Black, shadowy mist hovered around the figure, obscuring certain features like hair and eye color. The figure turned, and Mick felt himself sinking through the floor, being swallowed up in the fiery gulf of Hell as his own face stared back at him through his phone. The video shook as the one holding the phone staggered back once being seen. The frame blinked out for a second but returned after a gut piercing female scream broke out, rising above all others, as Mick's face filled the screen, eyes, nose and mouth all leaking black tar. The phone tumbled to the ground, and landed with a perfect view of what transpired directly above it. Mick's body, inhabited by an eldritch presence not of this world, was holding a woman up in the air by the throat, blood running down the side of her face, caking in her blond hair as her eyes, wide and wild with terror. She looked to be about in her mid-twenties, her makeup smeared. She wore the bloodstained tatters of what had been a witch costume. Black shadowy mist shimmering around the arm that held her up.

Through sheer force of will that left him on the brink of passing out, Mick managed to tear his eyes away at the last second, just as the sounds of bones and sinews being pulled apart commenced. A sharp scream was suddenly silenced by the mortifying sounds of gurgling and choking, and then the phone was silent. The silence that filled the room, seeped and penetrated into Mick's flesh, wriggling inside of his bones, burrowing into his marrow as hot tears fell down his cheeks. His face was contorted into a wrathful snarl, and he felt like he would burst a blood vessel as he looked at the creature in front of him.

"Such power...Much death...You deceiving yourself little hunter. Blood of monsters not washing away blood of people you slaughtered."

Mick lashed out, kicking his feet in a vain attempt to strike the creature, which in a blink of an eye was suddenly not standing where he was before Mick's outburst.

"Ironic coming from a vampire!" Mick screamed, his chest heaving in and out with rage as he hung there like a limp fish on a line, ready to be gutted.

"Yes. Conjure power within you! Strike me down, like girl in video!" The Collector taunted, pocketing Mick's phone once more and folding his hands behind his back. At the mention of what he just watched, Mick felt all energy leave his body. He hung there, swaying back and forth like a hunk of meat in a slaughterhouse. The Collector turned his attention toward Rufus and Oscar.

"Now heal with no scars..." he said, gesturing toward their throats. Oscar was growling again. Mick's body slowly rotated on the chain until he came into view. Eyes still feral, his face looking like it might be boiling just beneath the skin.

"I have gift for you," the vampire said as he waved one hand about the room in an exaggerated fashion, like he was clearing away dust with a rag. Their eyes suddenly all zeroed in on a small human form that none of them had seemed to notice before in this relatively small and empty space. How had they not seen it? Or would their minds not let them see it? Mick had no idea. It was huddled in one of the dark corners. A lanky boy that looked to be about nine or ten years old sat hugging his knees to his chest. He looked to be of African descent, his curly hair caked with damp dust. His skin was of an ashen paleness that made him look utterly sickly and emaciated—and then Mick saw why. The boy's eyes were blacked out. His ears were gnarled points that jutted out on either side of his head, and his teeth, all of which were slightly tipped with a sharpened crown, sported unnaturally longer canines on top and bottom.

The boy began crawling toward them, his teeth barred, revealing a receded gum line. His nostrils flared as his clawed fingers pawed at the ground with each advance.

"Or rather...*You are* gift to him." The Collector said as he turned away and began walking toward the door.

INFORMANT

Sunny sat at the table with four other officers, sipping coffee and thinking of all the nasty things she would say to Mick when she saw him the next time. She had been stuck working with the research department, giving details about the night the tall, deformed creep was apprehended. Talking about how fast he moved, the fact that he had been drinking blood of some sort. Her knowledge of certain occult practices shined through in her interviews, particularly blood magic. The fact that Tregorr had been drinking blood might be a possible link to some kind of occult practice, which brought up all kinds of rabbit trails about what these kids were possibly having done to them. All things she didn't want to delve into any further.

Sitting here answering questions about the occult and its uses wasn't her idea of fun when the guys were out doing real work. She had tried making them see reason in her going, not as an undercover agent, but more like a covert stealth infiltrator who could slip in and out of the building to look for clues without getting caught. One thing that she had loved learning in her training was the art of stealth. It was part of the reason she used a bow. But now she wasn't getting to use that skill, and she was almost bored to tears sitting here talking to complete strangers about her skills and knowledge that she *wasn't* applying at the moment. It seemed like a slap in the face. She had spent the better part of three years learning these things that helped her become one of the most important parts of her team, and now she was stuck playing twenty questions with these cops! She thought at least Rufus, and surely Oscar would have backed her up, but even they seemed to side with Mick, and then Pallacios had to throw in her two cents! She picked up her pencil and began drawing little doodles of Mick falling off a cliff, or getting hit by a bus. That seemed to help her a little bit. She was shaken out of her thoughts when another officer entered the room and knocked on the door frame.

"Yeah, Cole?" Officer Westerman asked. Sunny looked up. Officer Cole's face was drenched in sweat, his gray tainted face looking like that of a ghost.

Sunny listened to their conversation. She could hear their whispers across the room. She had exceptional hearing. It was one of the things that made her so dangerous to the enemy; she was able to hear them, but they couldn't hear her—sometimes.

"A man walked into the station just now…B-big guy. Long white hair. Never seen em before. But he's asked to speak with her."

Sunny's skin prickled when she tried to nonchalantly notice the officer pointing past Officer Westerman's shoulder toward her.

"Did he give his name?" Westerman asked, suddenly sounding put off.

Cole shook his head, "He just said he needs to talk to her. He smells like an open grave and he's uglier than sin. Please…I already got the Sergeant out there talking to him, and the Receptionist is in the ladies room bawling her eyes out. Just, please man. I need her to come with me."

Before she could be beckoned, she stood up, folding her note up and pocketing it as she approached Cole. The man's cheeks were slick with tears. The mask of sheer, primal terror that he wore sent her nerves jangling to full alert as her skin continued rippling to life.

Cole turned toward her, "Miss are you armed?" He asked, wiping his eyes. Sunny nodded, patted the pistol she had holstered on her belt and said cheerfully, trying to offset the man's terror, "Yep! With a real gun and everything," she finished with a flashy smile. The cop gave an appreciative half smile as he turned and motioned her to follow.

Sunny had a hard time keeping her questions to herself as she followed Officer Cole down the hallway. Sergeant Boland met them, with Pallacios hot on his heels, and they joined them as they went down the twist and turns of the hallways in the Denver Police Department. With each step, Sunny felt heavier. A knot in her stomach that she didn't know was there until just now, became tighter. No sooner had she noticed it, than they had reached the door to the interrogation room.

Officer Cole opened the door, revealing the one who had came calling for her. A large man, wearing old, weather worn clothes that were probably stolen from a Big and Tall store, with an oily, black stained gray hoody. The shirt he wore looked snug, the fabric straining over his big barrel chest. He sat drumming gray, clawed fingers on the table as his eyes, with large pupils that nearly took over the entire eye, looked up at them and locked on her. The small spaces around the enlarged pupil were blood red. Long stringy white locks fell down to his shoulders, slicked back, probably by gutter slime or rain water. She tried to stop her nostrils from flaring involuntarily when the smell hit her. Like a dead cat that had washed up out of a sewer drain after a flood. He looked at her and smiled in an attempt to be pleasant, but apparently the guy hadn't looked in the mirror for some time. His teeth reminded her of a piranha, or a great white shark.

Pallacios butted her way past Cole, turned to him and instructed him to leave, and he enthusiastically obliged.

"Hello sir, my name is Agent Della Pallacios," She started and stuck out her hand. The man rose and extended his large hand and smiled.

"Name's Hank. It's a pleasure," he said, turning his eyes toward Sunny and offering her his hand, "Sorry for scaring the shit outta your cop friend back there. I'm just so damn handsome people don't know how to handle me. I hope the secretary is okay. She seems like a sweet girl."

Sunny nodded and shook Hank's hand, gooseflesh traveling up her arm as she squeezed his hand firmly. It felt like shaking a slab of frozen meat, but one that could squeeze back.

"Sorry, cold hands, warm heart, ya know?" Hank said as he sat back down.

"So," Pallacios started, folding her hands in front of her in a business like fashion, "You wanted to see us? What can we do for you Hank?"

Hank smiled again, looking over at Sunny. Oddly enough, though his smile and overall odor was off putting, she detected no malice, or attempt at intimidation in it...Not even hunger. She could tell by making her eyes bright enough to peek into the higher dimensions surrounding them all, that his aura was a swirling vortex of dark gray, bordering on black...The kind of colors surrounding a corpse. Her eyes traveled slightly behind him, looking at a shape that stood there, ghostly and transparent. It had a face, one that looked remarkably like Hank. Still gruff, but with far more human like features. Whenever Hank spoke, the apparition behind him spoke as well, as if speaking through him.

Sunny swallowed and placed her hands down flat on the table, sat with her back straight, and returned the smile.

"Well actually I'm here to speak to her," Hank said, lifting a finger in Sunny's direction, the ghostly, more human version of him mimicking the movement. Sunny couldn't help stealing a glance at Pallacios out of the corner of her eye, and smirked. The Agent's face fell in a confused manner, but she quickly recovered, catching the edges of her slipping professional mask and pinning it back to her face.

"Understood sir, but seeing as how she is under my authority at this time while aiding with a federal investigation, whatever information you pass on to her will be brought to my attention. Sooner, rather than later."

Sunny let her eyes rest a second on Pallacios, noting the flickering grayish brown, hazy outline the rimmed her body. Despite her professional tone, Sunny could see just by her aura that she was afraid. Her wording also indicated that her possessiveness was asserting itself.

"Well," Hank said with a playful snap of his head back toward Pallacios, "I suppose you have a point. Full disclosure, and I'm sure you could tell just by looking at me, but I'm obviously not human."

You don't say? Sunny thought, keeping her smile up like she wasn't surprised in the least.

"Second, little girl, I have some information about your friends. I and a colleague of mine have been watching y'all since you rolled into town."

Mick watched, his eyes transfixed on the gangly form of the boy as he crawled toward them. Those blackened eyes, drilling him with a mesmerizing stare as he crawled ever closer. A painful, sharp sound was coming from the boy as he crawled toward them, sounding like painful gasps for air, followed by shallow exhales as his bony limbs carried him closer toward their hanging bodies.

"Mick," Rufus said calmly.

Mick, still transfixed on the horror crawling toward him, managed to hear the voice of his friend, "What?" he almost yelled, reflexively kicking one of his feet out toward the kid's face.

"That's Morgan Harris."

Mick felt the world screech to a halt at those words. He didn't dare remove his eyes from the creature trying to drag itself toward them, but he couldn't wrap his mind around what he had just heard either.

"How the hell do you know that?!" Mick shrieked as the kid managed to stand upright, his back hunched.

"Magic trick! I'll explain later." Rufus said.

"You're doing your thing right now?! How?!"

"Damnit Mick shut the hell up!" Oscar roared, his voice sounding like a growl that zapped Mick's nerves into compliance.

"Morgan," Rufus said calmly, "look at me amigo…Look up here…" The boy's wide, blackened eyes roamed over toward Rufus, the teeth still bared in a hungry snarl.

Rufus kept his words calm, his breathing steady and his body as relaxed as he could be. He had never attempted his trick under such circumstances, but he knew of no other recourse. He kept his eyes steady on the child he knew to be Morgan Harris, the one they had come to rescue. He held an image in his mind of what the kid might have looked like before this fate had befallen him. A tall, athletic boy with rounded features, a charming smile that wasn't comprised of razor sharp fangs. He pictured him happy, running with a football out in the full light of the sun. He let his muscles relax as he felt his mind lifting out of his body. The overwhelming tingles he felt nearly caused him to jerk as he hung there on that chain, but he resisted with every ounce of willpower he had. He thought of Mick and Oscar hanging there next to him. He knew Oscar wasn't helpless. He could change and bust out of his chains easily.

He thought of Sunny and how frustrated she was that she couldn't come along on the same mission they had been given, and how utterly adorable she looked when she tried to convey her frustration. With those last thoughts, he successfully freed himself from his fleshy confines, slipping back into a realm he had spent the better part of nearly two decades navigating. *This* was his home. He looked back at his body, hanging there by the wrists, seeing the blueish silvery cord that ran from his stomach to his astral form. He stepped out onto the concrete, covered in writhing fungus that formed fingers that followed the soles of his boots as he approached the ghostly impression of the same boy, huddled in the darkest corner of the room. The boy looked exactly how he had pictured him while departing from his body.

"Hey mijo. What brings you to this rotten place?" Rufus asked, sinking down onto his haunches. The ghostly apparition of the boy snapped his eyes up to meet Rufus's gaze, and he backed away further into the corner, trying to melt into the wall.

"Hey, hey…easy. I'm here to help you little brother. Can you tell me how you got here?" Rufus said, holding out his hands in a gesture of peace. Morgan's eyes flashed around nervously, looking at each and every corner like something was watching.

"I-is he listening?" Morgan asked, his voice on the verge of giving way to a hysterical sob.

Rufus looked around, an exaggerated show but one that got his point across, "I don't see or hear anyone else but us."

"If he's listening I can't talk to you. I'm sorry!" Morgan said, springing up and trying to dash away. Rufus closed his eyes and when he opened them, appeared right in front of the fleeing specter of the frightened boy.

"My name is Rufus, and I'm here to help you." He said, catching Morgan by the ethereal arm and halting him. Morgan looked down at his arm, eyes wide with shock and terror as he looked back up at Rufus.

"W-wha…How? No one else can see or hear or touch me but him! How are you—"

"Shhhh," Rufus said, lifting a finger to his lips, "Then if he can hear you, speak quietly with me please. You see mijo, my friends and I are about to be torn apart…by your body. But if that happens, we can't help *you*. I need you to try and take control of it for me."

Morgan was shaking his head, "I-I don't know how Mister…I'm sorry." He said, and even as a phantasm, Rufus could make out faint traces of ghostly tears as they fell from the boy's eyes.

"It's okay little bro. It's easy. You just walk up to it and touch it. Like tapping someone on the shoulder when you're trying to get their attention."

Morgan's eyes looked down at Rufus's exposed stomach, and his ghostly face was illuminated by a silvery glow as he noticed the cord running from Rufus's stomach up to his physical body. Then, just as quickly as he noticed it, Morgan took a deep breath, trying to hold in his sobs as he looked at his physical body. There was no chord leading from his form to the thing on the other side of this veil.

"I…Why don't I have one? What does that mean?!" he cried, "I'm dead aren't I?"

Rufus's face fell as he joined Morgan's gaze, looking at the quivering thing that used to be his living body. It looked like it had stopped to observe its prey, trying to suddenly figure out what they were. "I know this place is scary. But I need you to listen to me," Rufus said, taking Morgan's face in both of his hands, "I don't honestly know how to answer that question yet. I don't think either of us would be ready for the answer. But I need you to walk over, and touch your body on the shoulder. Just like I said. Try to get its attention. I'll help you but you've got to trust me!" He said, nudging Morgan in the direction of his body. The boy's ghostly form was moved ahead rigidly, slowly like he was about to try and feed an animal that could take his hand clean off.

"Just touch it?" He asked again, "I don't say any magic words?"

"No magic words…But there is one word you can speak." Rufus said, "It's actually a name. It got me out of here a few years ago. Ask for a guy named Yeshua. He'll hear you and he'll help you." Rufus said, willing the ectoplasmic essence of the astral plane to coalesce into the form of a business card with the name Yeshua emblazoned on it in gold letters.

Rufus caught a twitch of movement out of the corner of his eye. He looked to his right and his inside's chilled. Oscar's restraints were falling to the ground, the shattered bits of chain links clattering to the floor as he landed on his feet. He saw Oscar's human disguise tear away in a bloody shower as a lupine muzzle exploded fourth from his head, ears elongating and eyes ablaze with the untamed fury of an apex predator. He was diving for something.

The body of Morgan Harris was latched onto Mick's suspended form, teeth buried into the tissue on the side of his throat as he flailed and kicked, trying to shake himself free from the thing's teeth that were now embedded into his flesh, and Oscar, who was lunging for his hanging body.

Rufus didn't even remember reentering his own body. But as the tingling sensation that rippled across his skin softened, he hoisted his body up on the chain, locking his legs onto the beam he was chained to. He leaned back, feeling every muscle in his body tense as Light surged through his veins and into the chain links. He looked over at the carnage Oscar and Morgan were causing to one another, both of their claws slamming into one another with raw animal fury. Mick's body hung limp, a fresh coat of blood drenching his twitching body and cascading down to the floor.

With an effort that felt like trying to pull a MAC truck through the Grand Canyon, Rufus let out a scream of raw, primal rage as he suddenly felt one of the chain links snap, their molecular structure flaring to illuminating brilliance that no mortal eye could behold without damaging their retinas. He felt himself falling, and tucked his chin inward as his shoulders absorbed the impact of the floor, cutting himself on metal shards. The chain that was wrapped around his wrists burned like white hot metal taken from a smith's forge as he rushed the two beasts.

Swinging the chain about like a radiant metal whip, he slammed the heavy links into Oscar's back, causing his demonic, wolf like head to snap back around as he roared.

Morgan scurried back further into the shadows of the room, shielding his eyes from the radiant light.

"Tranquilate, o te voy a partir la madre!"

**Stand down Oscar, or I'll kick your ass*, Rufus snarled as he loosened the chains from around his wrists, and wrapped them over his hands like a pair of knuckle dusters. His eyes flared to a fiery white, and his breath shot out from behind his teeth in a white hot gust of burning steam.

In a defiant howl, the beast threw out its arms, as the bones in them cracked and elongated even further. The claws at the end of each digit extended another two inches and Oscar's head rose to nearly touch the ceiling as the frenzied eyes looked down at Rufus.

"Maltido!"

**You little shit!* Rufus growled as Oscar dug his claws into the concrete and reared back to strike.

CHAIN AND CLAW

Rufus focused the Light through his flesh, fortifying his bones, fueling his veins with divine adrenaline.

The beast lunged. Rufus ducted, flanking left as the beast's claws mercilessly cut through the air where his head would have been. He felt a warm trickle coming from the top of his head and down the side of his face. He didn't have time to whip around before he felt claws digging into his ribs. The pain didn't even register at first, not until he was airborne. He felt the soles of his boots leave the floor, and he hit the wall behind him. Chunks of the wall behind him rained down on his body as the air vacated his lungs. The Light rushed to the damaged tissue, surrounded and inflated his lungs. It surged through him to such a degree the chain links wrapped around his hands had white smoke trailing off of them.

Oscar lunged again, and Rufus dodged the next swipe. He stepped in and drove his fist up into the base of the ribcage like a piston. The beast let out a high pitched yelp as Rufus brought his fist away, the chain links having burned perfect indentations into his abdomen. Bits of fur were singed at the ends. With the beast's bent over, he followed up with a right hook. Its massive head flew to the side as Rufus's fist traveled through it, the searing hot chain links melting the skin and fur off of that side of its face.

Oscar rolled backward, claws digging into the concrete to help stop his momentum. It was all the beast needed as he sprang forward, muscles taunt like a thick spring ready for release. Rufus attempted to throw himself to the other side of the room, yet fire raked the right side of his muscular torso as claws and fangs bit down hard into his flesh, dragging him to the floor. The points of the fangs demolished his nerve endings, separating the muscles from his rib cage and ripping sinew and veins out like old wiring in a computer. Oscar's head then reared back, and lunged to clamp down onto his face.

The pain was gone. Energy surged through his limbs in a shockwave as Rufus screamed in fury. He threw his arms up and caught Oscar's gore smeared jaws by the searing hot chain. Oscar's bloody maw tried to bite through the chain, a primordial *need* to snap through it consuming him as the links sizzled through the edges of his wet canine mouth. Rufus knew not to take his eyes off of the thrashing head of the creature that a few moments ago had been his friend. The Light in his veins began to flicker. Yet in spite of this, he felt his grip on the chain beginning to tighten. His muscles, already stressed to the point of exploding, were unyielding as they filled with lactic acid, screaming for a release.

He could let go. This beast would be quick about its work. He was laying here, trying to hold back the hurricane fury of this beast with the laughable strength of a broken twig by comparison, with only the fading strength of this burning hot chain holding the storm back—and it was only then that he noticed the beast's eyes.

Oscar's eyes when he was in any of his various lupine forms were always a deep reflective golden color that shown bright in the darkness from a football field away. These weren't those same eyes.

The eyes that bulged from these sockets were a deep crimson, to the point of nearly appearing black, save for a single flash of red that vanished just as quickly as it appeared.

I see you too, comrade, the Collector's voice sang sinisterly through Rufus's head.

You amuse me, you live.

With those words, the crimson faded from those eyes, as if being sucked deep back within them like from a drain or a vacuum. The reflective gold came flooding back, and the expression on the creature's face became panicked as it tried to spring up and away from Rufus. He felt his arms jerk with the force of the beast trying to back away, but his muscles were locked in that rigid, unyielding tightness. Rufus felt his flesh burning as his vision blinked in and out from darkness to dim. He tried to focus the remaining reserves of Light he could conjure up to flow to the shredded muscles and splintered bones. He felt his vision going black as the burning cold spread throughout his body. His hands were shaking as he tried to find purchase on the blood slicked concrete floor. The sounds of cracking bones and an ear shattering howl that slowly blended into a human scream cascaded over him like a shower of liquid nitrogen, freezing his body even further as he tried to crawl with one arm, using the other to apply pressure to the area of his torso that was now gone. His vision turned completely black, yet he could feel his eyes still wide open as shock began to take hold.

There were words coming from somewhere. Hands rushing to help him up, and help put more pressure on the area.

"Oh God! Oh God Rufus I'm sorry!" Rufus felt the hot sting of moisture hitting his bald head.

"Stay awake! Please bro stay awake!" Oscar panicked, switching back and forth from English to Spanish. Rufus's body went limp. He wanted to tell Oscar that it wasn't his fault, and that he wasn't in control of his body. He tried moving his lips, but even that was too much for him. He felt himself slipping into unconsciousness. And then just as quickly, he felt a surge of power, engulfing the shredded flesh. The sensation made his organs vibrate. He felt air filling his lungs, felt a cocoon of icy heat encasing the damaged tissue. He could feel his cells joining back together as new arteries, blood vessels and muscle filled in the canyons carved out by Oscar's teeth.

His vision exploded into a blinding array of colors no human language could articulate, shimmering arcs of rainbow prisms that coalesced into a human form above him. The form was screaming as energy was released from it, and with the last surge, Rufus saw that it was Oscar, his eyes blazing like fire and every vein in his body lit up like a livewire as the Light traveled through him.

"Gracias…" Rufus said weakly. Oscar pulled Rufus up toward him, embracing him in a bear hug, his tears staining the side of Rufus's head. Neither of them said anything for quite some time as they held each other. Mostly because Rufus couldn't breathe. Oscar's arms were like the iron jaws of a big game trap as he sobbed.

"It's okay bro…It wasn't you." Rufus said.

"I can still hear his voice inside my head." Oscar sniffed as he finally let go.

"Tell em to piss off." Rufus groaned as he rolled over, catching movement out of the corner of his eye. Morgan was directly beneath the hanging body of Mick, his tongue unusually long as it lapped up the blood that pooled on the floor beneath his body. Rufus sprang up and dashed over to Mick, with no regard for the creature that was beneath him.

"Mick!" He grabbed the sides of Mick's face, looking him over. Blood had turned his entire right side crimson. His heart stopped at what he saw. The entire right side of Mick's throat had been ripped off, chunks of tattered flesh hanging on by threads of skin and sinew. His eyes were wide open, pupils dilated in terror. He felt Morgan's clawed hand pawing at his leg and he kicked it away without looking.

"Oh Dios…" Rufus breathed out as his throat went dry. He pressed his ear to Mick's chest and prayed for a heartbeat. But his prayers were met with silence. He felt his face tightening as heat traveled up toward his face in a rush of madness. His eyes burned with the sting of acidic tears as he looked down at the slobbering creature at his feet, blindly licking up the last traces of precious blood that had spilled down from Mick's body.

"…I told you what to do…" Rufus growled as the creature looked up at him.

He heard the sounds of the boy shrieking as his hands closed around his throat. But he didn't see a thing as his vision went black. Yet his hands were meticulous, guided by the blind sense of one who was skilled in the art of killing in the dark. He felt his fingernails digging into the dead flesh of the freak that had taken his friend and colleague from him. He heard the ear splitting screams that were trying to form words. He didn't care. This was no longer a child. He felt the fiend's claws digging into the flesh on his arms as he slammed it against the wall again and again, his screams drowning out that of the vampire's. And then he let go. For a moment, he was the man who had slaughtered hundreds in the streets of Broken Edge, and had enjoyed it. He was the man that had harnessed the other worldly power of a being who had imparted its own essence into his flesh and had given him the powers of a god. He was the man who held this creature's fate in his hands.

When his vision came back, he was standing over the cowering form of the little boy he had come here to save. He dropped down to his backside, away from the boy who was now huddled in the corner, trying to burrow his way into the wall of concrete blocks. Morgan's wretched form looked much more human this time, though the eyes were still blacked out.

"I-I'm so sorry Mister…p-please don't kill me…" Morgan whimpered. Rufus just sat there for a moment eyeing him as his thoughts began to slow down. The fact that this thing was now speaking was proof that Morgan had regained some form of control over his body from the other side, but not before tearing Mick's throat out. It was too little too late.

"No need to mijo…you're already dead," he said coldly.

For a long time nobody moved or spoke. It took Rufus everything he had to look up at Mick's hanging body again. Suddenly the irony hit him. Mick was a kid that very well could have perished in the Broken Edge Massacre. He managed to live through the chaos. Rufus had never said it to Mick directly, but he had implied numerous times that he looked at him like a little brother that he was responsible for. Mick survived the event that leveled his city, the one Rufus was a part of, only to die while Rufus failed to protect him.

"Oscar," He said as he slowly stood up, his body wracked with pain, "Help me get him down."

WHAT HAVE YOU DONE?

Mick woke up to a throbbing sensation that felt like a living thing was trying to swallow his entire skull. Like a squishy suction cup with razor teeth was trying to gulp down his brains. It was something he was almost used to, given his line of work. He pushed himself up off the ground, which felt slick with a type of green, fungal substance. That was weird. He didn't remember this stuff being on the floor before. Had he been moved to another location? He stood to his feet, feeling lightheaded as he tried to stand. He held his arms out on either side of him to steady himself if he began to fall. The air in here was much cooler than the other room. Funny he didn't even realize how the room felt until he had just remembered.

He looked around at the room, noting the similar, if not exact layout as the other one he woke up in. Only this one seemed to not have any electrical sources of light. Just an off putting, yet softly glowing greenish purple hue that had no discernable source. He looked down at his chest and wiped the green stuff off of himself, realizing the strange absence of something.

Hadn't I been scratched really bad? Mick thought as he looked down, examining his flesh like a teenager looking at their first patch of acne. Suddenly he felt his eyes watering as a stinging sensation emanated from the areas of his flesh where he remembered the scratches. He saw the flesh begin to puff up as it resisted the friction of some force, until his chest split open in four parallel gashes that soon filled with blood.

Mick screamed as the fire crept up on him, wrapping around the affected area as more gashes appeared in his flesh.

Suddenly Mick remembered the time he met Yeshua on the Astral Plane, recalled how when he thought about drawing his gun, it appeared in his hand. The realization doused the pain in his mutilated flesh to abruptly cease, and when he looked down, he willed the gashes he had manifested on his flesh to close up. He watched in fascination as the gashes sealed themselves. He was watching the entire healing process, seeing the blood clot in each gash until it hardened into scabs, which shrank as the flesh around it turned pink, until each scab was gone and only glowing white scar tissue remained.

Ok…so I'm not in my body anymore…what the hell happened, he thought as he noted the disturbing absence of the silvery blue chord that should have been running through his stomach. He looked up at the ceiling, down at the floor, noticing that the fungus was creeping up the walls as well. He approached the wall directly in front of him, which hadn't been overtaken by the fungus yet.

Please let this work, he thought to himself as he placed his fingers on one of the concrete blocks that made up this wall. The edges of his fingers were glowing with a sizzling of greenish white energy as he pressed his fingers against the wall and closed his eyes. He felt his fingers, passing through the material, felt the minerals of the concrete blocks passing through his incorporeal form. The feeling of the tightly packed atoms vibrating so closely together as he slide right through, over, and around them like liquid. At some point of phasing through the wall he had closed his eyes. He was instantly reminded of the fear he had of getting pool water in his eyes as a kid, and how he always kept his eyes closed when he was under water. He guessed it was kind of like that. When he felt his face shimmering out of the other side of the wall, he eased them open. Same room as the one he woke up in, but this one had a light bulb hanging from it, emanating that greenish purple glow. Two figures were slumped in one of the corners. After a while he recognized them. One was Rufus, who sat with his naked back against the wall, his head resting on his folded arms that rested on his knees. The second was Oscar, who was seated in a similar fashion but was completely naked.

Oh crap, Mick thought. Had Oscar changed? He wracked his brain to try and remember. Usually, unless he was able to run off and find a place to strip, Oscar went through a lot of clothes. He looked down at the shredded remains of some grungy jeans, old shoes that looked like they had exploded, and saw several broken chain links scattered all over the floor.

Where's my body? Mick thought, feeling his heart rate escalate as he turned around to the sounds of sobbing. He turned in their direction to see a tall black boy who looked like he was about nine or ten, wearing cargo shorts and a faded orange t-shirt with a logo.

Mick dropped to his knees, and as they made contact with the floor, it felt like they were going through quicksand. He remembered who this boy was. He remembered what happened to him. And Mick suddenly remembered the last agonizing seconds of his life as he felt the right side of his throat beginning to tear. His hand shot up to feel the loosely hanging bits of flesh dangling loosely through his fingers as blood raced down his chest.

Mister? The boy asked as he looked in Mick's direction.

Mick looked up, his eyes wide as he superimposed the dead, chalky white face of the thing that had attacked him, over the face of the kid that was walking over to him.

You're Morgan Harris? Mick asked. The boy nodded his head slowly, brushing tears away from his eyes with the back of his wrist.

Y-yes sir. What's your name?

I'm Mick. Mick Johnson. Those are my friends Rufus and Oscar. We're hunters, and we came to get you and your friend Wendy back h—

Before Mick could finish his sentence, he felt the air nearly knocked out of him as Morgan's arms encircled him and the boy buried his face into Mick's chest.

Where is Wendy? Did you find her?! Morgan chocked out, eyes pleading. Mick shook his head and placed both hands on either side of Morgan's head to try and calm him.

Wendy's safe okay? She's back with her folks. Mick assured him as he felt himself drawing Morgan deeper in to return the sudden hug. When Morgan was able to compose himself enough to communicate without his voice teetering on the verge of another sobbing breakdown, he let go of Mick, his expression rigid and cold as stone.

It was my fault we got took. I had a picture I had drawn the night before that I wanted to show her, but I forgot it on my way out the door to catch the bus that day. I told her we should lie to our teacher and say we were gonna ride the bus when we were really gonna just walk to my house so I could show it to her.

Mick nodded, listening intently to his story. Hearing the guilt and the blame Morgan put on himself for their situation as he recounted it.

Well, Mick began awkwardly when Morgan was silent for a moment, *like I said, she is back with her parents now. We just gotta figure out how we're gonna get out of here and back into our bodies.*

Morgan's eyes looked away, and he closed them hard like he was trying to hold back another wave of tears as his arms shook.

Buddy, what's wrong?

Morgan's left arm came up and pointed behind him to two more figures that Mick hadn't noticed. In one of the far corners of the room, in a section where the otherworldly light refused to illuminate, a gaunt, bony thing was hunched over another body that was shirtless, wearing tattered and ripped jeans. The figure had its wrist pressed against the mouth of the shirtless body, whose own hands were both wrapped around the creature's wrist as it suckled.

Mick knew that he was incorporeal at the moment. He knew that when he looked down at his "body," it was a spiritual reconstruction of what he remembered himself looking like. He was pure energy on this plane. Yet he felt like if he had blood here, it would have run like an icy river, embracing him in a frigid blanket of biting cold. He had found his body, and it was drinking blood.

Morgan what have you done?

Morgan backed away, his eyes pleading, *Mister I'm so so sorry. I did this to you. I'm the one that brought you here. You didn't deserve that.*

Neither did you! We're both victims here kid! Mick said as he swung his arms out in an exacerbated fashion, causing Morgan to flinch.

My pa always says if you screw up…you gotta make it right. This is the only way I know how to make it right! This way you can go back to your friends and help them! They need you! Morgan shot back, stepping up to Mick.

Mick looked passed him at his body. The legs were twitching with a life of their own as the mouth—Mick's mouth—continued to suck from the creature's wrist. The creature he knew was Morgan's physical, now vampire body. He looked over at Rufus, who sat there as solid and unmoving as a statue. His eyes moved toward Oscar, who was beginning to stir as Mick watched his ears twitch, saw his shoulders roll and his fingers curl.

Okay Morgan, I'll go with that, Mick said as he began walking over to the two figures in the shadows. He saw his face as he stepped closer. Eyes wide and as black as that of a shark, with a reddish hue glancing off of the surface of the eyeball.

Mick stretched his hand out over his face, snapped the fingers, waved them in front of his eyes. Nothing. No movement of the eyes to follow the motion of his hand.

Your bald friend told me to just touch it. Like this, Morgan said as he stepped over and touched the shoulder of his body. The creature looked up, blinked its eyes a couple times, and looked around the room warily. Its gaze darted over to Oscar, who was starting to look up and around.

But you gotta hurry! Morgan urged.

Mick went to reach down to touch his body on the side of his head but then looked up, *That's really awesome, but can you enter back into your body completely?*

I can't! I've tried, and this seems to be the only thing that works on them!

Mick looked up again at Oscar, who was starting to crawl towards them, his features shimmering and blurry from this side of the veil. But Mick could see the ears beginning to stand up. See his limbs contorting and breaking into legs of the beast he truly was.

I guess this'll have to do for now, Mick said as he reached down, grabbed his body by the side of the face and squeezed. It felt like plunging his hand into a vat of liquid nitrogen, and the chill that engulfed his form stole any form of breath he might have been simulating in those incorporeal lungs.

He knew he was sitting up, in a dark corner somewhere in this room. He touched the floor, knew his fingertips were making contact with it, but he could not feel the texture of its surface. There was no registration of temperature, only vibrations as something stirred on its surface. The sounds of cracking bones were filling his ears, though they sounded muffled as if his head were in a drum of water.

He fumbled along the floor, feeling the tips of his fingers dragging the surface. He felt at least that much. He staggered to his feet as a rush of vertigo nearly lifted his head from his actual body, trying to hold himself up by fumbling for the wall, when something caught one of his arms. He looked down to see a child sized shape, trying to hold him steady.

"Mick?!"

It was a voice from somewhere in the room. Was that his name being called? He turned his head sluggishly, as he saw a man with no hair, standing next to another form that buckled and twisted on the floor into a new, four legged shape. The human shape on the floor had turned into something with a charcoal gray coat, now coated with blood and gore. It stood up on all fours and shook itself clean. The animal backed up towards the bald man, keeping his golden lupine eyes on the two of them as a floor rattling growl shook the room.

Mick, that was what the bald man had called him, held up his hand—somehow. He wasn't sure how. His arm felt like a rigid board tied to a string.

He tried to speak, his vocal chords cracking from what felt like an eternity of disuse.

The bald man's hands were held up defensively, his legs bent slightly at the knees.

The child sized shape next to him was talking, his voice distant. "Mick," raised his other hand up to feel his mouth and drew it away with something moist and sticky on it. Dark crimson trailed away on his fingertips as his attention was drawn to the lively puddles of blood on the floor. He could smell the sweet metallic richness, flooding his nose with sensory pleasure. His eyes glanced off of the orb of light, seeing the individual glowing coils housed within the glass bulb. His eyes saw the rainbow prisms exuding from the lightbulb in such radiance that he had to look away.

Bald Man and Child Shape were yelling, each pointing toward him as the animal on growled. The child shape was bearing a mouth full of fangs, and was clinging to Mick like a life raft while the animal was standing there with its hackles raised. The sensation of sounds, their voices clashing, was only audible in his ears as blurs of sound. He could barely make out any words as his senses were slogging through the haze of rigor mortis. He felt weightless as he looked down at his feet, only to see they were firmly rooted to the ground.

The thing the people in the room kept calling Mick made a dry croaking sound, the noise tumbling out over parched lips.

Bald Man's eyes shot towards Mick as it tried to speak, his expression bordering on homicidal rage and utter shock. Like he was something unnatural that needed to be put down. A name was starting to take shape in his murky awareness. A name that felt right to associate with this Bald Man. Had this Mick, known him at one time?

"Rrr…Rrrrufus," the Mick creature tried to say.

"Mick…can you hear me?" the Rufus thing finally asked. It took Mick a couple seconds to reply, his mind processing the question slowly as it bubbled into his awareness. He swallowed, tasting the staleness of his own tongue in his mouth as he looked down at his boots.

Mick nodded, its head moving slowly.

Rufus looked at him with a grim expression, his face like a stone wall as his eyes traveled from Mick down to the kid that was now hiding behind him.

"Can you remember anything?" Rufus was asking. Mick looked up at him and then down at the animal at his side, who was eyeing him intensely with those golden orbs. He stood there for a moment, blankly trying to recall some detail he could latch onto. Disjointed fragments began swimming through the wasted landscape of his mind, winding and twisting their way further towards oblivion as his vision began to go red. There was a vital component he was missing, and he had to have it. The red haze was growing thicker as the animal shape began to growl and emit quick explosions of sound into his ears.

The thing they kept calling Mick dove for one of the crimson puddles on the floor, and lapped at it like a dog.

HANK'S STORY

Sunny sat at the stop light in the SUV they had all driven up in, her passenger in the seat next to her starring out of his own window with a blank look. She didn't realize that she was tapping her thumbs on the steering wheel, one of many nervous habits she hadn't noticed she had until a couple years ago. She stopped when she noticed she was doing it, and upon stopping, Hank chuckled.

"I was listening to that. You have nice rhythm." He said, a deadpan smile coloring the bottom half of his face.

Sunny smiled and nodded as the light turned green, and she pressed her foot to the gas and went through the intersection.

"I tried playing the drums once when I was ten. I gave up after three lessons, but I really liked to sing. After me and my brother were taken in by—" She paused. She was about to share sensitive information with a complete stranger.

"Our foster family," she corrected, avoiding any mention of her time involved in a dark cult and the being she had devoted herself to, "I decided I wanted to pursue other hobbies." She concluded, adding a bit of edge to her voice, just enough to let Hank know that pressing was off limits.

He only nodded, "I understand. Kids change with time, same as everything else."

She sighed in relief, thankful she had avoided dragging up anything that could tie her to the one she had called Father. Her mind drifted back to the interrogation room where Hank had awaited her. After divulging that he had transported Mick, Rufus and Oscar to another location, he said he wanted Sunny to help him and his associate scout out the perimeter and break them out. Their cover had been compromised by Ronald Tregorr. Hank confessed to rounding Mick up for a meeting in the one called the Collector's office, but only after he had been instructed by the Collector to move them did he find that Tregorr snitched on them. For now he was appearing loyal to the Collector, while his associate, the one Wendy had called The Doc, was secretly attempting to rescue abducted children before they could be presented to the Collector. Some of them he was successful in rescuing without blowing his cover or appearing suspicious, others, not so much. Hank snickered with an evil grin when he told them that Tregorr's brains had been blown out during the skirmish in the office.

He revealed also that the missing child the authorities had been after, Morgan Harris, was being held at the same location. Pallacios was adamant that their next course of action should have been to storm the premises with a SWAT team, surround the building, go in and rescue Morgan and the hunters.

"That might work," Hank had said, examining the crusted dirt layers under his claws, "If the place wasn't already being patrolled by several of my kind, and housing other supernatural creatures that the Collector keeps locked away in that building. You go in like that and you will get yourselves killed, not to mention your friends. My kind know how to cover their tracks. They will sick the Collection on your SWAT team so fast they won't know what the hell hit them, and then flee the scene and watch from the surrounding rooftops before any dash or body cams can spot them."

Hank never even raised his voice, never rose from his seat. But Sunny was watching the wrinkles in Pallacios's face deepen with every word he spoke. She swore she could see the roots in her hair turning a chalky white, and when the agent balled her hands up into fists at her sides, she thought she might fall over. Sunny had stolen a nervous glance over at Hank's eyes after he finished speaking, and for a heart stopping second, she felt a small glimpse of what Pallacios was feeling. Those eyes were transfixed on her in the same way a starving person might look at roadkill—a marriage of sadistic indifference and lustful hunger that seemed to reach out, take hold of her face and violate her with the very cadence of its voice. Pallacios, demoralized and reduced to a near fight or flight mindset, struggled to tear herself free from where she stood. Sunny watched as her muscles twitched, as if attempting to run for cover. But she stood frozen, her once balled hands now clutching the back of the chair she stood behind for dear life.

"I thought you would see it my way," Hank had said to her with a smile.

Sunny put on her blinker and changed lanes when Hank told her she would need to make a left at the next stop sign. She stole another glance over at him, and was disturbed when she caught herself thinking that he actually looked handsome from a side view. Almost as handsome as his ghostly counterpart, whose phantom hands were now burrowed into the back of Hank's skull when she looked.

"So, what's your story?" Sunny asked him, feeling like she was walking out onto a ramshackle catwalk above a tank of sharks. Hank's expression didn't change as he turned his head in her direction, his neck stiff like a mannequin.

"Little girl, this car ride isn't long enough for that." He stated. Sunny shrugged, "Give me the highlights then."

Hank eyed her for a couple awkward seconds, and then pulled out a tin flask from inside of his jacket. The stale stench of wet copper was overwhelming, and made her eyes water as Hank took a long swig out of the flask. He drew the flask away, a small bloody ring around his lips where the opening had touched his mouth, which he promptly licked clean.

"You wanna know how I was turned?" Hank asked, and she noted the exhausted tone in his voice, like he had told this story far too many times.

She shook her head, "No, I was just curious about your life before."

He sat there for a second, digging the tips of his claws through holes he had worn through his jeans. He closed his eyes and drew his head back as if to recall.

"Well…I was a part of the 3rd Marine Division stationed in Dong Ha Combat Base in Vietnam in 1968. Me and my brother Trevor survived an attack on our ammunition dump. Not sure how I survived having three pounds of shrapnel embedded in my gut. My brother got sent home after having to have his left leg amputated below the knee." Sunny thought she heard a hint of emotion there. When she looked over at him, he was staring into the floorboards with an odd smirk on his face.

"That dumb little shit…" Hank chuckled, "I take three pounds of shrapnel saving his scrawny ass and the little fucker has the nerve to still lose a leg."

Sunny felt a wry smile creeping up the sides of her face as Hank reminisced, allowing himself to simmer in the moment before he started again.

"After his amputation Trevor got to go back to the States. It took about four surgeries to dig all that metal outta me though…" His voice trailed off as he stared, transfixed on the floorboards. Sunny didn't press him as he sat there lost in his memories.

"Then it came in one night…" He said, his tone taking a grim shift. Sunny felt the muscles in her arms tense when he said those words, feeling the cold venom that seethed into each word.

"I was in recovery from my second surgery. I woke up one night during a thunderstorm. I looked up and saw it. I thought it was one of my guys cause it was wearing a uniform. I couldn't tell if it knew I was awake. It wasn't even looking at me. The only way I noticed it was when the lightning flashed just right. It lit up the room long enough I could see it, just standing there." He said, his voice nearly dropping to a whisper.

"This thing, was wearing a uniform?" Sunny asked, for clarification.

Hank nodded, "Had the rank of a Private. I couldn't make out anything else that identified it. But…It looked like that uniform didn't even fit. I had never seen anyone with such long, frail looking arms…Such a long neck. It just stood there, watching, and I think its eyes passed over me once. After a while it began shuffling through the room, stopping at the beds of each person in recovery. The damned thing was sniffing each one, muttering to itself. I blacked out. When I woke up the next morning, I asked anyone else if they had noticed anyone come in. No one saw or heard anything. I kept seeing it. Almost always at night, but…" He stopped, claws digging into his jeans as the memories washed through him, the residual energy coating his rigid frame as he moved his head toward her.

"I saw it once in the daytime too. By then it had been about four months since my last surgery. I was getting ready to be sent home. Was gonna be shipped out two days later, when the damned thing attacked me in my barracks. I got the hell outta there with my life. I had a wife to go home to. There was no way in Dante's Hell I was gonna try and fight that thing, not knowing what it was."

Sunny nodded her head sympathetically, waiting for him to continue, all the while trying to figure out what it could have been Hank had seen. Part of her wondered if it had been another vampire, but she dismissed that idea, mostly on the basis that seemed far too obvious.

"When I got home to my Laura, she had told me of…some strange things that had happened around the house while I was away overseas. At first it was just little things like her car keys moving around the house. But when something started biting her, she called the police and stayed with a friend at their place. Now keep in mind this is happening in the late 60's. The world hadn't accepted the existence of monsters under the bed as a tangible reality yet…I don't know what I was thinking," He said, his voice trailing off like a runaway cart down a hill. Sunny let him respond at his own pace as he visibly looked like he was trying to gather himself now. The stoic exterior had melted into a mountain of a hollow man wishing for the sweet release of tears that would eternally lie beyond his reach.

"I spent the night in that house. I told her to stay at her friend's house across the street. I was going to get a look at what had attacked her and send the goddamned thing to its maker. She said she could hear it moving in the walls. After what I had seen in Nam, I wasn't about to doubt her." He stopped and looked up, a visible wave of relief washing over him as he made eye contact with her.

"Take a left up here and go straight for another block. Pull into the alley on the right and then kill your lights." Hank said.

Sunny nodded her compliance and got into the turning lane as she simmered in the silence, waiting for him to continue, but he never did.

They both exited the vehicle, stepping out into the darkness of the alley. As she felt the thud of her car door, Sunny realized for a quick second how Mick must feel in cramped areas as she looked at the three feet of extra space she had between her, the SUV, and the building on her left. Hank, being so big, had to shimmy his way out on his side because he couldn't get his door open all the way. The sight was briefly comical as she offered to help, to which he politely declined.

"You sure know how to show a girl a good time," Sunny said once he was out, looking up at the buildings that shot up from the concrete on either side of them for a good sprinting distance. Hank snickered.

"Are you worried I'll try something?"

Sunny shook her head, "I want to say that if that was your intent you would have done it already, but then again now is the only time we've been alone. But honestly…I can't say I'm too worried."

Hank nodded, "Thank God. That gets old, every mortal you reveal yourself to thinking you wanna use em as a slurpy all the time."

Sunny nodded, "Oh I can imagine." She said looking past him at an approaching shadow, one she hadn't even heard approaching, even with her exceptional hearing. Hank was already turning toward the approaching shadow, hands stuffed casually in the pockets of his hoodie.

The two looked like they were talking, but even as Sunny listened she could hardly make out any of the exchange. The other figure now looked like they were looking passed Hank toward her. Soon Hank was motioning for her to come toward them.

"This him?" She asked.

"Sunny, meet my shithead little brother—Trevor, the one the little girl called the Doc." Sunny saw the Doc's head turn toward Hank from beneath his hood, and then back at her, "I like that…Doc. Sounds so much better than shithead." Doc said, his voice sounding like a smoke inhalation victim trying to sing. His voice was a tenor compared to Hank's bass though. He stood only about three to four inches taller than Sunny, which made her all the more aware of how hulking and tall Hank was. The Doc—Trevor—stuck out his hand toward her, clawed fingers shooting out of fingerless gloves that looked like they had been fished out of a dumpster.

She steeled herself and grabbed the hand with a hearty shake. She studied his face. He appeared much younger than Hank did, not quite as gnarled around the edges, but his face had a sharp, angular quality to it. As she looked closer, she noticed the exaggerated ridges that adorned his face, which managed to accentuate the fact that the man she was looking at was not human.

Trevor extended out his other hand, like he was motioning her to follow him on a grand tour of this alley. Hank was already starting off in the direction the Doc had come from.

"Shall we?" he asked.

ESCAPE

Mick sat huddled in a far corner of the small room on his haunches, his hands dripping with dark crimson fluid. At some point, all he saw was red, and Rufus had said he had licked up most of the blood on the floor. Plastic pouches of blood had been brought into the room as well, and Mick held the shredded remains of one such container in his claws right now. His hands shook as he battled with his eyes to not look at his hands, not to look at the shredded bag that only a moment ago, contained a substance he had never known the bliss of consuming. He gritted his teeth, his swollen gums feeling their pointed tips carving into the side of his cheek. He felt his face tightening into a snarl as his hands closed around the remains of the bag, and he threw it forcefully off to the side.

Without thinking he shoved his fingers into his mouth, slicing the flesh of his fingers, yet his mind reeled at the taste of the intoxicating blood that they were drenched in. To feel the splash of life essence coating the insides of his mouth, down his throat, was, dare he say, orgasmic in a way. It was when he heard his name being spoken off somewhere in the dimming light of this room, that he flinched like he was being smacked. He looked up, his eyes adjusting again out of the haze his brain had entered.

Rufus, that's what the bald man had kept saying his name was, had tried to bring Mick up to speed. Apparently the animal that kept growling at him was named Oscar, and was something people called a werewolf. The child in the room with teeth like Mick's name was Morgan, and they were all friends who had come to a place called "Denver" to rescue him.

"You gonna be alright?" Morgan was asking, shredded blood donor bag at his feet as well. The boy sat with his knees hugged against his chest. Mick didn't respond right away. Not until he heard his name being spoken again by a different voice.

"Hey vato, the kid asked you a question." Rufus said. Mick turned to see him sitting on the ground across the room from them, Oscar lying down on his belly, his wolf eyes ever vigilant in his quadrupedal form.

Mick shook his head, "I think so." He said, and wiped his hands off on his filth ridden jeans.

He tried standing up again, and nearly toppled over as his muscles propelled him upward, faster than he remembered he could stand. He almost felt he would experience vertigo, but that didn't happen. The room's features were sharper than he remembered them being.

He reached up and touched his skin. He could feel the sensation of his fingers touching it, but something felt off. Like his skin was detecting the friction of his fingers dragging along the surface, but no texture. The more Rufus and Morgan spoke to Mick after he came to his senses, the more he had the feeling that he had been like them at one point. Images filled his head of a place they called "New Broken Edge." They seemed to switch between that place, and a place called "home." Mick finally figured out that they were the same place. Rufus told him of another companion they had, named Sunny. He tried to remember what she looked like. Rufus had said it was a she anyway. Rufus was speaking again.

"They bring those blood donor bags once every two or three hours…Been keeping track in my head. Nothing better to do really," Rufus said, his eyes drooping as if he would fall asleep.

Morgan spoke up from his corner of the room, "They have a metal doggie-door they been shoving em through."

Rufus nodded, "It only opens and locks from the outside though, I checked it out a while ago before Mick revived."

"Maybe Oscar could get out through the doggie door," Mick suggested. Oscar's eyes shot toward him with an unamused look. Mick stared at the creature, marveling how expressive its face looked. He had vague recollections of what the animal had looked like wearing its human mask.

Rufus pushed himself up and motioned for them to follow him down the corridor part of this room. Once they got there, Mick noticed a twin set of large lights set in a metal casing above the door, one a deep red, and the other dark green. The red light lit up as they approached, bathing them all in a warm glow.

The doggie-door Morgan spoke of was two feet by two feet in diameter. If Morgan scrunched his shoulders in, he might be able to fit through. Mick bent down and inspected the door for himself. He saw the outline of the door, but noted the visible absence of hinges on this side. Oscar lowered his head down, his nose fervently sniffing out the edges of the door, his tongue periodically shooting out along the door's surface as he did so.

"Got about another hour before they open that up again," Rufus said.

Mick looked up at him over his shoulder, "What if one of us waits here by the door and grabs the hand of whoever opens it?"

Rufus shook his head, his eyes drooping, "And do what? Pull them through the tiny door and make them give us the keys?" Rufus asked.

Mick's face fell. He wasn't sure where his plan would lead but he figured it was something to build off of at least.

The glow from the red light above the door suddenly went out, and the small corridor they stood in was pitch black, save for the weak light coming from the main room behind them. All eyes turned toward the lights resting above the door, just as the green one came on and a metallic click resonated in Mick's skin. Everyone looked at the green light for a few seconds, and then at each other.

Oscar let out a soft *whoof*, and stood on his hind legs, pressing his fore paws against the big metal door. Mick stepped back out of respect for his size. On hind legs, and in the form of a normal wolf, Oscar was still huge. Tall enough now to wrestle a six foot man to the ground.

Oscar leaned back on his hind legs and bounced his front paws off of the door's metal surface, and Mick felt the hairs on his arms flare when the door actually budged outward.

No words were needed as they joined Oscar in pushing open the huge metal door, the green light flooding out of the room and illuminating what lay beyond in a ghostly hue. Oscar stepped forward, now walking on all fours again, and stepped down into a dark hallway seemingly constructed of metal. Each of them followed, stepping down into the extending hallway, noting the odd tread of the floor. Grooves running parallel from the step they had taken down from their room, all the way to—Mick's eyes widened.

Ahead of him, another ten feet or so, was two double doors about twelve feet high, with thin slivers of light coming from the other side.

Before anyone could say anything, the darkness was flooded with a violent surge of light as the double doors were flung outward, blinding them all as they felt a powerful force shoving them to their knees. A tall figure stood silhouetted against the now seemingly sterile white environment behind them. But the red eyes were unmistakable. The claws of the outward stretched hand twitched as Mick and the others strained and twisted under the seemingly growing pressure that was forcing them down to crawl on their bellies. The eyes of the Collector turned towards Morgan, flashing with an unreadable glare as he stepped forward, and plucked him up by the throat with one hand.

"I give gift of food. I give playmates to entertain, and you think to leave?" He scolded, his voice sounding more like an irritated parent. Mick saw out of the corner of his eye, Rufus trying to rise, fists raised to lay into the Collector as the Light in his veins flared to brilliance. Yet with his other hand the Collector stretched out his fingers and Rufus was slammed back onto his knees, the Light in his veins glowing brighter as if it had nowhere to go.

Oscar's growls were suddenly turned to human screams as the lupine form on the floor began to violently thrash. Mick still had enough movement in his hands that he could attempt to shield his face from the giant paws and their threatening claws, but the attempt was feeble. Only after the screams turned to a choking gurgle could Mick see what was happening. The wolf like body was turning more human as the nude form of Oscar appeared. Oscar's hands went for his own throat, as waves of blood began gushing from a throat that seemed to be mauled by an unseen attacker. Rufus gasped and screamed as bite marks appeared on the side of his throat, drenching the left side of his chest in fresh blood.

But that's when Mick began to feel it himself. He felt something hit him square in the chest with the force of a battering ram and he flew backward. He felt a wave of energy become solid as he was struck across the face, and then he felt gashes appear in his flesh. That's when he remembered. They were reliving the injuries that had sustained earlier in the Collector's office. The places where he had touched them and healed them earlier in that cell.

Amidst the sounds of tearing flesh and gurgling chokes, the Collector stopped, his eyes burning into Mick as he dropped Morgan, limp on the ground.

"Your blood is changed." He said through his thick accent as he stepped over the writhing bodies of Mick's friends and knelt down. Mick had to fight to keep his vision from blurring over as the Collector got closer.

The Collector smiled through his beard, his eyes suddenly looking at Mick with an odd mix of amusement and predatory delight.

"You have changed. But not turned." He said.

Mick could only shiver as one of the Collector's clawed index fingers traced a line from Mick's bottom lip all the way down to his stomach, where the rest of his fingers suddenly flared out like a giant spider and hovered there. Mick felt an overwhelming tingle suddenly vibrate through his stomach region, his bowels, and the other organs in the surrounding area. He tossed his head back and began to convulse.

"The boy changed you, little hunter. But you are not turned. Still too much of the old you left inside." The Collector smiled as he placed his clawed finger under the soft flesh of Mick's chin, and stood up. Mick felt himself standing up with him, as if the weight of his entire body was being supported on that one claw. He felt the thick red blood stinging his eyes as he began to cough up globs of dark red liquid. He felt his limbs moving in unison with the Collector, as the two stepped over the now limp bodies of Rufus and Oscar.

"No! What are you doing to him?!" Morgan screamed as he tried to stand back up, fists raised and fangs bared to come to Mick's aid. The Collector flung him back into the metal wall with a flick of his wrist on the other hand.

The bright overhead lights flooded Mick's vision as they stepped out into the almost pristine white expanse of whatever this place was. Mick managed to rotate his head on that claw just enough to make out that they had just exited a massive shipping container, one of several in a seemingly infinite row. There were just as many facing him on the other side as the Collector threw him forward into one headlong. The world turned upside down, rotating at a whirlwind speed as his senses exploded upon impact with the container he was slammed into. He briefly heard the sounds of inhuman, otherworldly shrieking coming from inside the crate, and that's when it clicked for Mick. He was called the Collector, because he collected other monsters.

"Awoke too soon. Old fluids, organs, tissues still inside. No longer need those comrade." The Collector said, and flicked his wrist again. With that, Mick's head shot to the right, and expelled an unnamable jet of multicolored bile. Dark red, black, brown, and gray, all seemed to mix together as Mick flooded the floor to the side of him with a putrid, water-like consistency that stood out in stark contrast to the seemingly sterile white of this place.

Mick fought through the haze as the indescribable stench of whatever he had just vomited out assaulted his nose, threatening more explosions of bile as the tingling intensified and he rolled over, clutching his stomach and chest in a vain attempt to regain control over his own body once again. He saw the blurry shape of the Collector now entering the open shipping container once more, looming over Oscar's body.

Mick crawled forward, trying to get up, trying to channel the blood to his limbs as if…as if he had done that before, in another life. But his feet staggered, sending him tumbling down onto the floor. His head spun as he began to hear the rising cries of other creatures, their gut wrenching screams, howls, chitters and wails reaching his sensitive ears from inside their own containers.

The Collector reached down and picked Oscar up by the shoulders, nearly cradling him in his arms as he touched the exposed larynx of his friend. Mick watched as the flesh instantly knitted itself back together. He released Oscar, laying him back down, stood and did the same with Rufus. The torn flesh of Rufus's neck became whole as soon as his finger's brushed the surface of the bloody tissue.

Then his wild, predatory eyes landed again on Mick and he stepped forward, ignoring Morgan. He bent toward Mick, his clawed hands tenderly brushing his face as a stampeded of boots hitting the floor, filling his vision with the sight of armed men in Kevlar. Before Mick could smirk or come up with a clever one liner, he saw that these guys weren't SWAT. He noted the absence of the sound of sirens. He didn't hear the beating of helicopter blades overhead. No, these men had the Counter Non-Human Coalition's logo on their shoulders. Each one of them surrounded him and the Collector, their automatic weapons trained on Mick. Their eyes were vacant. Not dead, but eerily still. No unconscious eye twitches. No pupil dilation, nothing. Like Tregorr's eyes.

"Gentlemen," the Collector began as he stood to address them, "please escort newest collection back into cell."

Mick suddenly felt an array of gloved hands forcefully hauling him to his feet. He saw a small group of men going for the shipping container, brandishing electrified riot batons that buzzed and popped with an unknown voltage. He saw Oscar and Rufus convulse when the device made contact with their bare skin. Three of the amour clad vampires wrestled with Morgan, one holding his kicking legs fast while the other two grabbed an arm each. Rufus and Oscar were hauled up onto their feet and herded back into the shipping container with Mick.

UNLIKELY ALLIES

Thankfully, the smell of blood was semi contained within the blood donor bags Hank and the Doc slurped from, but the musty, dampness of the small storage unit seemed to counteract that small blessing. The stench from the accumulated pile of empty donor bags in the open trashcan next to Doc's wheeled office chair was beginning to gag Sunny's airways, and every breath she took, traces of the stuff wafted into her nose, down her throat. She winced and pulled her shirt collar up over her nose from time to time. Neither Hank or the Doc seemed to take notice, or even care as their eyes stayed glued to the desktop that was set up on a small card table, the power cords plugged into a small, cordless electric generator. A police scanner rested on the concrete floor, crackling with the voices of officers relaying information about break-ins.

The monitor was split between four different screens, each displaying camera feed from different buildings in the city. Buildings that the Collector owned. Whitehaven, the one the boys had been stationed at as homeless guards, was one of them. The other three were warehouses.

"This is how we keep track of when a kid goes missing," Doc explained as he motioned vaguely toward the equipment. Sunny's eyes looked at the wall to her right, just past Hank's bulk. A cork board with a map of Denver was tacked up, along with trails of red yarn marking locations of victim's last known whereabouts. The wall behind her sported a modest weapons wrack. Two survival machete's, a .223 caliber hunting rifle, a Remington 870 shotgun, a Beretta 92F and a 1911 .45 pistol, both with suppressors on the ends were all hanging above a stash of various ammunition boxes, and a small wooden crate containing flash grenades.

Her eyes returned to the screen displaying the camera feed Doc had enlarged. It was the warehouse Hank had said he was instructed to take Mick and the others to. A large, fifteen passenger van had arrived about twenty minutes ago and had been let in through a garage door on the east side of the building.

"You couldn't have put cameras on the inside?" Sunny asked as her heart rate increased with each passing minute. The suspense of waiting for any signs of activity were driving her to nearly pull her hair out as that garage door remained shut, taunting her.

"Nope," he said flatly and then punched Hank in the arm, "That's why I have him. Hank's my eyes on the inside."

Hank gave a pleased grunt, and then said, "Since your friends and the boy are the newest additions to his collection, he will be spending a lot of time here."

Sunny closed her eyes and took a deep breath, trying to get the uneasiness in her stomach to stop with the nervous tremors. She knew asking her next question wouldn't help ease her mind, but the more she knew, the better she would be equipped to handle the situation. At least it sounded good in theory.

"What all does he do with them?" She asked. Hank turned to her.

"His collection?" he asked.

"I probably don't wanna know, but, yes. Why does he collect them?"

Hank looked down at his blood donor bag in his hand, and then his corpse eyes turned toward her, "The Collector considers himself to be a connoisseur of the blood. His pallet has acquired the taste for not just the different blood types of humans, but other non-humans as well. He gets a particular kind of charge from drinking the blood of shape shifters, anomalies, magic users, and anything else he can get his hands on, something human blood just doesn't provide him."

Sunny stood there, quivering anxiously as he spoke. She looked down at her hands. She could see the flesh glowing red beneath her skin as light began to pulse through her veins.

Doc was motioning toward the screen as the garage door began to open. Sunny's eyes locked with the screen as the door raised higher, revealing the same van as armor clad figures wielding military grade weapons were loading up alongside a tall, gaunt figure with long, jet black hair, and a long dark beard. There was an abrupt glitch in the feed right where this man was at all times, even though he never stood stationary. The glitch moved with him, creating an effect that at times had a vague humanoid shape, and at others, was just a blotch of multicolored pixels that were struggling to reconstruct themselves in the right order.

"Hey zoom in!" Sunny asked Doc. He nodded and proceeded to zoom in on the garage door. She watched with baited breath as the van pulled out and left the parking lot quickly.

"Time to go," he said, scooting his chair back and stepping past Sunny toward the weapon rack.

He handed the crate of flash grenades to Hank, gave Sunny a wink, and lifted up the garage style door.

"Let's get moving ladies," Doc called as he sprinted toward the vehicle.

Two blocks away from the warehouse they had observed the Collector leaving from, Sunny brought the SUV to a stop in a back alley behind a row of stores. She parked next to a row of dumpsters below a metal scaffold on the side of one building where a ladder reached up to the roof.

She looked at Trevor through her rearview mirror, watching him fiddle with the prosthetic leg, tightening buckles, securing clamps, and then he rolled his pant leg down. She caught herself wondering just how old he was when he had turned. He looked so much younger than Hank. She herself was only eighteen. Trevor might have been twenty three at most when he was turned. Only when she reminded herself that they had both fought in Vietnam did she remember that Trevor was old enough to be her father. Seeing someone preserved in a state of perpetual agelessness, though by all accounts, clinically dead, was something she had never witnessed before. She found them both fascinating.

Sunny and Trevor exited the vehicle, while Hank got out, came around the front of the SUV and squeezed into the driver's seat.

"You ready for this?" Trevor asked her from beneath his hood.

She nodded, "let's do this," and with that, the handcuffs came out, securing her wrists.

ALL ACCORDING TO PLAN

Hank and Trevor's iron grip on each of her arms was cutting off her circulation. On the other hand, they were both as sturdy as iron, enough to brace her weight when she bucked, kicked, thrashed and cussed. Had circumstances not been so dire, this would almost have been fun. She felt very dainty, kicking between the two of them. But her arms from her biceps all the way down were going numb. It wasn't long before the two had made their way through the parking lot, with many of the CNHC hunters whistling and jeering in her direction as they escorted her inside.

Thankfully, with their betrayal not made known to anyone working for the Collector yet, their plan was quite easily the most straight forward. Hank and Trevor's idea to bring her in as a new part of the Collection was, suicidal, to say the least. In her head Sunny had seen at least a thousand different ways this could go badly. The simplified version of the plan involved letting several of the creatures housed at this location out of their cells, while Sunny would be safely reunited with her friends in the cell they were being kept in while the guards got overwhelmed by the sheer variety and numbers of the creatures here. Then at some point, Hank and Trevor would use the confusion and mayhem to their advantage while they snuck everyone out. It seemed half baked, but it was crazy enough to possibly work.

The only comforting thing though, was that if things did go south, at least she would be with the boys. They had fought their way out of the jaws of death together before.

"You sure you know the passwords to unlocking all the cells?" She had whispered to Hank between displays of kicking and screaming.

"Unless they changed em, yeah."

That was less than reassuring. She had hoped for a response of "Like the back of my hand," or however Hank would say it. She hadn't considered that the passwords could have been changed.

Before she could have a chance to think any more about that though, one of the guards was approaching, a key card in his gloved hand. His eyes looked hollow and lifeless, his face gaunt as if deprived of nutrients for weeks. His gray complexion bordered on almost pail white. He handed Hank the key card and then his eyes turned toward her, and he smirked. Trevor had explained that these were the blood addicted servants of the Collector. Not vampires, but as close to the still living human equivalent as one could get. The Collector found the term Ghoul to be less than fanciful. He preferred to call his human associates his Thralls instead.

"Tonight's been quite a hall for him hasn't it?" the man asked.

"Two hunters and a werewolf, and with this broad it makes three hunters," Hank chuckled.

"She's pretty," the guard said, eyes traveling the length of her body with hunger. The chill that exploded down her back sent her eyes to illumination as she spit right in the guard's face.

The guard smiled, shook his head as he wiped his face clean with his glove.

"Sweetheart I hope that's not all you've got." The hunter smirked.

"Oh trust me, there is a lot more where that came from." She growled. She heard the door beep after the guard punched in the code, and a mechanism was heard unlatching with a metallic click.

"Right this way," the guard said, leading the way with his weapon casually pointed to the ground.

The door opened up to a near blinding, crystalline, almost sterile white interior. The only thing that broke it up and seemed to dampen the effect was the stark contrast of the large shipping containers laid out in what seemed like a football field's worth of length. Maybe longer. The sudden shift hurt her eyes. Her eyes watered hard as she tried to blink away the moisture and the annoying discomfort stabbing into her retinas from the sudden shift in light. When she could finally bare to look at her two escorts, Hank and Trevor were keeping their heads down, their eyes all but closed.

"So you're hunters too?" Sunny asked. Her response was met with the cold touch from the barrel of a pistol pressed against the back of her head, as suddenly, another set of footfalls joined them. Where had this one come from? It's not like there were any shadows to hide in.

The one she had been talking to simply ignored her as he led them further down the cavernous line of shipping containers on either side, walking passed many other, similarly clad hunters, many standing guard at individual containers. Suddenly the steady momentum of Trevor and Hank's gate came to an abrupt halt as the hunter leading them stopped at a shipping container that was a sickly green color. She felt Hank tense up as he held up the key card in the other hand.

"This is the wrong cell," Hank growled as he flicked the small plastic key at the guard. His reflexes were a lot quicker than Sunny had expected, as the hunter plucked the keycard out of the air before it hit its mark.

"It's one of the few empty cells we have left at this location. Take it up with the boss," he said and he held the key card up to the sensor. It turned from red to green and Sunny heard a loud, echoing clang as the container's doors unlatched.

"I did you brazen little fuck! And he said she's to be put in the same container as the others from last night." Hank said, and Sunny watched his eyes. The same look he had when he spoke to Agent Pallacios. The same hungry look that conveyed to the one being spoken to that a beast was addressing their primal self, appealing to their need to flee with a flash of its fangs. The hunter turned slowly towards them, his eyes now gleaming with an arrogance Sunny hadn't seen—or rather, felt, since her time bound to Father.

"Ya see, now that's odd because when we get a new addition he tells us personally where he wants them," the hunters said. His voice dropped and Sunny saw his gloved hands tightening around the handle of his weapon, "And we haven't heard shit about this girl."

Other hunters were starting to approach them, their muscles shifting under the weight of their high collared Kevlar vests. They were all gripping their weapons in a ready fashion, not training them on the group, but held in such a way as to guarantee that as the next step.

"You boys don't know shit. She goes in the same cell as the others from the recent hall. Additions that I dropped off myself," Hank said, his voice gaining more of an edge. Sunny looked at him, saw the crimson tainted black of his eyes expanding to take over the milky corps white of those orbs.

The hunter with the keycard twitched an eyebrow, "Has she been presented to him yet? You know he doesn't like the catalogue being updated without knowing what's been brought in first."

"We just came from Whitehaven. This isn't the first time I've brought in last minute hauls for him," Hank growled.

Sunny felt the tension in her stomach as it coiled like a serpent. The hunter and Hank locked eyes with one another for what felt like a lifetime.

"Is there a problem here?" Another hunter who approached from behind asked, his face entirely obscured by a helmet and a gator face covering. The way his voice carried, the way he walked, Sunny guessed he had more authority than most of the ones here. Something else about his voice bothered her. It sounded familiar.

Hank turned to face him, releasing his grip on Sunny's arm. She was instantly thankful for the small rush of relief she felt on that side of her body. Until Trevor's other hand clamped down on that arm and jerked her around to where she was on her knees, both arms now twisted at such and angle behind her back she could hardly picture how he was holding them. She let out a legitimate gasp as the pain racked its talons deep into her muscles, and tears sprang to her eyes.

"We're going to have a problem if this little welp isn't going to let us put her where the boss said to!" Hank replied, pointing a meaty, clawed finger at the hunter with the keycard. The hunter with the commanding voice shot his eyes toward the one with the keycard.

The Thrall beneath all the armor drilled his underling for a moment before he spoke, his voice now carrying a definite edge to it, "Williams," he began, "you will escort these men to the container they desire. Is that understood?" He said, and as Sunny watched she swore she saw a shock of illumination from the corner of the man's eye. She blinked and it was gone. Again, that voice! It sounded almost like it was carrying a small hint of a Hispanic accent.

She looked up slightly, her eyes still having to squint because of the nearly overpowering lights. She dared not use the Higher Sight in here with such extreme lighting. While it helped her to see into the dimensions that coexisted alongside the material, it was also glorified night vision, and using it in this area would fry her eyes right out of their sockets. So she did the next best thing. She extended her senses out from her, reaching with her psyche to try and see passed any barriers that might give her a glimpse at the man's aura, a trick she had learned how to do from Judah, the right way.

She gasped as another lightning rod of pain shot through her muscles. She was being hauled up to her feet again, and shoved like a rag doll further down the line as the cluster of guards parted for them. She tried craning her head behind her to get one last look at the vampire commander, but it was no use. She felt the jagged edges of her nerves in her neck protest and it was too much to try and keep fighting against them.

A dull, puke green shipping container labeled 18-F34 looked up ahead, and with it, the sudden smell of putrefied remains, mixed with the scent of bleach flooded her nostrils as her eyes were drawn to an out of place stain that covered a massive area of the white floor. A hunter with a gallon of bleach was scrubbing the surface vigorously, trying to lift the large stain out. Her curiosity was quickly put down however when she heard the telltale beep and the metallic clang of doors being unlatched. Hank and Trevor manhandled her inside, ripped the keycard away from the guard who had just been put in his place, and proceeded further into the blackened maw of the metal container. They were approaching a solid reinforced steel door with a small opening at the bottom.

In spite of the pain she felt, Sunny drew in a sharp breath as new kinds of tears sprang to her eyes. This monster Hank and Trevor called the Collector had hurt her friends. Hurt her family. It had been a few years since she had felt so much rage swell up inside of her that it burned her eyes with tears. If she ever got her hands on him, she would channel the Light through every object in the room, turn the entire building he was in into a death box! She had no idea how she would do such a thing but she added it to the list of feats to add to her arsenal.

The metal door was open in a matter of seconds, and Hank and Trevor shoved her inside, closing the door quickly behind her. She massaged her arms and shoulders, tried rotating them in her sockets to get some circulation and ease the cramps that were burning through her like lava.

She stood in a dimly lit hallway, constructed of cinderblocks within the shipping container. Already the shuffling of footsteps was approaching.

She forced a little bit of the Light to her eyes, just enough to cut through the dimness as a figure came into view. It was stalky but muscular, shorter than Rufus. The face gave it away for her immediately as she rushed toward her friend.

"Mick!" She squealed as she rushed to embrace him, and then recoiled in horror at the sight before her when the Light revealed more.

REUNION

She felt her insides crystalize as her nerves seized in every inch of her body. She blinked rapidly, subconsciously trying to convince herself that what was standing before her wasn't Mick! Wasn't her friend. Until it spoke.

"Are you Sunny? They told me about you. I won't hurt you. Please don't be afraid of me." Mick pleaded as he held out his hands, slick with blood. His face had been coated in a dried brown crust, that went down his shirtless chest. His eyes looked sunken, and glassy. Uncannily like that of a mannequin.

A semi human form was writhing on the floor, its dimensions and limbs cracking and squelching into new forms, like it was struggling to decide which form to take. Oscar's face gasped for air as his body twisted into a flesh warped mockery of what he actually was. A human face on a wolf's body that was trying to stand under its own uneven weight. Her insides reeled at the sight. The thing before her was trying to speak words, which escaped in a series of gasps that tore her heart out.

Within a few more awkward seconds of horror, the face, as well as the rest of the head, had finally managed to rearrange itself into a somewhat normal looking wolf. It looked like a diseased, mangy thing as it limped toward her.

"Oscar," she trembled as she reached out her hand toward him. Oscar responded by wearily sniffing her fingers, then his tongue shot out as he affectionately licked them.

Rufus's body was lying in a corner, seemingly being guarded by another shape. The one resting next to him was a nine year old black boy, whose features were angular and sunken like Trevor's, and a mouth full of serrated fangs.

"This is Morgan Harris, the other kid we were sent up here to rescue," Mick stammered. Her eyes scanned the boy cautiously, her skin now awash in a cold sweat.

The boy Morgan looked up at her, his face contorted as if he might be crying, but his cheeks and eyes were dry.

She knelt down next to Rufus's body, her hands trembling, and Morgan moved to give her space, all the while shaking his head, "I didn't do it miss. He's not like this cause of me."

She nodded as she acknowledged him, "It's okay. No one is mad at you," she said.

Rufus's eyes were rolled into the back of his head, and his head twitched as she went to touch his cheek.

"What's wrong with him?" She asked, turning to Mick.

"We almost broke out. The Collector stopped us, messed all of us up. After they shut us back in here, Rufus said he could feel you coming. He's been like this since," Mick said, his hands shaking.

The whites of Rufus's eyes flickered like small lanterns in his head.

Too much was going on all at once for her to take in. Mick had been turned. The other child they had been sent to return home was now a vampire. Oscar had been severely weakened, and Rufus was immobile.

Suddenly Rufus's head jerked violently to the side and she jumped, as his voice came spilling out of his mouth, "Williams…give me that keycard, now. You two, with me."

She shook from head to toe, spasms of shock and confusion crawling through her like worms. Suddenly realization donned on her. She felt the floor spinning out beneath her as she finally realized where the voice of that one hunter had come from.

She knew of Rufus's expanding psychic abilities ever since she began working closely with him. His ability to jump into the memories of victims was something he had used many times in their investigations when they gathered intel from survivors of creature attacks. It was something she had asked him to teach her to do. He had tried a couple times but she just couldn't reach the same level of trance necessary to accomplish it. But she had no idea that Rufus was capable of jumping inside of another's body!

A metallic clang resounded down the dark hallway from the entrance. The thrumming of boots, as Hank, Trevor and the masked and armored Thrall entered the cell.

Morgan retreated into a corner, Oscar let out a low warning growl, and Mick stood up.

"You!" He said as he attempted to rush Hank, who reached out one of his large hands and effortlessly pushed him aside into the wall.

"Mick stop! They are on our side!" Sunny yelled.

"They set us up!" Mick countered, his voice rising with fury and eyes turning a frightening blood red, "Took me, Oscar and Rufus to meet that…thing!"

"Mick se sienta! Sit down!" Rufus's voice came out of the guard, freezing Mick in place. He backed up against the wall, and slid down to his rump, his eyes looking from Rufus's actual body to the one he was borrowing.

"Your friend here has a better alternative to our original plan," Trevor said.

Sunny's eyes, as well as Mick's looked cautiously toward Rufus's body, and then the armored hunter that was looking at them impatiently.

The Kevlar clad figure walked forward and said with a twinge of Rufus in its voice, "Alright, now listen up."

FREEDOM

An agonizing thirty minutes had passed. Thirty minutes of waiting that felt like a cold, serrated scalpel, carving calligraphy in his skin.

Mick paced nervously, his previous meeting with the Collector having unlocked the floodgates on his memory. He had begun remembering almost every detail now of his other life before waking up in this place. The meeting in the Collector's office, the vampire named Hank, and the fact Mick used to be able to control some kind of near divine light in the same way the Collector could control all of them. His friend Sunny, who he felt he was meeting all over again for the first time. He wrestled with the look he saw on Sunny's face when she came around the corner. Saw what he had become. The teeth, the eyes, the blood. Everything. That look of pure shock. The revelation that now, she had a reason to be afraid of him. But something else was screaming at him from another corner of his mind. A reoccurring nightmare that he had kept having before. It felt like it was such a long time ago. And the resemblance of someone in the nightmare that looked like the other guy Hank had come in with. The one in the grungy hood. Granted both that guy and Hank were dressed like homeless bums but the guy in the hood was dressed a lot like how Rufus had described the guy Wendy Matthews said had saved her when he saw her memories. Was he one of them too, a vampire? His mind kept pressing the rewind button, seeing the flashes of it in his nightmare. Were they truly the same person?

"So," Mick said to Sunny, "they your friends?"

Sunny looked up at Mick from the collar of her shirt, which she had pulled over her nose to help filter out the smell in here. She had been sitting with her knees pulled up against her chest, making herself small. "I like em. They helped me get back in here with all of you." She said.

"So if you can be friends with them…then is this," Mick motioned to himself, "gonna be okay?"

Her eyes softened and she crossed the room to him. She reached over and touched his shoulder, and her shirt collar fell to reveal her smile, "Mick…No matter what. You're family. Even if you need blood now instead of food to live."

Mick closed his eyes and nodded, relief carving a smile on his face.

"I'm sorry. Just the look on your face when you came around that corner is what got me. It felt like another piece of me died. I can't lose you guys, not now that I'm like this. I'm in bad shape here and I need all of you," Mick said, his voice raspy. Neither of them said anything for a moment. Their eyes just roamed around the room, watching Morgan as he guarded Rufus's body. Oscar limped along, looking like a stray dog that had walked a mile through the bloodiest reaches of Hell and come back to tell about it.

"Have you seen that guy in the hood before? Like ever?" Mick asked.

"The one that came in with Hank?" She asked. Mick nodded.

"Not since Hank introduced me to him tonight. That's actually his brother. His real name is Trevor. Turns out they are both Vietnam vets and are looking to get out from under the Collector as soon as possible." Sunny said.

Mick nodded as she spoke, "They know where they're gonna go when they do manage to get free?"

Sunny shrugged, "Just out of Colorado, that's for sure. They both said they will be safer when they are out of the Collector's domain. He only controls Denver, but after they are done helping us, they said they would probably never set foot across the Colorado state line again."

"Maybe they could come with us. I'll need someone to help me figure out how to manage this new condition," Mick said, and then he looked down at the floor.

Mick closed his eyes again and began to think. Think about a cracked mirror. A blood soaked floor. A woman's screams…

His ears pricked when he heard the heavy metallic swing of the cell door, and the heavy, tromping boot steps of the body Rufus was piloting entered the cell, with Hank and Trevor on either side of him, and an excess of five other armored hunters behind them. One was holding a muzzle.

"Let's move! On your feet! You're being moved back to Whitehaven!" Rufus barked.

More memories were floating up to the top of Mick's mind like cargo from a shipwreck. In his line of work, he had become used to being shoved into a van with a bag over his head. He found himself recounting all the times he could now remember. The time when the hunters rescued him from Terrance, the "Tick," Miller. There were so many others to recall, and now, he could add this one to the list. One time, he, Zach, and Parish had all been sent to investigate a rash of disappearances in Houston, TX. As they all awoke with bags over their heads in a boiler room under a university, their captors turned out to be a cabal of slashers working with a tribe of subterranean dwelling throwbacks they had managed to strike a deal with. Hunt victims to slay on a college campus, feed the cannibalistic creatures that dwelt below the leftovers.

It suddenly struck him how absent mindedly he was recalling these memories, before he remembered the feeling of the bag enshrouding his head, cutting off his airways as it shrank ever so smaller. But something strange happened then. He realized that he hadn't felt the need to breathe since he violently vomited all over the floor earlier. That realization sparked a chain reaction of other things to be aware of. If he hadn't had to breathe, then what did it matter if that bag was shrinking over his head? He tried breathing just out of curiosity, feeling the blood rush around his lungs. He felt them expand slightly as the blood massaged the airways, coated the lungs and flooded the muscles around them. But after doing that about three times, the effects began to wear off, to the point breathing seemed far more trouble than it was worth. His claustrophobia now seemed like a hollow echo, like everything else about him now. He began to count down in his head from one hundred again, trying to muster the feeling of dread he felt when his job thrust him into tight spaces. The feelings surfaced as distant whispers of a lifetime ago. He realized there in that moment, he could indeed play the part of being terrified of small, enclosed spaces, but it would be just that—a gag. His claustrophobia had died…along with the parts of him he had puked out all over the pristine white floor. Mick didn't know whether to shout for joy, or cringe in horror at the realization that his fears had been laid to rest at the cost of his humanity.

Regardless, as the van pulled away from the compound, Mick knew that in time other fears would indeed arise to replace those old ones. The chief among them, being obvious. How could he stay with the Reclaimed, and continue in this state? Would he try to hurt any of them? Or worse, did any of them have what it took to put him down if he did lose it? He knew these hunters he had embraced as family well enough to know they would rather summersault through moving hoops of fire for him before they ever considered that as an option. He didn't want to die really. But then he remembered his lack of a pulse, and instantly had to rethink his wording. If he was already dead, in the clinical sense of the word, what could this existence possibly be classified as?

"Yeshua," he whispered, "I need you…I need you…Please don't leave me."

He felt a clawed hand pulling the black linen bag off of his head, and he looked back to see Trevor staring at him absently. Everyone else had had their facial coverings removed. Trevor's gaze then shifted as his hands began working to remove the muzzle around Oscar's lupine face.

Mick knew, now sitting in the same vehicle with him, that Trevor's face was indeed the face he had seen in the mirror in his nightmare.

"How did it happen to you?" Mick asked, trying to establish some common ground, but also prying in his subtle way for something that would confirm his suspicions.

Trevor's eyes moved towards Mick's as he slide the muzzle off of Oscar's face, "I appreciate the straight forward approach," he said, "but that's not something I'm willing to revisit tonight. You're Mick right?" Trevor asked, sticking out his gloved hand.

Mick nodded emphatically and shook his, "That's what they keep calling me. I don't feel like me though, that's for sure."

Trevor nodded a little, "Its jarring as hell trying to make the transition."

Mick nodded, "Tell me about it. I puked up half of my insides before you guys got here."

Hank snickered next to Mick, his eyes locking onto him, "That's one thing most of the movies never got right about us. Our bodies essentially die. A corpse eventually expels its fluids. Tell me you ever seen *that* in a vampire movie?"

"Hey so can you guys turn into bats?" Morgan asked from farther back in the van. Trevor let out a chuckle. Hank's laugh was much heartier.

"Hell no! Do we look like cheap Dracula knockoffs to you?" Hank grinned. Morgan shook his head.

"No sir."

"I like this kid," Trevor said, patting Morgan on the shoulder.

"Hey so," Mick cut in, "What else do the movies get wrong?"

"Well," Hank began, "when we awaken, we're a blank slate. We each have the basics—super strength, heightened awareness, ability to see in the dark. As we adjust we pick up other, more subtle abilities. We can use the blood to effect someone's mind, make them see shit that aint there. In most movies ya see vampires shape shifting, turning into mist or flying. That's strike number one. We don't awaken already being able to do those things. If you meet any other vampires who *are* capable of doing what the movies and books show, it's because they have spent centuries learning the magic that will allow them to do it. So you wanna fly? Turn into mist? Fine. Good luck seeking out an Elder who will teach you."

Mick sat there, taking it all in but also getting a little impatient. He needed to talk to Trevor about how he was turned. About the dead woman in his dream. Because as far as he knew, this was going to be the last time he might see either of these guys.

"So it's like leveling up in a video game? We start out as level one characters and then we get stronger as we level up!" Morgan exclaimed. Hank and Trevor nodded, a look of *sure kid, whatever you say,* passing between them.

"Alright kid, you wanna turn into a bat? A good place to start would be to study the magic of the Navajos. A vampire who shapeshifts basically has to do the same thing as a skinwalker. Only difference is you'll be mixing the power of your blood with your first few rituals and then if your blood is strong enough, you turn into a bat, or wolf, or fuckin Jimmy Hoffa. That's what some of the others still loyal to the Collector have said they've had to do." Hank said. Mick saw Sunny wince.

"He doesn't need to know how to do that!" She said, her voice as cold as a corpse. Hank stopped and looked back at her, looking annoyed.

"The kid just asked a question and I—"

"He does *not*. Need. To know. Magic is *not* something you mess around with lightly, little boy! *Especially* skin-changing! Take it from someone who has been there." She said as she looked passed Hank, Trevor and Mick towards Morgan. Her eyes were flaring up, lighting up the darkness inside of the van, and Mick felt compelled to look away. Mick heard her voice cracking as she spoke, and a luminescent tear fell from her eye as she finished. The rest of the ride was silent for another couple blocks before Sunny directed the vessel Rufus had commandeered to turn right into a narrow alley. When the van stopped, the body suddenly slumped back in the seat as Rufus's real body in the very back began to stir.

He sat up slowly, rubbing his eyes and bald head momentarily, and yawned so big Mick thought the man's jaw would come unhinged.

"You doin' okay mister?" Morgan asked as he tapped Rufus on the shoulder.

"Not doing bad little man," Rufus said, groggily.

"Is he asleep?" Sunny asked, pointing to the driver.

"For now." Rufus said.

"Any idea how long we have before this guy wakes up?" Sunny asked.

Rufus shook his head and eyed the man's prone form in the driver's seat for some time.

"No need to find out," he said, "I can make sure he doesn't wake up to follow us or report us missing. Wouldn't even have to possess him to do it."

Oscar let out a low 'whoof!' of support.

Before anyone could come to a decision, Trevor was speaking up, "Don't waste good blood. Not when there are only three hours until dawn and these two need to feed," he said, putting a hand each on Morgan and Mick. They both shot him a look of stern apprehension.

"Yes?" Trevor asked, annoyance growing in his tone.

"We're not feeding on that guy!" Mick said. He had had no problem licking up blood from the floor, or drinking it from blood donor bags, but that was when he was in a red haze. Drinking from a live victim was where he drew the line. It was a line Mick knew there would be no going back from. Stepping across it meant that now he couldn't keep his denial at bay. Yes he had changed, was no longer human. But to drink from a living victim in his mind would solidify the very thing he didn't want to admit.

"No way!" Morgan agreed.

"It'll be fine, me and Hank can take the first drink, show you where you need to bite to get the most—" Mick cut him off.

"Dude no! Hell no! I can't! We're not doing this!"

"You know you're already covered in dried blood right?" Hank snorted. Mick looked over at him, indignant. He hated how much of a point Hank was making, but he still had not overcome his revulsion at the idea of killing another person to drink their blood…no matter how sweet it tasted when he drank it earlier.

"From blood donor bags! You can't just expect us to—"

"Enough!" Hank roared, and everyone jumped. The van was quiet for a long time.

"Okay," Hank started, "Regardless, we can't let this guy live. So whatever the hell you're gonna do, just do it for fuck's sake! But if you both go into slumber during the day without having fed adequately, you'll wake up ravenous, and possibly hurt someone. You aren't experience enough to gain any control over your thirst when it hits. Not yet. In time you will. But do you want to wake up as a rabid beast tonight? A fuckin, mindless, blood-thirsty husk? Is that what either of you want?"

Mick sat there, staring at the floorboards. He closed his eyes. All his usage of what blood he had drank earlier was used up, and the longer Hank went on, the more images of him going off the deep end came flooding into his mind. Images of Valerie, Judah, Zach, Parish. Their blood pooling around their bodies from their mangled throats. Mick, down on all fours, lapping at their blood like a dog.

He looked at Morgan, and then back towards Hank and Trevor.

"Look," Hank started, his tone more level as something approaching empathy crept into his voice, "It's never easy your first time. With your background as a hunter, that comes with a lot of baggage. You kill monsters…Now you think this act will turn you into one and there's no going back."

The final ring of those words echoed loudly in Mick's ears, like a mallet delivering the final stroke of a nail into a coffin.

"You only become the monster when you don't take care of yourself first." Trevor said.

The following seconds that ticked by was filled with the unbuckling of seatbelts as everyone exited the van and got into the SUV, leaving Mick and Morgan alone with Hank, Trevor…and the sleeping driver.

PURGED BLOOD

The form of a small creature on the floor filled the Collector's vision as his shadow loomed over it. The thing had cartoonishly large, pointy ears, with two dull, pinkish red orbs housed within its misshapen head. The Collector's nostrils flared as the panic that emanated from the small creature filled his nose. The panic that was rushing through the goblin's veins right now.

The Collector stroked his beard casually as he looked at the creature with a mixture of hunger and something akin to pity. He knelt down, yet even in that position he still managed to tower over the goblin. The creature was exceedingly ugly, its jagged teeth almost chattering as it stood there. Its pockmarked face was slack and drooping, giving the creature jowls.

The goblin knelt down, spreading its clawed fingers out on the rug, bowing its head and muttering something in gibberish that the Collector had never heard before. The small frame of the creature shook fervently as it dared to look up. Once eye contact was made, it quickly dipped its head down again.

The Collector reached his hand out and stroked the bumpy skin of the creature, tenderly brushing its mess of oily, black hair to one side, smoothing it out. He reached into his inner breast pocket on his tweed long coat for something, and the goblin stopped its petition as his eyes traveled up to meet the Collector's gaze again.

The Collector felt the wool fabric give a damp squish between his fingers as he withdrew it from his coat. He unrolled it with both hands. The item was a long wool cap that ended in a frayed tip about two and a half feet long. It was stained dark brown, and as he inspected the item in either hand, a residue stained his fingers. He licked from his clawed fingers as one does after sampling a dessert dish.

"You want this?" The Collector asked, and the pitiful creature at his feet frantically nodded its head, ears flopping on either side. The Collector felt his mouth shifting into a grin as the door to his office burst open, and the tangled mess of footsteps invaded the quiet of his office. He turned to see Ralph man-handling one of the homeless under his charge to their knees. A man in his early fifties. A long, unkempt beard fell down his neck, his wrinkled face stretched with terror as he tried to look up through the blood that coated the right side of his face from the gash above his eye. Ralph had the man held firmly by his thinning hair, his head drawn back to expose his neck.

The Collector nodded to Ralph, who released his grip on the man's head rather forcefully. The man's eyes darted around the room in confusion as he tried to speak. To ask what he had done wrong, to beg. But his breath cut short when he glanced at the small creature that was now confidently standing behind the Collector, donning its long wool cap with the tip that fell to the creature's crotch.

"You have done nothing wrong," The Collector said calmly.

"But," he said as his eyes took on a darker red, and he looked back at the goblin behind him, "I must borrow you…for him." He said. The man's eyes, wide with unspeakable horror, were pleading for answers.

The Collector side stepped just as the goblin rushed the man, claws flashing as the man's throat was suddenly eviscerated. A fountain of blood splashed the goblin's face. Its gleeful chittering replaced by an almost drunken moan of pleasure as it continued to tear the man's throat out, and then proceeded to stuff the woolen cap into the fresh hole he had made. The goblin's hands shook with drunken delight as the cap soaked up the red fluid. The creature then proceeded to roll around in the man's blood, scooping it up in its hands and throwing it all around the room like a giddy child. The Collector smiled and lashed his tongue out to catch some of the droplets that hurdled towards his face. He smiled with contentment as he looked up at Ralph, who had moved as far out of the way as he possibly could.

"Happy little bugger aint he," Ralph observed, his bone tusks clattering against each other as he crossed his arms.

"He is," The Collector agreed casually.

Ralph cleared his throat to speak again, "Uh…Sir? Has anyone checked in with you about the new additions from sight three coming back here tonight?"

The Collector looked up, his face knitting together in an expression of content knowing, "I am aware those carrying my blood have been moved. It is not cause for alarm, comrade." He smiled as he said this.

"Is Hank checking in with you tonight?" the Collector asked. Ralph shook his head.

"Aint seen em all night."

The Collector nodded, as pieces began fitting themselves together in his head, "Unfortunate for him," he said, "His brother, Trevor, also shirking duties. The Matthews girl…"

The Collector's eyes moved off into the distance, visualizing Trevor for some time before muttering absently to himself, "It was as if…she having help." Then he shot Ralph a look that conveyed he was dismissed. The Aussie dipped his head, and stalked out of the office quietly.

He noted how bored he suddenly felt as his eyes looked at the gleeful goblin, now making, of all things, a disfigured blood angel on the floor as if it were a child. He deliberately closed the space between them in a blink, plucked up the bloody cap from off of the goblin's head in a flash. The goblin's expressions of glee quickly turned to horror as the Collector unhinged his jaw, and sank his network of serrated fangs deep into its belly. The sounds of his swallowing filled his already keen ears, as the syrup textured blood that flowed from the creature's abdomen filled his guts. His vision began to fill with sparks of radiant colors from across spectrums that didn't exist in the material realm. His body was wracked with the same pleasure sensations he felt in the bathhouses of his Mother Russia when he gathered his followers to him. The same frenzy of ecstasy he had to work himself up in before his maker showed him the power of his own blood. That ecstasy washed over him, and through him now as the blood of the otherworldly filled his dead flesh. If only Makari, his maker, was around to know the pleasures of drinking from the otherworldly. The blood of humans still had its merits, but was comparable to a bland, unseasoned slab of—his mind had drawn a blank. He had forgotten the taste of mortal food, unable to draw any comparison.

He dropped the now motionless goblin, and it hit the floor with a wet slap. He regarded the blood soaked wool cap in his hand, then rolled it up in both hands, staining his chalky white skin further with fresh blood. And then he held the fabric over his unhinged jaw, and squeezed out the blood in a continuous, dribbling stream into his mouth.

Once he had wrung out every possible drop, he tossed the hat onto the creature's now lifeless body, and turned to address the presence that had just entered the room.

"You like to watch, no?" The Collector stated as his eyes landed on the tall column of writhing shadow in the corner. Its arms were crossed over its chest, which writhed in shadowy black tentacles that evaporated and melted back into its body the moment they sprouted. The guest inclined its head to the side as a chuckle burbled up from within.

"It filled me with a certain level of amusement." The guest admitted as it unfolded its arms and in a blink was standing over the two bodies.

Neither of them spoke for a time, their silence held in mutual respect for one another as each tended to their own interests. The Collector withdrew a handkerchief from off his desk, and began to wipe his mouth, and then dipped his clawed hands into a basin of water on his desk and ran them through his beard. The shadowy guest looked on the two bodies still, his eyeless gaze seeming transfixed upon them.

"A member of the Redcaps," The shadowy guest observed, looking at the goblin, "easy enough to come by when accompanied by soaring crime rates."

"It will awaken soon," The Collector said, observing the wool cap lying on the small creature's chest, "they cannot truly being killed, unless cap is desecrated."

The shadowy guest nodded, savoring the shared knowledge between the two. The Collector leaned back in his chair, held out a hand. One of the fine, high backed chairs his musicians sat in when they played came scooting across the floor near his desk.

"Forgiving my rudeness Father. Please, sit down with me and let us be catching up," he said. The creature that stood before him, nodded graciously and sat down.

"I am truly sorry that children here not satisfying you." The Collector apologized sincerely. Father nodded in understanding.

"Grigori," Father began, using the Collector's real name, "my rejection of your choice stock is not a reflection on the quality of the children themselves. I have come to inform you that I have already chosen vessels for my children to inhabit."

Grigori, the Collector, leaned back in his chair and stroked his beard, his red eyes betraying his interest.

"If you have made choice, then why telling me now?" the Collector asked.

Father leaned forward, his writhing, featureless face now perfectly level with Grigori's.

"As the one who gave your coven the means of bringing you back from the ashes, my disclosure of such information is at my discretion. As such, I no longer require your thralls to hunt down and abduct children on my behalf. Your efforts will not go unrewarded however," Father said.

The Collector's eyebrows raised as he listened intently.

"Go on," he prodded.

Father held out one of his hands, producing a small, billowing smoke column that gradually took the shape of faces. Faces of the new additions in the collection.

"I am aware you have stumbled across a new type of blood. Blood that has been...purged, of my essence," Father said.

Grigori was leaning forward now, resting his elbows on his desk as he studied the shifting shadow sculptures.

"I apologize to you and your kind for the way my essence has tainted the cattle. But what if I told you I know a place where my essence is being purged from the population? A city where you and your coven can find more of the purged blood."

The Collector folded his hands beneath his chin, eyeing Father intensely as he felt the blood he had just consume raging against his insides with longing. He had heard tales from others far older than him of a time when the Damned were practically gods in their own right. Feasting on tainted blood had reduced them to a hollow reflection of their former glory. It was something he had known since being embraced by Makari. Those among the oldest in their circles had not dared to sample the blood of other creatures other than mortal humans though. The stubbornness of the elders would see them continue to slink along through the shadows, not as true godlike predators, but as husks of their former selves. It was because of that, that the Collector would be the survival of their kind.

Father had been the one to pass on the knowledge to the Collector's followers of how to bring him back, of soaking his charred remains in the blood of other creatures. Blood of the wild things that changed shape. Blood of that which was made from the dreams of Faerie. Blood of those who practiced the magic arts. Tainted mortal blood would have never sufficed to bring him back.

The Damned would have to adapt to survive. Father was showing them how.

"The city of New Broken Edge can be your new haven, Grigori," Father said.

The Collector smiled as he nodded, "Tell me more."

UNRAVELING

Mick stared down at the near-bloodless husk of the man that he, Morgan, Hank and Trevor had just fed from. The man had been stripped down to his boxers. The perforated, mangled flesh glared up accusingly from the legs, where the femoral arteries had been burst open. The throat was a jagged mess that looked like to chewed up hamburger, the jugular vein and carotid artery now obliterated.

At one point the man had awoken from the feeding, thrashed violently, and then blacked out again when Hank used his massive fist to nail him between the eyes. The two veterans stood, using their fingers to wipe the remaining drops from around the bloody ovals of their mouths. Morgan sat hugging his knees to his chest, next to the dumpster they had thrown the body into. His eyes glowed with a feint reddish hue as he buried his face in his hands and shuddered.

Mick had to turn his eyes away from the poor kid, wishing he could say something to comfort him and make this nightmare go away. Kind of hard to give words of relief when he was stuck in the thick of it himself, with no immediate end in sight.

Mick had drunk much more eagerly than he thought he would, a fact that disturbed him greatly. The idea of feeding from this guy made him want to vomit again before it happened. But once Trevor opened up that first vein in the man's throat, and the smell hit him like a cartoon character with a giant mallet, every sense he had was dialed up to twelve, and he knew he had to feed. He couldn't turn down the blood as it beckoned to him. He swore he heard the stuff singing to him, and he hated to admit that it was one of the sweetest choruses he had ever heard. It was then that he remembered something Terrance Miller had said as he chased him through the old Broken Edge Mall. He had said, or Mick thought he heard him say, that he would hear Mick's blood. As far as Mick knew, Miller had just been infected with Wretch Syndrome, and nothing else. No hint of vampirism at all, but it made Mick wonder, does blood have a frequency that supernatural creatures and other freaks can hear?

Trevor was looking at him, and he returned the gaze. Hank was sitting down next to Morgan by the dumpster, his large hand covering one of the boy's shoulders.

Mick stepped forward, his eyes looking toward Sunny, Rufus and the wolf that were sitting in the SUV a few yards away down the alley. Then his gaze returned to Trevor.

"You alright?" Trevor asked. Mick shrugged.

"I don't know how I feel." He admitted.

"But you feel full, right?" Trevor pressed.

"Yeah."

Trevor nodded, a pleased look on his face, "That's what counts. For now that'll have to be enough." He said.

"Hey," Mick said, looking back quickly at his friends in the SUV, "I know this might sound weird, and I promise I'm not trying to be more weird this time, but..." Mick tripped, trying to think how to proceed, "Look I don't understand it, but I've had several nightmares with you in them before all this happened. In the nightmares, I'm you. I look in a broken mirror, and I see your face. There is a woman screaming and—"

Hank stepped in, "Let's go little bro," he said, his voice now sounding a thread away from volcanic explosion. Trevor looked from Hank to Mick, his face truly confused, yet also intrigued at the same time. Morgan was starting back toward the SUV. Trevor stepped forward.

"Look, leave after dark tonight. Sunny told us what hotel you're staying in, we can meet real quick before you leave and see you guys off." Trevor said.

Mick wanted to continue, to get some bloody answers, but Trevor's voice made it clear that they were done. He gave Mick a final look before he turned and followed his brother into the shadows.

10:51 AM,

Sunny sat slumped in one of the plushy arm chairs in her hotel room, trying to fall asleep. The bed in this room was too firm for her liking, but this chair had been a great substitute. The room she occupied by herself was heavily fortified with wards Judah and Zach had taught to her. Her mind drifted to the sticky notes she had taped up over the doorframe, with the wards written in various languages. Hebrew—to ward off demons. Gaelic, to ward off any unwanted visitors from the Fair Folk, and Latin for everything else. She concentrated, willing what little energy she had left into the words written on the pieces of paper. The salt line she had poured in a sweeping semicircle at the entrance to her room thankfully hadn't been disturbed either.

She had driven Morgan to the police station, where Pallacios had met with her to oversee the procedures of notifying Morgan's father and then reporting on what had happened. Sunny had told them Morgan needed to be returned to his father before dawn. It was a fact Pallacios had intended to throw her weight around on but when she took one look at Morgan, she was convinced otherwise. Arrangements were being made throughout the day to have blood transfusion equipment delivered to Morgan's house while he slept, and his father would see to feeding his son. In the next twenty four hours, Morgan, and his father would disappear into witness protection. Sunny had learned Wendy Matthews and her family had already been relocated.

She hoped the boys were doing alright. All of them, especially Mick, were probably all passed out, dead to the world. Hopefully they had each managed to get a shower before getting to sleep.

She jumped when her phone rang. The chorus to a song she didn't know the name of, but liked anyway, played as she dug the phone out of her pocket. The first thing she noticed was that her battery was almost dead, being on three percent. The second thing, was that it was Valerie calling. She answered it as she stumbled toward the bedside table where her charger was, and plugged in.

"Hey," she answered, trying to sound sweet but not bothering to hide the fact she was about to crater.

"Did I wake you?" Valerie asked.

"Nah. I'll sleep when I'm dead," Sunny said.

"Careful saying that in our line of work," Valerie said. Sunny sat down on the bed so she could talk while her phone charged.

"Sorry. Last night would definitely be enough to convince me I need a career change," Sunny admitted.

Valerie was quiet for a little bit, "What happened hun?"

Sunny's eyes were closing. She forced them back open long enough to get a full sentence out.

"So much has happened since we got up here. I don't think any of us will be coming back the same." She said, letting the silence simmer in the air before she began again.

"Both kids are safely back with their parents. But one of them is now a vampire…and so is Mick." Sunny choked out. She heard silence on the other end. She swore if she listened intently enough she could hear Valerie blinking. Whatever she thought she heard turned to a sigh and a deep breath before Valerie finally responded.

"I don't mean to question what you're telling me," Valerie said, "but you're sure?"

Sunny closed her eyes as they began to sting with tears, "I watched them both feed," She said, as the weight of this trip, and the last ten hours came crashing over her, crushing her under its weight. She realized now that with Valerie on the other end, she didn't have to be strong for the boys any longer. She could devolve into a crying mess, and no one would judge her for it, especially Valerie. And that is exactly what she did. She broke down. Told her everything. Told her about Hank and Trevor. How they had helped get the boys out. About Oscar and the state he was in when she saw him, trying to take animal form to cover his nakedness. The look of excruciating pain, shock and embarrassment that was etched into his face as he was trying to shift. Seeing Mick latch onto a man's body like a leech and suck him dry. Even if the man did deserve it, the fact it was Mick doing it was enough to cause all kinds of emotions to come roaring to the surface. Disgust. Resentment. Fury. Disquiet. Paranoia.

And Valerie listened to all of it without judgment, without interrupting. They both cried together.

"Do you think there is any way to cure Mick? Can he go through another Reclaiming? How does this work?" Sunny asked, trying to keep her voice in check.

"I don't know honey," Valerie admitted, her voice straining under the weight of her own emotions, "As far as vampires are concerned, they are still largely thought to be myth, since they are so good at hiding. There are a lot of hunters that know about them but when it comes to exposing their kind, proof vanishes, and hunters end up slaughtered. Occupational hazard. Plenty of other creatures to frame. So without any concrete acceptance of their kind, no one knows how to even treat vampirism. As for the Reclaiming," Valerie said, pausing, "Yeshua's hold on Mick is still as strong as it was the day he tore out of his tainted skin. Think of Brandon and Oscar. Both are creatures that any other hunter would kill if they knew their secrets. But they both choose to serve Him. I can't see why Mick's case should be any different. Yeshua won't abandon him because something happened that was beyond Mick's control. That isn't how He works."

Sunny felt her arm getting heavy as she switched hands, "What about the Light…Could he still use it? Or will it kill him?" She asked.

"Brandon and Oscar can still summon it, but I don't know how that would affect a vampire's body," Valerie said. Both of them were quiet for a moment before Valerie continued, "I'll need to run a few tests on Mick when you get back home. If what they say about vampires being reanimated corpses is true then it will be just like doing an autopsy…I hope."

"I hope you're right," Sunny said.

PARTING GIFT

Mick sat there on the edge of his hotel bed, putting on a pair of his own socks. The failed attempt at posing as a homeless guard, and then being treated as a piece of property, had left him longing for his own clothes, his own bed back home. Anything that he could with certainty say was his. He squinted towards the heavy tapestry of the blackout curtains in his and Oscar's room. He wanted to peak out of them, in hope that he could see the sun one last time. But he would have to settle for the tiny streams of light dancing on the floor under the curtains.

The clock on the table read 8:38 PM. The sun had all but set completely, leaving the sky a dark canvas of navy, with a small trace of pink and orange toward the west. He remembered vampire movies from before he was born, how some of them burst into flames, how cool it looked. He closed his eyes and rubbed his hands through his hair. Horror movies became a rare occurrence after the Broken Edge Massacre. After everyone knew the things that went bump in the night were actually real, no studio would risk putting out a horror flick for at least ten years. The fear of having a hunter or some other vigilante peg an actor in a suite as the real thing was very real. The occasional horror flick would come out but only as a low budget endeavor from an Indie studio that usually went straight to video. He wondered how future vampire movies would fare after their existence was revealed to the public. They would probably join the ranks of films who began with the tagline *"Inspired by true events."*

He looked over at Oscar, now in human form, sleeping curled up under the covers. He remembered the agonizing, bone jarring snaps and cracks of his body as it morphed back into human form in the shower. Mick had turned the shower on for him, and hung the 'Do Not Disturb' sign on the door when he heard Oscar yelp the first time. It was six in the morning when

Oscar finally came shambling out of the shower, looking like he had been assaulted in an alley, the towel barely wrapped around him as he fell into bed. Mick did his best to cover him up before he finally felt his eyes closing on their own. He closed the curtains and fell into bed just before dawn had fully illuminated the sky.

He had woken up at a quarter till seven, thankful for Hanks words and encouragement to feed before they parted ways. He didn't dare entertain the thought of going after one of his friends. But having fed, he was thankful the temptation wasn't there. He didn't know for how much longer.

He was almost fully dressed from his shower when he heard a knock at the door. He stood slowly and approached the door, looking through the peephole to see who was on the other side.

Trevor stood there, waiting patiently for him to open up. From the looks of it, he had somewhat cleaned up. He had ditched the grungy look and was now dressed like someone who had a job. Not a good paying job, but maybe a fast food joint. A black t-shirt with the faded image of a cartoon character's face on it. Probably Porky Pig or something. He wore what looked like jeans that had seen their fair share or paint and bleach stains, and a pair of Converse. He was carrying a Styrofoam pail with a plastic red handle in one hand. A familiar, metallic smell was coming from the container. Mick began to salivate.

Mick unlocked the door and opened it up to him, seeing that his pointed ears and bestial features had somewhat receded, making him look more or less like a cancer patient with a deformity than an actual monster.

"Hello there," Trevor said, smiling and sticking out his hand. As he smiled, his teeth did appear to look more human, albeit just very crooked, like he had needed braces early in life and had never been able to get them.

Mick shook his hand, "Do I need to invite you in? Is that a thing with you guys or no?"

Trevor snickered, "If you wanted to be polite then sure, but no, you don't have to invite me in if you don't want to." Trevor said.

Mick nodded, "Gotcha. Come on in."

Trevor nodded, and stepped across the threshold, the contents of the Styrofoam cooler screaming at Mick as Trevor set it down by the door and motioned to it, "That's for the road. It's the last of mine and Hank's personal stash."

"You guys didn't have to do that," Mick said, reaching for the container and pulling out a blood donor bag full of B+. Trevor helped him undo the cap on the bag and patiently waited for him to gulp it down.

After having sucked down the last of the stuff, Mick eyed the empty bag for a second, feeling the rush of energy that filled his body, making his skin feel like a network of livewires. He sat down on his bed for a minute, letting himself get oriented to his surroundings again before he heard Trevor speaking again.

"So," he began, "tell me about your dreams again."

Mick looked up at him. He ran through each instance of having the nightmares, recalling as best he could the details of each time, until he got to the most recent. The sight of the mangled woman, violated and left to die as she soaked in her own blood. The cracked mirror with Trevor's face, and how Mick saw everything through his eyes. Then finally he revealed the last detail of that hellish nightmare—The red, glowing eyes of the Collector, looming down on him as he tried crawling toward the woman, who in the dream he felt was his beloved.

Trevor sat there, in one of the guest chairs, taking it all in. Oscar began to stir. He sat up, gave a drowsy nod to Trevor and Mick, grabbed some clothes out of his duffle bag next to his bed, and walked like a drunkard toward the bathroom, leaving them in relative privacy.

"Is that why you asked me how I was turned?" Trevor asked Mick. He nodded.

"I don't understand it at all. But yeah I was wondering if maybe I was seeing the night the Collector got to you. I don't know why I even had these nightmares in the first place. I've never seen you before. I'm just trying to figure out what the connection could be. Maybe you and Hank could come to New Broken Edge with us." Mick said. He had meant to go on but Trevor held up a hand.

"Your team is going to have their hands full trying to figure out how to support you now that you are a vampire. I know Sunny has told us how open minded you guys are. You obviously have a werewolf on the team so a few vampires couldn't hurt. But they don't need to be burdened with our company. We can feed ourselves, we know how to find prey. But your team won't sleep easy knowing there are two vampires running around their city. It won't look good for you guys, even though we would stay out of your way. So no."

Mick hadn't thought about that. He sat there, looking down at the floor as he tried to formulate a response to that. The prospect of having someone around that could teach him how to handle his condition was sitting right here in front of him, but was unwilling. He thought back to how fortunate Oscar was to have Brandon. He wanted to ball his hands up into fists and scream. He needed to know how to handle being a vampire, and if neither Trevor nor Hank were willing to help him, then he, and the rest of his friends, would be better off if Mick just walked out into the sunlight.

"But I will tell you this," Trevor began again, and Mick's ears perked up, "the nightmare you've been having, it isn't about me."

Mick's mind went blank as he heard that. He looked up at Trevor, face crumpled into confusion. Trevor nodded, and began digging into his back pocket. He pulled out a plane, brown imitation leather wallet that was overflowing with cash, and pulled out an old, worn piece of paper and handed it to Mick. The paper was thick, and the back of it was faded yellow as Mick unfolded it. Beyond the crease lines that had worn away some of the details, Mick saw two young men, sitting in an open cab style Humvee. A hut, constructed of bamboo and straw was in the background to their left, and beyond that, a thick, dense wall of jungle foliage. One young man was undoubtedly Trevor. His face in the photograph was a much stronger, robust version of the sickly looking young man sitting before Mick now. He was wearing a helmet, the fastener straps dangling from either side like the two floppy ears of a dog.

The other young man, holding an M16A1 across his lap in one hand and victoriously holding up a bottle of what looked like Scotch in the other—had the exact same face. Mick looked up from the photograph, looking at Trevor, who was now looking at the floor. But it was unmistakable. The shape of the nose, the cheekbones, the shape of the eyes. Identical.

Mick turned the photograph over, seeing faded text written in cursive on the back—*Hank and Trevor Houseman, Dong Ha, Vietnam, 1968.*

Mick handed the photograph back to Trevor, his hands now shaking as the face he saw in the mirror came screaming back to him. Blond hair, now caked and matted in blood. The same shape of the nose, cheekbones. The same eyes.

"Hank and I are identical twins," Trevor said, "His transformation wasn't as kind to him. He mutated into a hulking behemoth of a man. The blood molds us, reacts to each of us differently. Some of us are lucky enough to keep a semblance of what we looked like in life. The wounds he sustained to his face on the night he found Laura healed, but somehow got integrated into his transformation…We managed to recover our grasp on our memories fairly quickly. Hank must be the one you were seeing in your nightmares. Not me."

Mick sat there for a second, trying to comprehend as he heard the shower in the bathroom turn off. He had been seeing nightmares about Hank and not Trevor? Granted, the picture he had just seen was proof enough to give credit to Trevor's words, but Mick hadn't seen that coming at all.

"But…the night that it happened," Mick started, trying to piece it together in his head.

"The Collector embraced me the same night he sent his Thralls to Hank and Laura's house. I died, and he bled into my carcass. We all lived in the same town. I reawakened the next night, drenched in my own filth. Me and Hank were both chained to hospital beds that were being hauled in a semi-trailer with some other new additions to his coven. Once we got to Denver, and had enough blood in us to think coherently, Hank told me what happened to Laura, to him. We played along with all his games until we were strong enough to start plotting how we were gonna get out from under him. And here we are. As soon as you guys leave town, we're gonna be right behind you." Trevor said.

"But you won't come with us," Mick said.

Trevor nodded, "Correct."

Mick could feel his ire rising, "Did it ever occur to you that you might need protection from the Collector?"

Trevor shook his head, "Once we are out of Denver he can't touch us. This is his domain, and our laws forbid him or any other vampire from proceeding with a blood hunt past the borders of his domain."

"And you trust him to stick to those laws?!" Mick jeered.

"There are other vampires higher up the chain that he will have to answer to if he violates them. They aren't laws he laid down himself." Trevor said, "Each territory is kind of like its own sovereign state, with each ruler capable of enforcing rules as they see fit. But there are a few laws that are universally kept amongst all our kind, across the world. Breaking one of these risks full exposer of our kind, and there would be swift repercussions to him if he tried to attack us beyond Denver."

Mick shook his head, "It's still too damn risky. What about his Thralls? Do those laws apply to them?"

Trevor nodded, "They do, but since they are basically pawns, they are able to get through the loopholes a little easier. Problem with that is, the Collector's blood is what sustains them. Keeps them younger, faster and more agile than the average human. Most of the CNHC hunters have been here in Denver since he kicked the old coven out before World War II. Once monsters started coming out of the woodwork, he saw an opportunity to insert his Thralls inside of the organization. If the CNHC goes after and destroys one of our kind, they can cover it up as being some other creature capable of taking a human form. They can fabricate evidence framing other creature types and linking them to our crimes. I've helped em do it."

Mick shook his head, trying not to sound annoyed, "So why not come with us? My friends could help protect you guys! That's what I've been trying to say."

Trevor stood, put his wallet back in his pocket, "Sorry, I was getting to that. Their source is here in Denver. They won't risk hunting us down if it means being away from him for more than a week. We're leaving tonight. As far as everything is going, they might be suspicious of me and Hank by now, but by the time they order the city swept for us, we'll be long gone."

Trevor stuck out his hand again, "It's been a pleasure getting to meet you Mick. I know you want someone to show you the ropes. It's obvious. But it can't be me or my brother. Not yet." He said as Mick grabbed his hand, shaking it while feeling deflated.

"See ya around. Don't risk sunlight, it burns like a bitch." Trevor said, as he turned and walked out of the door.

AWKWARD

The door clicked behind Trevor, shutting Mick back into the hotel room with the cooler full of blood. He eyed the container, feeling defeated as his cold hands shook. He ran his hands threw his hair a few times and then rubbed his eyes as he walked over to the cooler, undid the red plastic clasps, and lifted up the lid. He eyed the fat blood donor bags for some time, each of them looking like red, bloated grubs. That image was enough to make him lose his appetite, but he forced himself to reach inside of the cooler and grab another one. One bag was about the length of his forearm. The single bag Trevor expected him to drink might not be enough to last him. Not knowing for sure, Mick thought it best to stock up.

"No, it can't be me or my brother to show you the ropes," Mick said absently to himself, mockingly trying to mimic Trevor's voice. "Never mind the fact that the Collector is a freakin psycho!"

Mick forced some of the blood left inside of him towards his lungs, to the muscles surrounding his heart, as he let out a long sigh. He wondered how long it took any vampire to learn to master their condition. Channeling blood to certain areas of the body at will seemed as easy as breathing used to be. Then again, Mick had had plenty of practice doing that very thing with the Light. He forced himself to breath, closing his eyes as he held onto the blood donor bag.

Just breath…In, out…In, out…

He finally felt the organs in his chest begging him to stop, to let the blood settle to other areas that didn't require so much effort. He opened his eyes, feeling the floor spin under his feet. He looked towards the mirror and noted his reflection looked to be a hint more colorful than it had a minute ago. He tried one more time, forcing blood to disperse around various organs and to his other extremities as he expanded his lungs one last time. The labored effort left him feeling weakened from the task, but he noticed his face becoming pinker by a shade or two. He looked more alive now for certain, but he looked like he was sick, tired and exhausted, lacking any sign of vibrancy. It was enough to force him to recall his gray reflection before his Reclaiming.

A twinge stung him in the back of his skull, like a dirty fingernail digging through his brain, and he stopped. He looked at the blood pouch, opened it up and began to greedily drink it down. It felt like drinking heated molasses, the overpowering taste of liquid copper transmuting into a sweet tasting fullness that filled him up. He drew his mouth away, feeling his lungs expand and his heart rate accelerate as the endorphins flooded his brain. He wondered how that was possible, wondering if drinking blood itself could make his organs function like normal. But the thoughts were drowned out by the overpowering taste that nearly sent him doubling over with pleasure. It became too much. He drew his mouth away feeling like he was breaching the surface of the water for air. He could feel his fangs extending all around his mouth, and he felt his jawline readjust to accommodate. He brought the bag to his mouth again, and drank like a man dying of thirst.

The sound of the bathroom door opening startled him and he drew the bag away from his bloody mouth, as he turned to see Oscar standing there in the doorway of the bathroom, dressed and groomed. His face was a mask of shocked embarrassment as he saw Mick standing there with the blood bag behind his back as if he had been caught looking at a dirty magazine.

"Sorry Mick I didn't know you were…" Oscar said, stammering, trying to look away.

Mick pulled the blood donor bag out from behind his back, looking at the remaining contents. His hands once again were a bloody mess, and he didn't even want to venture a guess at how bad his face was.

"Guess I know how you felt," Mick offered, "ya know…when your mom walked in on you and you were eating raw hambru—" he stopped, closing his eyes as he realized he wasn't helping. Oscar stood there in the doorway to the bathroom, nodding.

"So they leave already?" Oscar asked, as he stepped into the room towards his duffle bag, pulling his tooth brush out.

"Yeah. Trevor said they had to leave Denver tonight just like we're going to." Mick said.

Oscar's head snapped upward, and a growl rumbled from deep inside of him as he tipped his head back and sniffed the air. At the same time Mick's nostrils flared with a familiar scent. Something moved from the corner of his eye. His eyes darted toward the window just as Oscar dropped his toothbrush and he began to get bigger and hairier. Oscar was going towards the window! Mick saw the explosion of glass before Oscar's body collided with the white, humanoid form that had torpedoed itself inside of their room.

He recognized the face of one of the Collector's musicians, the cello player, as he and Oscar wrestled to the ground in a blazing storm of claws, fur and blood. The door to the hotel room burst open just as another form was crawling through the window.

"Well, well, what a nice room! Our accommodations weren't good enough for you? "

Mick instantly recognized that voice with the Australian accent. Ralph walked in, wearing a blue V-neck and a nice leather jacket, the telltale clattering of his enormous tusks accompanying him.

Mick grabbed the edges of the comforter off Oscar's bed, ripped it off and flung it toward Ralph in a fluid motion. The heavy comforter landed over the Aussie's head as his arms attempted to catch the thing and yank it free from his face.

Before Mick could tackle him, he felt a battering ram hit him in his side, one with arms that enfolded around his waist as he went sailing onto the bed. He felt icy hands encircling his wrists as another cold, white face came into view. The crimson eyes of the violin player locked with Mick's as the vampire unhinged his jaw and gave a throaty hiss. The stench of stale blood mixed with a garbage heap assaulted Mick's nose as the sounds of people screaming out in the hall were filling his ears.

"The Collector wants his property ba—!"

A gunshot went off in the room from somewhere. Ralph dropped to one knee and cussed as the bullet hole from his back dripped burning liquid Light.

Rufus ran toward Ralph as he was attempting to stand back up, kicked one leg out from under him and drove a glowing blade straight at his throat.

Ralph caught the hand and flung Rufus over his shoulder. He landed on his back onto the other bed as Sunny rushed in, bowstring drawn, and let one fly. Ralph's hand reached out and plucked the arrow from the air, the tip just inches from his face.

"Alright mates, wanna do this the hard way do ya? Fine!" He said, ripping the tusks from his belt and jamming them into his mouth.

There was a sudden jolt of exploding glass. Mick looked over to where Oscar and the vampire had been, only to see the broken out window, the sounds of them free falling out of the second story window down into the parking lot, still tearing into each other.

Rufus took aim at Ralph and squeezed off three more rounds as his mass grew. The clothes he wore were shredded off of his body like paper as his skull cracked and broke under the pressure of its new form. His face elongated into a boar's snout, as he let go of the tusks and lunged with enormous meaty hands at Sunny, omitting a high pitched squeal like a wild boar.

Mick saw the vampire he was wrestling with producing a long, sharpened piece of wood from inside of its jacket.

You've got to be kidding me!

He felt pressure exploding from inside of his chest as the stake entered him, and all went black. The only sounds he could hear were the panic of the other guests screaming to call 911, Rufus shooting at a demented wereboar, and Sunny's furious screams.

PERSUASION

The dark clouds of the night held the light of the moon hostage over the Riverside Cemetery in Denver. Graves from many families who had occupied Denver's earliest days were here, propagating the belief that Riverside was the city's oldest cemetery. The graves, varied and unique as they were, were all in fine condition for not having been polished or weatherproofed in who knew how long. Wild roses, yucca, sage, as well as numerous other types of flowers and plants were growing throughout the area, creating natural decoration between the rows of graves as well as growing over some of them. This place, as it served as a home to many fowl, coyote, and squirrels, was a beautiful haven, even at night. Though many did not frequent cemeteries at night, those who dared to venture into this one would say the same thing. A pond with a family of ducks was nestled in a corner of the cemetery, with a stone outbuilding nearby. Many worn paths near the pond led into a grove with many trees in desperate need of trimming, some either fully, or half-dead. Those paths, assumed to have been worn down by the wildlife of the area, were being trod by two-legged visitors this night.

The Collector, waited by a fallen tree that rested in the grove. His dark eyes spotted the first of his kin who walked up the paths leading into this forest sanctuary. Their footsteps made not one single noise as they tread over dead leaves and twigs that had littered the paths.

These were the oldest of his kind he had ever met. Certainly not the oldest in existence, but those approaching were old enough to recall the time when Babylon was merely a concept in the minds of its founders. The procession of primeval Elders approached silently, his maker, Makari, being amongst them. Seven soon stood before him, with one of them leaning on the phantom form of a beautiful woman, trailing mist behind them in a blanket of ethereal fog.

The Collector bowed, taking Makari's out stretched hand, and kissing it tenderly as he looked up into the gnarled, ancient face of his maker. He bore all the telling physical traits of his bloodline. The pointed ears, a face full of fangs more suited for tearing through a throat as opposed to delicately puncturing arteries, and an ever aging, yet perfectly preserved face that masked a timeless thirst, forever held in check by an eternity of patience. The others gathered, all bore differing physical features. One of the eastern Elders, the one that was being escorted by a spectral female form, looked like a newly arisen corpse with silvery eyes, the pupils only a mere pin prick of black. He swayed slightly like a stiff board, his limbs wracked with rigor mortis in the fine suite he wore.

"You said your message was urgent, my child. Speak, so that we may all hear." Makari commanded as he stepped away from his progeny. The Collector rose to his full height, dwarfing his maker as he looked down to meet his gaze.

"I remember stories you tell me, of time before history. Of time before taint. Of old blood…I have found it, Makari." The Collector said fervently.

Makari's eyebrows raised, his recollection of the tales seeming to surface to the forefront of his mind. The Collector heard the papery thin brow become knit as his maker looked at him amused.

"Grigori," Makari said, his voice tender as if speaking to a child, "such blood was lost to this world long ago. You are mistaken, I'm afraid."

Silence hung in the air for a moment. Not even the sounds of insects buzzing or chirping could be heard in the grove as the dead eyes of the Elders bore into him.

"This," the phantom Elder said in an Scottish accent, jabbing an ethereal finger toward Grigori, "is what feeding from other creatures of the night has done to your progeny, Makari. He seeks to convert your pallet toward the blood of werefolk, and the bile that seeps through the veins of the under dwellers, instead of that of mortals! His bravado for capturing them and holding them has gone to his head!"

Makari addressed the accusing Elder, a woman who's hair floated in a cloud of mist as her icy blue face became solid. A flowing white gown of mist clung to her lithe body, yet barely covered up anything from her chest up. The only thing truly concealed was her legs, which through the contours of her gown, appeared as if they might be triple jointed. The mist around her seemed to rush toward her, forming the rest of her dress. She stepped forward, her face as blue as a corpse pulled from the ice. She was solid enough to touch.

"Elder Alana, how he governs his domain is no concern of ours, so long as he does not reveal us to the world at large," Makari growled.

"It was blood of other creatures that brought me back, Baobhan sith," The Collector said, addressing the shimmering phantom woman that seemed to float more than walked toward him.

"Mind your tongue!" Makari scolded, and then looked back at him, "If what you say is true, where would this old blood be?"

The Collector smiled as he looked Makari in the eyes, "Part of it lies with me, in my collection. The rest of it lies outside my domain. In city called New Broken Edge."

Makari's eyes, as well as the eyes of the other Elders, all narrowed at him, "And how do you plan on bringing it back? You make a lofty claim. If the old blood is returning, and if it warrants our knowing, how will you pay your respects to the Elders you have summoned here this night? Our pallets have never tasted of the old blood. How are we to know it is true?"

"By going to New Broken Edge. Spreading out there. It is unclaimed territory. It—" Makari cut him off with a wave of his hand, and the Collector felt his lips tighten together under the weight of his maker's stare.

"Your domain…is here. The way you handle your coven is efficient, your utilization of local hunters to cover your tracks—brilliant! You have learned so much since your short time as Tsar during the First World War. But your success has once again gone to your head Grigori. The circumstances around your assassination have already made you a legend. But you cannot and will not jeopardize our existence to the public just to find something that no longer exists!" Makari hissed. The Collector felt the blood in his limbs congealing as the words of his maker washed over him, encasing him in rigor mortis. His eyes glanced toward the Elder Fai, the vampire who's limbs were stiffened to the point of needing Elder Alana's assistance. The Elder's silver eyes gleamed with delight as he watched Makari use a trick that Elder Fai had taught to him.

The other four Elders watched snickering, their designer suites seeming to absorb the darkness from the night. The Collector smiled as he watched them, seeing the shadows beginning to encircle their cold bodies.

"If you wish, you may taste of them, all of you. What I have, I share with each of you," Grigori said.

"I refuse to drink from your deplorable stock of counterfeits, whelp!" Alana said, her eyes drilling him with an icy stare.

The Collector nodded in resignation and then looked up, into the shadows of the tree grove, "I wished to share amongst you power I had found. You have made choice."

At those words, the shadows that appeared to be clinging to the other four Elder's clothing became a solid, amorphous black shape that suddenly enveloped the flailing bodies that struggled to get away. One Elder moved so quickly he appeared to have teleported away from the shifting mass of shadow, only when he reappeared, was entrapped by sleek, black tendrils that stabbed into his undead flesh and pulled him apart from the inside out. Another one that looked to be more or less a living regular human with brown hair was hurled through the air like a rag doll, and the Collector heard every bone in his back shatter upon impact with a thick tree. Before he hit the ground, he was plucked from the air and impaled on a broken tree limb through the chest, his body reverting back to a corpselike appearance. The others shrieks were cut off as the black mass of living shadow suddenly began to walk toward Makari, Elder Fai, Alana and the Collector.

"Elders," the Collector began, "I give you, one who promises old blood."

Alana had reverted back to her ethereal fog form, now coating the ground in her essence where they all stood. Elder Fai's limbs stretched out with a deafening crack as he forced blood to his extremities and, with a look of great pain on his face, began to move and back away. Makari stood to meet the now human shape of Father as it stopped its approach, the head looking down to meet the eyes of Grigori's maker.

"Good evening to you all," Father's voice snaked out.

Alana's spectral hand lashed out at Father's shadowy body, her claws hardening into talons capable of felling a tree. Her hand passed through his shadowy form.

"My dear, I am far older than yourself. You cannot harm me." Father said, turning to look down at the maiden, who now was dissolving into a thick, wriggling carpet of fog to blanket the ground once more.

"Father here has told me of New Broken Edge. The taint is purging there. I and my spawn will travel there, and we will drink of old blood. My domain will expand. Elder Makari, Elder Alana, Elder Fai...Please, join me in restoring our kind to power we once held in times before ancient taint." The Collector pleaded.

Makari looked at his spawn, eyes burning with the ire of this betrayal. Elder Fai hobbled forward on unsteady legs, holding his arms out slightly for balance. The blanket of thick fog that was Elder Alana growled like a ravenous beast.

"You toy with demons, Grigori! How can you trust this creature?!" Elder Fai hissed, working with some effort to point toward the shimmering black shape of Father, who was towering over him.

"He knows those who carry purged blood, quite intimately. It is he, who burn original Broken Edge to ashes with his hordes." The Collector replied.

Makari's face slackened as his eyes traveled from his progeny toward the towering form of Father, his lips forming the word 'you!'

"Yes, Elder Makari. It was me. I understand that when I pulled my stunt and revealed myself and other creatures of the dark to the masses, it endangered your existence. After all, if other monsters exist, then it was only a matter of time before the cattle got smart and discovered vampires exist as well. However, here you are, your kind still existing in relative peace. Now, the existence of other monsters plays in your favor. Many of your kind now know how to mutilate a corpse to look as if it was attacked by something else. A practice your kind has been employing for millennia but now there are plenty of other creatures to blame for the bodies that turn up in rivers, landfills, and dumpsters. As it stands, it seems I have done your kind a sizeable favor."

"A favor none of us asked for!" Makari spat.

"Perhaps we should hear him," Alana's voice slithered out from the fog. The Collector smirked at her words, her stance now changed once she saw she could not reduce him to a bloody heap as she did with her countless male victims.

"You cannot be serious!" Elder Fai said.

"Tell me, do you not wish to return to the days when you ruled over the cattle and were worshiped and revered? I can give that to you." Father said, cocking his head to the side.

Grigori, the Collector, watched the three remaining Elders, reading their movements. None dared to attack.

"And what is it you require in return?" Makari asked.

"I only wish you to reclaim your rightful place among the cattle. That's why I made an example of Broken Edge. It was but a small step toward reclaiming the world spoken of in myths and epics. The purging of my taint is a gift—" He was cut off as Alana's voice shot through the air.

"Your taint?! So it started with you!" She screamed, rage exploding from her voice as the trees around her suddenly became laden with ice.

Father turned toward her, seeing the frozen corpse visage of the vampire, now fully tangible and wearing her fog gown.

"My being here in your world has had its repercussions for the cattle, I will admit. It helps to keep them blind and subjugated long enough for your kind to rise up," Father said.

"And in the meantime, they build weapons of war capable of wiping out whole populations!" Elder Fai said, his canines beginning to elongate.

Father nodded, "Elder Fai, there are wonders yet to behold. Their toys are of no consequence. The purging of the blood is a gift. New Broken Edge is a breeding ground for the old blood. You are being handed a banquet. It would offend me greatly, if you did not partake. What say you?"

TAG

The ebony curtain of darkness slowly pulled itself back from Mick's awareness, only to reveal yet another layer of pitch black that encased him. He wasn't sure at what point any awareness had crawled from the trenches of that black abyss he had fallen into, covered with icy sludge and shivering. He wasn't even really sure if he was awake or not. He hung in the awkward twilight between sleeping and waking, where dream specters could still reach him before he stepped over the threshold and into the waking world completely. But one thing he did know, was there was something touching his face. When he had the thought to reach up and remove whatever it was, his arms never responded.

...Okaaaay?

He thought about blinking. But his thoughts produced no action of the sort. He thought about trying to move his arms again, but the correspondence between his brain and his extremities was nonexistent. He thought about wiggling his fingers, his toes, trying to sit up, only to realize none of those things was going to happen. Did he still have fingers and toes to wiggle? He tried again to raise his head to look, only to be reminded that such movement wasn't possible. Every limb, muscle, and joint was locked up tight. He was a prisoner in his own flesh. He couldn't even move his eyes. The texture of whatever dark womb had encased him felt like thick plastic, or rubber, he couldn't tell which. The fact he could feel texture, even if it was just enough to know something was touching him, was a small victory he would have to claim.

He suddenly felt the part of the substance that was on top of his face open up with the sound of a zipper. It parted, his vision now flooded with a dim, fluorescent light that flickered somewhere close by. Dingy, rotting ceiling tiles hung just overhead, their crumbling remains looking like a strong sneeze could dislodge what was left of them.

All of those details only served to enhance the unspeakable urge to flee when he saw who had opened the zipper.

"How we feelin' mate?" Ralph taunted, his face only inches away from Mick's frozen, catatonic visage.

Oh shit oh shit oh shit.

"Can ya hear me in there?" the Aussie chuckled as he brought a calloused hand up to the side of Mick's face and slapped it a couple times. Mick's eyeballs, frozen in their sockets, did not budge. He could feel the stale air, which now was trying to smother him now that the zipper had been undone, caressing his eyeballs.

Does he know I'm awake? Maybe not. Just don't move, Mick thought to himself, and only after did the irony hit him. He suddenly felt pressure on his nose as Ralph pressed a finger into it.

"Honk, honk!" Ralph sneered and then stood up and chuckled heartily, "Oh Christ I've always wanted to do that."

Okay that wasn't weird at all, Mick thought.

"I think you *can* hear me," Ralph said as he leaned down into Mick's face, his breath smelling like chewing Tabaco that had been scrapped off the bottom of a corpse's foot.

"Between you an me, I was told the boss thinks you're defective now. Something about your blood being special but now it's useless to em. You being turned was an accident from what I hear. He's got some bigwigs coming to take a look at your friends. You being an accident, well, he's not too eager to be showin' ya off. So you an me, well, we're going to have a bit o' fun. You see, you can't move with this wedged in your chest." Suddenly Mick felt a light tapping on something in that area. The friction of something splintery against his insides. Suddenly the fight in his and Oscar's room came flooding back to him. He remembered the vampire who wrestled him down effortlessly, Ralph busting in through their door, Oscar tumbling out of the broken window with the other vampire. He remembered Rufus and Sunny storming in, getting thrown around like ragdolls. The stake being plunged into his chest, and then, darkness.

"But see," Ralph continued, "If I were to remove it, well then you might be able to participate. So I scratch your balls, you scratch mine. I take out this giant splinter you've managed to acquire, and then you participate in a little game of tag."

Go fuck yourself! Mick screamed in his head.

"So if you really wanna play, then Simon says, be quiet," Ralph chuckled and then put his ear to Mick's breathless lips, as if listening intently.

Go bathe with a toaster!

"Well…I never!" Ralph said, his eyes watering up as he put a hand to his mouth, "I never had anyone actually agree to play along! Thanks mate!"

Mick suddenly felt agonizing pressure on his insides as he heard a wet, sticky *shlunk* sound. His back arched along with the upward pull of force. Soon he felt air filling a spot on his chest where there was now a large, cavernous hole. Within seconds, he was able to blink again. He felt his eyes moving around in their sockets, like rusty ball bearings in sockets of dried bone.

"You must be thirsty," Ralph said, dragging what sounded like the edge of a blade along the surface of a table somewhere else in the room. Mick tried to move his eyes to follow the sound. His neck was still stiff. Ralph suddenly loomed over him, blade pressed against one of his palms.

"I would offer you something stronger, but I'm fraid this is all I got," he said as he raked the blade down his palm and squeezed his hand tight. Dark crimson oozed between his fingers, and dribbled down his palm. Mick felt the first few drops hit his cheek, then his lower lip, until finally some got into his mouth.

God no! Stop!

But he felt the muscles in his throat working against him as he involuntarily swallowed Ralph's blood, greedily gulping it down as the steady stream of fluid that coated his gullet, revitalizing the atrophied tissue of his throat.

He sprang up like a bullet, an inhuman roar tore from his throat as he slashed at Ralph with outstretched fingers, curved like talons. Ralph side stepped, caught one of Mick's hands, and flung him off of the gurney, and onto the floor at Ralph's feet. The confines of the body bag twisted around Mick's feet as he slashed through what remained of it.

"Yes! Now we're having fun!" Ralph roared as Mick saw the carved bone tusks come out, one in each hand.

Mick lunged at Ralph, crouched on all fours like an animal. Ralph laughed as his boot came up and connected with Mick's face, kicking him back down. The laugh soon turned to a guttural groan that turned into a swine-like squeal as Ralph dropped to one knee. Mick watched as his flesh rippled and writhed, like a blanket covering a bed of snakes. Ralph's flesh split as his muscles bulged, bones breaking as he stood. When he rose to his feet, the final product was that same, nightmarish pig face, the tusks shimmering in the flickering light like heat coming off asphalt in the summer. Bloody tatters of human skin clung to the behemoth, swaying and falling off like shredded curtains.

Ralph was now well over seven feet tall. His hands came down off the tusks, fixed in his mouth where he had jammed them into place. His ears flicked about, twitching as if to shake off imaginary flies. The snout flared as a smile managed to creep across the boar's face, resembling an uncanny marriage of human and animal. The sound that came out from the throat caused the hairs on Mick's arms to bristle. It almost sounded like a voice, but a voice choked by a wet, hungry squeal.

"Well, guess I'm it!" Ralph squelched as his enlarged meaty hand flung a table out of his way before he put his head down and charged.

Mick screamed as he just barely managed to fling himself out of the way. He hadn't realized what was behind him until Ralph's head smashed through it like a battering ram with a deafening screech of metal warping and hinges breaking. There had been a door behind him the whole time! He could have made a run for it!

He didn't have time to blame himself for that. His eyes quickly began scanning the room for something he could use.

He saw shelves to his right, boxes to his left and an old table in between the two. He ran over toward the shelves just as Ralph was standing back up and stumbling back in through the now upgraded doorway.

Mick's hands clumsily knocked off various sharp implements, tools, and other objects he dared not ask about, before his eyes landed on the mother-load. He reached with both hands for the chainsaw on the top shelf.

He didn't have time to check the fuel tank. As his hands enclosed around the handles of the nightmare power tool, he fumbled for the rip cord. The chainsaw belched as the motor rumbled, but not enough to start the thing. He pulled again, desperately praying the stupid thing would work.

The saw began to vigorously shake in his hands as the motor roared to life, and the sharp, ear splitting sound of the chain running along the track filled his ears. Mick looked up just as the hulking form of the creature was barreling toward him. He yelped again, reflexively jumping out of the way, his lower back crashing into a table with various torture devices and other leather accessories.

"Come on pigzilla!" Mick taunted as he squeezed the trigger on the chainsaw, causing the blade to rev even louder. Ralph's enraged squeals overpowered the tool as he lunged away from Mick, and with both hands, grabbed onto the gurney, and flung it toward him.

The gurney tumbled through the air toward him, and he ducted and rolled beneath it. The improvised torpedo crashed into the wall behind Mick, catching the flickering fluorescent light and shattering it. The clang of the light fixture mixing with the deafening crash of metal and sheet rock sounded like a car crash. But it wasn't until he came up on his feet again and was face to face with Ralph that he noticed one problem—he had dropped the chainsaw when he dodged the flying gurney.

The only mercy he could think of now, was that the room was bathed in fresh darkness, veiling the wretched face of Ralph somewhat. Mick felt himself becoming airborne as Ralph's hands closed around his throat, lifting him up off his feet and smashing him into the shelving repeatedly.

He felt his back get punctured by splinters of wood and sharp pieces of metal. He found himself wishing he could black out, but Mick also realized in the next second that as a vampire, he didn't need to breathe.

"When you play tag," Ralph squealed in his face, spittle flying off his uneven teeth, "You're supposed to RUN! Not Dance!"

Mick struggled to reply as his feet dangled there a good four feet off the ground. The creature's hand was so large, Mick found his jaw was practically wedged shut, his fangs piercing his gums.

"Wasn't…trying to tango until you threw the gurney at me," Mick said through gritted teeth.

A sudden burst of light flooded Mick's vision as the creature rammed its head into Mick's face, square between the eyes. He felt himself falling to the floor, the roar of the chainsaw growing louder as he tumbled down.

When his vision stopped spinning, he looked up, seeing Ralph's colossal foot coming for his face.

He rolled quickly to the left as the foot came crashing down with enough force to crush Mick into jelly. As chunks of concrete rained down on Mick from the crater Ralph had just put in the floor, he was suddenly aware that now, there was another source of light filling the room from somewhere—and the chainsaw, though still roaring hungrily, wasn't on the floor.

Ralph squealed out a curse just as a tall, human shape rushed him. Mick scrambled up, trying to get out of the way as a glowing chainsaw blade slammed into the bicep of the wereboar with a meaty crunch, the glow from the hungry tool now illuminating the blood spattered, bald form of Rufus as he channeled the Light into the blade.

Rufus held on as the blade ripped and chewed through Ralph's bicep. The wereboar thrashed and jerked as muscle and tendons were stripped from his arm in a crescendo of liquid crimson. Ralph stumbled backward, falling onto the remains of the table he had flipped out of the way earlier, clutching his arm and squealing in maddening agony. Rufus advanced, taking the chainsaw to Ralph's left leg. The creature thrashed as the blade chewed through the muscular flesh of the thigh. Mick heard the sickly crunch as the blade hit the bone. Rufus withdrew the blade from the creature's leg, and plunged it into the soft belly, shredding it's innards as the blade chugged deeper and deeper. Rufus had to jump back when Ralph twisted and writhed onto his newly opened belly, nearly taking the chainsaw with it.

The body on the ground began to shrink. It's mass bubbled beneath the surface as steam started to emit from Ralph's flailing body. The individual limbs, those still attached, shrank until they looked like the scrawny limbs of a human again. The clatter of tusks hitting the concrete was audible as Rufus shut off the chainsaw, stepped over Ralph's mutilated body, grabbed him by the shoulder, and forcefully turned the man over onto his back. Ralph's eyes were wild and unfocused as his teeth chattered.

Rufus grabbed one of the tusks, held Ralph down by the throat, and rammed one of them through his sternum. Ralph's body thrashed and jerked as Rufus pushed the tusk through the flesh with a wet squelch.

As blood shot from Ralph's mouth. The veins on Rufus's arms, and his eyes were glowing brightly beneath the skin, visible through the blood that coated him like war paint. The tusk lit up in his hand as he pressed it in even further.

After several agonizing, long seconds, Ralph's body finally stopped twitching.

REBELLIOUS COLLECTION

Mick stood up, his eyes fixed on Rufus, whose body had been completely covered from head to toe in blood and bits of flesh.

For a brief moment Mick caught himself wondering why he wasn't convulsing with thirst at the sight of all that blood, but in the next second realized that after Ralph had basically given him some of his, it had tasted like stale sewage water, with only the faintest traces of anything human tasting remaining. Mick caught his insides roiling with disgust as he realized that he had even been thinking any of this.

"You alright mijo?" Rufus asked, his voice raspy as he tossed the tusk down at his feet.

Mick blinked a couple times, looking at the pile of gore on the floor that used to be Ralph, and then looking back at Rufus, who looked like a slaughterhouse worker with glowing eyes, "Y-yeah. I'm in one piece."

Rufus nodded, stepped over Ralph, and began rummaging around, looking through some objects that had fallen from the shelves and onto the floor. He came up with two machetes in one hand and a crowbar in the other. He tossed one of the machetes to Mick. His reflexes were quick, but not accurate. His shaking hands fumbled with the handle in mid-air and it clattered noisily to the floor.

Rufus hung the curved end of the crowbar from one of his belt loops and grabbed a rusty survival hatchet, and stuck that into one of many side pockets on his tactical pants.

"You know where we are? Where Oscar and Sunny are?" Mick asked.

Rufus nodded as he stepped forward, "We're underneath Whitehaven. They had me on the first floor. I woke up right as one of those blood suckers was prepping me for an IV. I played possum and overheard where they had you, Oscar and Sunny. When I heard all I needed to know, I killed me a couple leeches, and came down here. It wasn't hard to find the room you were in. I just followed the sound of your screaming like a little girl." Rufus chuckled. Mick nodded as he followed Rufus out into the hall.

A checkered pattern of bloodstained, grimy tiles covered the floor. The ceiling was an arch all the way down the hall in either direction. Flaking, blue chips of paint and wall texture coated the crumbling walls, infested with mold. Streaks of pale light cut through the darkness in eight foot intervals from behind the doors that lined each side of the hall, sparsely lighting the way. The hallway was scattered with gurneys, a few flimsy looking metal shelves, and bulging, soggy garbage bags, the contents of which filled Mick with a horridly pallid stench that permeated the area.

He didn't have to breathe, he realized that now. But he also knew that as a vampire, using every sense he had at his disposal would be vital in finding their friends. So he channeled the blood to his lungs, massaging them in a way that let them expand as his nostrils flared to take in the scents of the area. He smelled nothing but the stale, unmoving hallway around him. He smelled the dirt, the dried blood, the things in each of their cells, and the contents of whatever was in those garbage bags. But he didn't smell Oscar here in this hallway.

"Where did you hear them say they were keeping Sunny?" Mick asked as they walked.

Rufus crept up to one of the metal doors, looking in through the small six inch window at eye level, "They said she's supposed to be on the third floor."

"Ralph mentioned something. The Collector has some important visitors coming to 'take a look at us,' whatever that means," Mick said as he followed Rufus's lead, looking in through the small windows located in each door on his side. Though being a vampire had robbed him of certain abilities that his human body had once possessed, he could still feel his stomach drop. He supposed that was a good sign, an indicator that his humanity hadn't been entirely stripped away. But at the sight of what he saw, he found himself almost wishing he could turn it off and on.

Standing there in one cell, was a man about a foot taller than Rufus. He stood there, shivering, his shirtless body seemingly held together with sutures, staples, twine, and bolted in certain areas with metal bracers that looked like they had been crudely welded. A few thin tubes were sticking out from various gaps in the flesh where the shoddy stitch work had failed to close up the tissue. An off colored, brownish fluid was moving through the tubes.

Is that what I think it is? Mick kept asking himself, wondering at what point he would cease to become shocked. Images of Mary Shelly's *Frankenstein* kept flashing through his head. The thing turned its head just enough for Mick to make out the eyes—two sickly, reddish orbs with yellow pupils roamed around in the eye sockets. The thing twitched and jerked as if certain limbs attached to it wanted to rebel.

Mick ducted before the creature could make eye contact with him, and he noticed Rufus was already at the end of the hall, peeking in through the last door on his side.

Mick crept up beside him quickly, and as he did, he noticed various sigils and glyphs painted on each door in blood. Though dried, he had grown intimate with that smell on a whole new level since his turning.

"Why are there other monsters down here?" Mick asked.

"I guess this is where the rebellious ones in the collection go. These sigils are to keep them contained," Rufus offered after a prolonged look into the last cell, his eyes still burning in the darkness like torches.

Mick took that in as Ralph's words came back to him. According to Ralph, the Collector had said his blood was useless to him now. So if the useless ones he no longer had any interest in were turned over to Ralph for whatever he wanted, then what in God's name could he have possibly done to Oscar?

At the end of the hallway, it separated into two different paths, one to the left and right. The one to the left stopped about ten feet from where they stood, and was blocked by a metal, rolling shutter. The one to the right went further into more of the same scenery as the hall they stood in. More cells, more trash.

"If I collected monsters," Rufus whispered, "I would want to keep my Theriomorphs and Lycanthropes separate from everything else. Keep them in their own category. Even the useless ones. And I would want to keep them in a secure wing."

"Why?" Mick asked.

"Organization. The reason you can't even find anything at home," Rufus smirked as he took the path to the left and inspected the heavy metal shutter.

"I'm very organized when I want to be," Mick retorted.

Rufus grinned but the seriousness returned in the same instance as he sank down onto his haunches, "Looks pretty sturdy. Wouldn't hold back a pack of werewolves, but it might take a single one some time to tear through this." Rufus said as he began running his fingers along the edge of the bottom, feeling for some kind of purchase.

"I'm gonna need your help," He said, looking up at Mick.

"Okay, let's do this," Mick got down on his haunches and dug with his fingers until they found leverage. On three, they lifted, Rufus channeling the Light through his arms and back, and Mick, channeling what blood he had for the strength he needed.

Even with the help of the Light and the blood, the door still felt like it weighed a ton. Mick had seen Parish use the Light to help him rip the door off a car to free an elderly woman whose vehicle had been t-boned at an intersection one night when they were out on patrol. But this shutter was no car door, and the strain of simply trying to pry it up was causing little droplets of blood to form over his pale skin.

When they had gotten the door up about three feet, Rufus, breathing in a controlled fashion, instructed Mick to roll underneath, and hold the door from his side so he could roll under. After an agonizing two minutes of lifting, holding and rolling, the metal door rolled back down on its tracks as the two hunters stood on the other side.

Mick saw Rufus's eyes begin to water. He held up a finger to signal he needed a second, and he turned his head to bury his nose in the bend of his arm. Rufus said a few unsavory words in Spanish and English before he managed to look up at Mick.

"You smell that right?" Rufus asked, once he noted that Mick wasn't reacting. Mick shook his head, "No. Not needing to breathe helps." Mick said, and then added, "If he's not here, I swear to God Rufus, after all that work with the door, I'll find a way to kick your ass," Mick said.

Rufus chuckled, said something in Spanish, and continued walking.

Mick concentrated, causing the precious life fluid to stimulate the dormant receptor cells in his nose, as well as his lungs so he could try to get a beat on Oscar's scent. The smells gradually mounted, starting as unpleasant, until they became unbearable, amplified to levels humans normally didn't reach. The smells were starting to transmute into tastes as they stalked forward in the dark. Like spoiled, slimy meat. Congealed and rancid. Off. That made Mick's gag reflex spark back to life as he felt the blood trying to force itself up through his esophagus. He tightened every muscle he could think of out of reflex, trying to keep his only source of fuel from spilling all over the floor. He wasn't entirely successful as he felt a trickle falling from behind his teeth and down the side of his mouth.

"Oh God…Oh God I smell it now," Mick gagged as he bent over onto his knees.

"You okay?" Rufus asked. His own face was still bearing the disgust of the new area.

Mick shook his head, and after several long moments of struggle, he finally managed to calm the reservoir of blood inside of him, what precious little he had left.

"I guess vampires can puke too," Mick said as he leaned against one of the walls for support. The effort of keeping down his only supply of energy left him feeling like his limbs had partially atrophied. He knew that wasn't the case but he now felt extremely weak.

"Do you smell Oscar?"

Mick shook his head, "Can't. Too many other smells. I don't know if I can isolate them."

Rufus stepped forward, "Okay. Do you need to rest or you think you can go on?"

Mick nodded and forced himself to keep going. Sunny and Oscar needed him, and the more time they wasted trying to find one, who knew what was happening to the other?

"Let's go."

To their left they found another path to take, one with old fashioned, prison style bars for a barricade. The barred door stood ajar, almost half way. The path ahead ended in another heavy shutter door. After the work it took to get the first one open, Mick doubted Rufus wanted to try for another one, and he didn't blame him.

"Guess we go left again?" Mick offered, knowing the answer as Rufus pushed passed him and slid through the open door. Mick followed his lead, crouching as the two came to a long, glassed in window where light was dimly washing through. They peaked their heads up to peer inside, mostly to be sure they were still alone for the moment. The window was dingy. Dirt, bugs and who knew what else had become encrusted on the outside.

The inside was illuminated by fluorescent light tubes that burned a little brighter and steadier than the ones in the room Mick had awoken in. A stainless steel table was in the middle of the room, covered with a bloody, formerly white tarp. It was surrounded by cabinets of medical equipment, and old, rusted carts where surgical tools were kept, complete with waste buckets. A sink was built into a long countertop that ran the length of the wall that was parallel to the long window they were looking through.

Mick felt the blood inside of him, moving like an amorphous, sentient presence as his eyes scanned the room. He felt it lurch in revilement as his eyes spotted what was propped up in a corner. Hanging on hooks from the ceiling in one of the corners, stock still like a scarecrow, was the bloody, matted fur hide, of a werewolf.

SILVER BARS

"We're too late," Mick found himself slinking backward at the sight of the fur hide. Rufus turned, a finger pressed to his lips.

"Mick, it's not him."

Mick looked at Rufus, dumbfounded. All the mental flashes of Oscar being tortured to the point of lashing out, transforming, and then by some alien means, having his hide pulled from his body as human screams mixed with primordial howls of agony and rage were starting to swirl on the screen of his mind's eye.

"What?"

Rufus motioned toward the thing in the room, "Mijo, look. It's not him. His fur was charcoal gray."

Mick blinked, and looked at the hide, hanging on the hook like a discarded towel. The fur of the creature, though caked with dried blood, was a deep brown. Mick would have breathed a sigh of relief if he had ben capable in that moment. He rested his head against the glass as hope flickered dimly in the plunging depths of his mind.

"Don't they revert back to their human appearance when they die?" Mick asked.

Rufus nodded, "Si. Whatever they did to this one, the hide was taken while it was still alive. They must have found a way to neutralize their healing factors so the hides could be removed."

Mick stared at the thing as the utter revulsion of that prospect crawled up his brainstem like an army of insects.

"Come on, we've got to find him before he ends up like the one in there."

The only two Lycanthropes Mick held any positive regard for were Brandon and Oscar. There was no love lost between him and the species as a whole, though in reality they were the only two natural born ones he had ever met. But even he had morals. He believed in putting the creatures down quickly and efficiently, if in the instance he ever had to hunt a pack of them. A fate like whatever had befallen the creature in that room, he would not, could not fathom doing such a thing. The Reclaimed weren't above using some ethically questionable means of obtaining information out of a creature if it meant saving someone else. But the evidence of what he saw in that room was sadistic. The mark of someone who took pleasure in torture. Something the Reclaimed had not exhibited even on their worst day.

The silence was literally shattered as shards of glass rained down on Mick's head, and a slippery, meaty hand closed around his throat. Rufus turned too late, his eyes flaring as the Light lit up the blade of his machete.

Mick found himself being hauled up and over the wall and through the shattered window before Rufus could get to him. He was smashed down onto the floor with enough force to crack a living man's skull as the deafening clatter of stainless steel supply carts went flying through the air or crashing into a wall.

Standing before Mick was the naked, human form of a feral man. Long brown hair hung in his face, obscuring everything but his golden colored eyes. Patches of skin looked like they were trying to regrow over his nude body, desperately trying to knit themselves back together over the muscular landscape of the red muscle tissue.

An indescribable growl of fury escaped the man's throat as his hair flipped back out of his face, revealing something between a mouth and a wolf's muzzle, half formed, skinless, and full of fangs.

"Nnnnnosferatu!" The creature growled as its claws slashed the shirt on Mick's chest, cutting through his flesh like paper.

"You take my hide! I take your head!" The creature screamed madly, as Mick scrambled away, going for the machete he had dropped when he landed. His hand closed around the handle just before he felt claws digging into his back. An inhuman shriek erupted out of Mick's mouth, something that sounded like a cat's yowl and a dying rabbit. The shock of hearing such a sound come out of his own mouth propelled him as he forced himself to turn around, and he embedded the blade into the side of the creature's neck, severing the carotid artery. The creature lurched as it hauled Mick up onto his feet, eyes still locked onto his. He looked like he hadn't even felt it!

The glowing blade of Rufus slammed into the other side of the creature's throat, the Light now seeping into the flesh as both major arteries on either side of its neck gushed blood. The blood on Rufus's side was mixed with illumination as the creature sank to its knees, claws dragging down Mick's chest.

Mick's eyes locked onto the image of the dying creature. Rufus stepped up and with a couple good yanks, wretched his blade free. Mick stepped closer. He didn't realize until now just how deep Rufus's blade had gone. He saw through the sizzling canyon the blade had created, and chipped fragments of vertebrae. Rufus's blade had damaged the creature's spinal column below the jaw. The sizzling energy from the blade burned indefinitely. It wouldn't be healing from a wound like that.

"You alright?" Rufus asked.

Mick nodded his head emphatically, and began walking towards the door to this room. He unlocked it and opened it with a loud scrapping of metal.

"Keep your damn eyes and ears open Vato," Rufus chided, "we can't play around anymore."

The halls throughout this section of Whitehaven's underground labyrinth of slaughterhouse rooms and tanneries wound on and on, each room showcasing more werewolf hides. They didn't stop to investigate any of the rooms longer than it took to identify the hides. None so far had belonged to Oscar.

Mick found himself theorizing along the way what kind of shapeshifter Ralph might have been. With Brandon and Oscar being the only two natural born ones he knew, he quickly began to discount Ralph as being a natural. Images of Sunny before her Reclaiming flashed through his mind. On the night the hunters had done their Q and A session at the high school, and Valerie driving like an action star to get him as far away from the building as possible, they had encountered Sunny on the road, wrapped up in an animal hide. He remembered how it had twisted and morphed her body into a humanoid parody of a dog and a woman.

Ralph had needed his tusks in order to change. He tried to recall what category of shapeshifter Sunny had called those kinds. Skin stealers? Skin shifters? It was something with the word 'skin' in the name. But in Ralph's case he didn't need the skin of a boar. He just needed tusks. He wondered if in reality all one needed was a piece of the desired animal for the magic to work. A bone, a feather, a patch of fur, an eyeball. His eyes studied the hanging werewolf hides as they went deeper and deeper. Perhaps Ralph had been planning to use the skins of these werewolves as part of his wardrobe. A wild, raging wereboar one day, a savage, flesh hungry werewolf the next.

"Finally," Rufus said, "a change of scenery."

Mick looked up. He saw the sign over the entrance to another area which read, "A-Block." He had been so lost in his thoughts that he hadn't even noticed, just walking forward as if on autopilot, not processing his environment. As a hunter, it was a habit that had nearly gotten him killed. The place they had just entered looked as big as a basketball court. Dull and depressing as it was, this space was very well lit compared to the rest of the basement. Bars lined the walls on either side of them, looking like a cell block in an old prison. Mick caught himself wondering just how many purposes this building served back in the day.

An agonizing shriek of pain stabbed into Mick's ears and he and Rufus both flinched. It was coming from one of the cells. It started out as human, but soon blended into a canine-like yelp. The kind a dog makes when it tries to walk on a broken paw. In an instant, Mick felt the burn of hope radiating from inside of him somewhere. Because that scream, when it sounded human, had sounded like Oscar.

"Bingo!" Mick said as he and Rufus raced over toward one of the cells on the right. Not wasting any time inspecting the contents of the other cells, they went straight toward the source of the painful howls.

Oscar sat curled up on a wall cot, dingy padded mattress torn to shreds underneath him. He sat hugging his knees to himself. He was barefoot and shirtless but otherwise still wore the shreds of the jeans he had been wearing when he transformed in the hotel room.

Mick caught a glimpse of the bottoms of his feet. They were burned to a flaking crisp. He had patches of scorched flesh on his back, his arms. He sat there, handfuls of hair in each hand as he rocked back and forth, sobbing.

Mick thought he caught the faintest sounds of Yeshua's name in there, but it was drowned out by the growling, rage filled sobs.

"Oscar!" Rufus called out to him, raising his voice to compete with the volume of Oscar's sobs. Oscar's face shot upwards at the mention of his name, his golden eyes wild and his face half transformed. His nose, flattened into a wolf's snout, was scorched and sizzling. Mick noticed the door to the cell was ajar, ever so slightly. From inside the cell one might not have noticed, especially in Oscar's condition. Yet it was closed enough to appear to be fully shut.

He could have walked out any time he wanted. What was happening to him?

"Oscar, you need to get ahold of yourself. Talk to us," Rufus said calmly. Oscar swallowed, the fur coating his face bristling as he shook.

"The floor," he choked out in a voice that sounded like a growl, "the bars... The walls. It's all *silver!*"

Mick blinked. Rufus's eyes flared up in an instant. Mick did the same, forcing the blood to his eyes as he had done with the Light when he was alive. He saw Oscar, huddled on his cot, but encapsulated in a dancing fire of yellow, orange and red. The inferno crawled over him, flaring up the strongest on the areas of flesh that had been scorched. It was in that instant that Mick wished he had Judah with them to explain what those colors in his aura meant. Judah could even see them without the Higher Sight.

"Oscar," Mick said, "There is no silver in that room. You're not allergic to silver. That's a myth."

Oscar's lupine eyes flashed towards Mick, his expression like that of one who was just hearing such words for the first time. The lesson Brandon had taught him about silver had been one of his first ones, and he had not been a negligent teacher.

"Y-yes there is! Look at me!" He roared, turning more to reveal his chest, streaked with parallel burn marks like he had been pressed against a flaming grill.

"Oscar, listen up. This cell is made of concrete and iron. There is no silver anywhere near you. Your mind is under attack," Rufus said as he grabbed onto the iron bars of the cell, and pulled the door open. It rolled along its track with a noisy, clanging rattle that caused Mick to glance around anxiously to make sure it hadn't attracted company.

"I…I can't walk out there," Oscar sobbed, holding out his hands insistently as proof. He shifted on the cot, and yelped when his back touched one of the chains. Mick and Rufus both watched as a fresh, second degree burn spread across the affected area. The flesh blistered up instantly, reddening around the edges.

"Shh shh shh, hey…Easy," Rufus said, grabbing Oscar by the sides of his face and holding him so their eyes met.

"Remember when Brandon had you hold a piece of silver in your hand? He had you touch your tongue to it, and nothing happened." Rufus said. Mick remembered that. He remembered it was not even a month after he had started his training with the hunters, and Brandon had called him, Rufus and Sunny to watch the proof of that lesson. As hunters, they needed to see firsthand that the stuff had no effect on the creatures. Brandon had placed a sharpened piece of silver in Oscar's hand. He had held it for over a minute with no adverse effects. He touched his tongue to it, and nothing happened. Then without warning, Brandon took the sharpened piece of silver, and nicked Oscar's arm with it. It shocked and surprised him more than anything. His blood trickled out of the nick on his arm, but otherwise, it began to heal at the same rate Oscar's other wounds did.

"He even cut your arm with it and you were fine," Rufus went on to recall as Oscar's face trembled in his hands, tears wetting the fur around Oscar's eyes.

"T-they…t-told me…" Oscar tried to say, as his face began to melt back into his human one, "that the w-walls were silver…They told me it would kill me if I m-moved." He closed his eyes and threw his arms around Rufus like a scared child, and held on for dear life.

Rufus returned the embrace, holding him just as tightly. Mick saw a gleaming stream of tears begin to fall from Rufus's eyes as they began to glow brighter.

"Who told you?" Rufus pressed.

"The vampires."

Mick recalled legends of them having mesmerizing powers over an individual. He wondered if, when under a vampire's mesmerism, if the power of suggestion was amplified in the victim's mind to the point of flat out erasing memories of prior experiences. He knew that Oscar knew silver wasn't deadly to them. He made a quick mental note how useful that could be under the right circumstances, and cursed quietly to himself as he was reminded that he didn't have anyone willing to teach him.

Mick watched as the two embraced each other, Oscar holding onto Rufus like a life raft. He watched with amazement as the burns on Oscar's flesh began to heal and mend before his eyes as his memories came back.

LIKE A PET

She could feel something cold resting against her skin, on each wrist. Something that was connected to needle-fine intrusions. Her eyes fluttered open weakly, as if her eyelids weighed about five hundred pounds each. Her awareness was slowly starting to inch further toward her extremities, returning in the form of an icy chill that started from her face, and wrapped her in frost all the way down. Sunny tried to move her fingers, and winced at how stiff they felt.

Forcing her eyes to stay open, she let her surroundings creep into blurry view, as if she were viewing them through a piece of wax paper pressed against her eyeballs. She managed to lift her head enough to look down at her arms where the numb, dull pain of something fine stabbing her was. Two IV needles were protruding out of her wrists, held in place with tape from a standard first aid kit. The thin tubes connected to the needles ran out on either side of her to two blood donor bags resting on scales. She winced as she reached her hands toward the needles on each arm, trying to undo the tape holding them in place. Her fingers were clumsy and felt like ice as she painfully managed to remove the invasive things. She slowly looked around the room, noticing the first aid/medical supplies resting on a tarp over a filthy countertop. Rusted cabinets lined the top half of the room. A dim fluorescent light hung lazily overhead, subtly humming.

She slowly, and with great effort, pushed herself off the table. She misjudged the distance from her boots to the floor however, and when the shock of that split second before actual contact with the floor had been made, she flinched and crumpled to the ground in a dizzy heap, letting out an enraged whimper that sounded pitiful. Her heart was hammering in her chest as she crawled toward the counter, trying to get her feet under her. She didn't care to speculate exactly how much of her blood had been syphoned out of her. She knew she felt like a husk, and wanted to collapse on the floor again.

She finally managed to make herself stand, and thankfully she was only a couple feet away from the counter as she did so. She held onto it for stability with one hand, and with the other tried to find something with which to bandage herself. Her fumbling fingers had been less than kind to the insides of her wrists when she tried removing the needles. A sickly brownish purple bruise now colored her skin after she removing the needles. She tried, painfully, to wrap gauze around her wrists, her hands shaking terribly as she used a pair of surgical scissors to cut the fabric and then cut strips of tape to keep them in place. She was too weak to try and apply much pressure. The best she could manage was the pressure from the bandages so she tried to wrap them tight.

Something blue caught her attention. She hadn't noticed it until now, but in the sink to her left, was a Tupperware dish with a blue lid, a banana, a cup of what looked like yogurt, an orange Gatorade with a straw poked through a hole in the plastic lid, and a bottle of water. She reached for the Tupperware, inspecting its contents. She realized what she was seeing was a salad. Someone had made her a salad, and left it here for her to find along with some fluids. Her mind tried to wrap around why in the hell food and drink would be sitting here in this sink. Was it poisoned?

At that thought a throbbing wave of recollection hit her square between the eyes. Vampires wrestling with Oscar and Mick, a shapeshifter who looked like a wearboar charging toward her. She slowly turned around and looked at the two bags containing her blood. She didn't recognize this room, didn't trust this food. Not if she had awoken in the lair of those things that attacked her and her friends.

She looked down at her wrists, seeing the little red splotches on the gauze wrappings. Her bleeding from the needle pricks had stopped thankfully. But if she was in a building with vampires, she reasoned they had the same smell for blood that sharks did. At least it didn't seem unreasonable.

She caught herself, against her better judgment, lifting the container out of the sink. Thankfully, the lid wasn't sealed. The effort of opening that with weak, clumsy fingers would have been enough to make her scream. A small plastic fork was in there. A salad made entirely of kale, spinach, nuts, berries, and strips of steak. The smell of the food greeted her as she held the container.

They're trying to take care of me…so they can bleed me again, she thought as she looked at the salad. She hated to admit it to herself, but it looked really, really good.

She tried to force some Light into her eyes, just enough to see if there had been anything added to the food and drinks, chemicals, powders, anything. The effort left her eyes to water as that familiar surge of chilly energy she felt encapsulate her eyes when she manifested it was no longer present.

Damnit! She thought, *the Light travels through the blood stream. What was I thinking? I'm too weak. I can't use it now…Not until I get my strength back.*

She eyed the salad, painfully reaching for the plastic fork. Her logic finally started to work as she considered the food before her. They wanted her for her blood. It would make sense they would try and take good care of her, almost like a pet. So poisoning the food they gave her made no sense. It would spoil the taste of the merchandise.

Sunny hated herself for what she was about to do. Eating food from her captors was degrading. It made her feel like a rabbit in a cage. But her survival instincts were starting to win out over her pride. She couldn't find the boys if she was this weak. Honestly, the effort of standing against this countertop was starting to get to her. To her knowledge she wasn't going into hemorrhaging shock… yet. She took inventory of her body as quickly as she could. Her stomach didn't hurt, wasn't swollen. She looked down at herself, checking herself between her legs. There were no blood stains on her jeans. Her chest was beginning to feel tight as she tried to breath, and her heart was still hammering like a jackhammer.

She picked up the fork, and made herself eat everything in that container, consequences be damned. She was getting out of here! She was going to find her friends and leave this hellhole, and wouldn't be coming back to Denver if she could help it!

It took her less than ten minutes to consume all the food they had left her and drink down both of the bottles of liquid. She hated orange Gatorade, but given her circumstances, being picky was off the table. It took her another ten minutes of just resting, sitting with her legs hugged against her chest, before she felt a little surge of energy. She stood up, her heart still beating rapidly. At least her steps were surer this time. She found herself not needing to hold onto anything for support.

Take the small victories, she told herself. Her eyes scanned the room for something she could use as a weapon. She spotted the cabinets again, and a brief spark of hope welled up in her chest, only to be shot down. There was no way her captors would be so stupid as to have put all her gear in one of those. As far as she knew, her bow, arrows, her sidearm, her knives, and anything else she carried on her person for hunting was gone for good. She reached up slowly, and with a little more strength, pulled open all the cabinets. Shiny, stainless steel surgical tools, neatly displayed on a towel, lined the interior of one cabinet. Whoever worked in here was neurotic to the point of OCD it seemed. Each tool was laid out symmetrically, in descending order of size, width, and blade length. She closed them and moved to the next one. Power tools, a large Craftsman drill, an electrical sander, were displayed amongst several drill bits that were displayed in much the same order as the surgical tools. She couldn't use any of those. Sure the drill was cordless, but it was noisy, and there was no guarantee the battery pack was charged. She moved to the next cabinet, her hope draining further with each step, her body feeling weaker.

An assortment of hammers, screwdrivers of varying sizes, wrenches, obsessively arranged in the most symmetrical patterns greeted her, and she felt her eyes widen with fresh determination as she grabbed the biggest Philips screwdriver she could find. The thing was as big and sturdy as a survival knife. She hoped as her strength continued to return, that she would be able to channel the Light into the object to make it lethal against the creatures. Her eyes scanned the other contents of the cabinet. Swinging a hammer or wrench in her present state would be a mistake waiting to happen. The screwdrivers, she could use like daggers for thrusting and stabbing. She grabbed another, smaller flat-head and tucked it into her back pocket as a backup, and then turned toward the heavy, rusted steel door.

She pulled the heavy door open as far as it could go before it started scraping against everything that was on the floor in this room. She was small enough that she squeeze through into a dark hallway. She was still shaking, and it was annoying her. Though now the reason why didn't seem to be so much as from blood loss, and that was what annoyed her the most. She had been so fearless in that cleanup of the St. Andrews back home. She remembered other missions where she seemed more die-hard than even some of the guys. She ranked right up there with Valerie, Judah, Rufus, and Brandon, she thought, or at least hoped, on a good day. But this was different. She stood alone in the messy hallway. Without her companions, those whom she had drawn such strength from in the past, she was haunted by the gnawing realization that she was now alone.

No...Not alone, she kept reminding herself, recalling images of the towering presence of Yeshua. The night when he had said her name—her real name, and had reached down and pulled her from the blackest ocean that her soul floundered in, never left her. The night when she was counted among the Reclaimed. He had never manifested to her since that night, but she hadn't needed him to. Not like she did now.

Yeshua, she thought, *Walk with me through here. Because I'm not leaving until I find my friends.*

She stood in the darkness of the hallway, letting the darkness wrap itself around her like a blanket. She could see rectangular outlines to her right. Boards, covering up shattered windows, kept the steady pattering of water droplets from getting in. She smelled the rain, the moisture seeping through the walls right before the thunder shook the building with a sudden boom that sounded like a cannon. She steadied her breathing and let the sound of the wind and rain hitting the boards on the windows speak to her. As she steadily walked forward, she let the prickles on her skin overtake her, wrap her in a shawl of crawling dread. She had learned to let the shivers overtake her. Not to fight them, but to ride them like a current. She realized as she stepped out into this hallway that she didn't have a choice. It was freezing out here.

The hallway turned left, and after a short distance, opened up into a large room lit by a construction lamp over in one corner, with the beam of light pointing directly up at the ceiling. The room was full of bunk beds, crudely welded together out of junk yard materials. The mattresses on each were thin to the point of practically being likened to a thick blanket. Each bunk bed had some sort of tray, or small table next to them upon which rested various items. Loose change, toothpicks, a random cigarette lighter, needles. One over on the furthest end toward the construction lamp even had a hand gun laying on it. The slide was open and the clip was lying on the tray. She couldn't tell from where she stood if the clip was loaded or not though. Over in one corner, an electric generator hummed, sitting next to an old washer and dryer that appeared to be from the eighties.

She found herself holding her breath as she stood at the mouth of the hallway, feeling naked and exposed with nothing to hide behind. Her eyes scanned the bunk beds for signs of movement. Each one, at least from where she was standing, appeared vacant. She knew not to rely on false hope, especially now. Looks were almost always deceiving.

Sunny flexed her fingers around the green handle of the massive screwdriver in her right hand, tried as best she could to relax her breathing, and crept forward into the naked exposure of this room. Even the collection of bunk beds, all eight of them from what she could see, didn't offer much in the way of cover. Not unless she hid underneath them.

She felt her face twitch as she slowly, quietly, dropped down onto her belly, and army crawled underneath the first bunk bed. She looked in the direction of the other side of this room, where the washer and dryer rested next to an open doorway. She could see her exit, and it exhilarated and terrified her all at once. She felt a sudden head rush as the excitement faded, soon being replaced by another wave of fatigue. She lay there, breathing shallowly as the sensation slowly subsided.

Go, she heard a voice say in her head. She obeyed, quietly slinking out from under one bunk on her belly as quietly as she could. She quickly managed to tuck her feet under the second bed when she heard whistling, coming from the door she was headed towards. She froze as the whistling got louder, and a pair of boots came into view as the door squeaked open. Then the whistling stopped. The boots stayed there in the door for what seemed like an eternity until they took a step forward, slowly, then another and another toward her bunk. She froze, trying to quell the hammering inside of her chest. She could feel her heart thudding so hard she swore whoever this was could also hear it. She clasped her hands over her mouth to try and muffle the sounds of her own, labored breathing.

The pair of boots stopped directly in front of her face, and the next seconds were filled with gut twisting tension as she tried not to pass out from lack of oxygen. The mattress above her creaked and groaned under the weight of whoever was on top as the person sat down.

A clatter of something metallic chimed from down the hall she had come from. She almost screamed as her insides violently jumped when the figure on the bed stood abruptly at the noise, and mechanically and methodically, started toward the hallway entrance.

Go, she told herself, and she quickly scrambled toward the next bunk, the heavy boot falls of the stranger tromping off behind in the opposite direction.

I have to get to that gun at least, she thought, and then wondered in the next second if her hands would even be strong enough to hold it. Her thoughts were cut off when she heard the footsteps of the stranger stop. Not gradually fade away—but stop altogether.

She was almost under the third bed when she felt something icy trap her ankle, and pull her out from under the bed. She felt her shirt sliding up as she was dragged on her belly out from under the bed, the cold tiles electrifying the flesh of her abdomen. She turned over, with strength she barley had, and flung her other leg into the pallid, chalky white face of what had grabbed her. The heel of her boot connected with the thing's lower jaw and she heard a definitive *crack*. She saw the stranger's black eyes flash with flecks of red and a vein bulging from their bald head. The gnarled, pointed ears twitched as its face leered toward hers, teeth shaped like spears. Clawed hands went for her throat.

"Can't escape, you can't escape. I can't let you escape," the thing murmured over and over again, as she gripped the screw driver still in her hand and launched the pointed end toward the vampire's temple. The tip of the enormous Philips head missed its intended mark, but found the soft fleshy part of the cheek and punctured it with a dull wet *pop*. She snarled with fury and pressed the screw driver even further in until the point exploded out of the other cheek, dislodging part of the jaw in the process as the thing twisted away from her.

It was standing up, gripping its head in both hands as it tried to yank out the screw driver. She twisted back onto her belly, and pushed herself up with a burst of new strength as adrenaline flooded through her. She wasn't ready for the momentum though as she found herself stumbling under her own weight.

But she was closer to the bunk bed with the gun next to it. She forced herself to stand just as the wet sound of bloody metal scraping against bone filled her ears as the vampire dislodged the screwdriver.

She grabbed the small end table on the bunk next to her, and flung it over. She heard an annoyed roar escape the vampire's maw as she raced toward the table with the gun on it. As she advanced, her heart hammering faster and faster, she could finally see that the clip did in fact contain bullets. She slammed the clip into the pistol, closed the slide and flicked off the safety. She spun on wobbly legs and took aim, expecting the fiend to be on top of her as she did so.

But the vampire was crouched down on all fours like an animal, hunched over the mess she had made when she flung the table over. The annoyed shrieks were forming cusswords and other words she couldn't understand as the thing hissed through its teeth. It hurried to pick up each item that had fallen off of the tray, the change, the scattered cigarette butts and the shattered remains of a ceramic ashtray. It was then that it clicked in her mind that this vampire was probably the one who had arranged the tools in the room she woke up in.

She squeezed the trigger as she felt the welcome chilling tingle swallow her eyes, and her veins on her hands lit up around the gun. The pistol barked its orders, and the bullets found their mark, smacking into the vampire. Its body lurched and twisted as she put round after round into its flesh. Steam sizzled out of each luminescent bullet hole. Light flowed through the creature's veins as it jerked and sizzled, until it finally fell on its knees. The glowing veins beneath the creature's white skin flickered and went out, just as Sunny felt her grip on the gun starting to slip. She stumbled backwards onto the filthy bed just as she heard a stampede of footsteps approaching from the door she had been trying to get to.

Her hands shook as she held up the gun, trying to recall quickly how many bullets she had used up. She vaguely remembered pulling the trigger six, maybe seven times. She did some quick math, realizing only eight rounds remained. She prayed that would be enough as she weakly attempted to sit up just as three figures emerged from the doorway, all of them instantly putting their hands up.

"Sunny, whoa! Hold on!"

She recognized those voices! All of them! She blinked as she felt a sudden surge of tears spring to her eyes. She lowered the gun as Mick, Rufus, and Oscar came into view, each of them scooping her up and embracing her, enfolding her in their strong arms.

Not alone sweetheart, the voice from earlier spoke through her head as each of them hugged and kissed her on the cheek, the nose, the forehead, each of them embracing her with bear hug ferocity as she embraced them in return.

You'll never be alone, Yeshua said.

CORNERED

Reunited, bloodied, humiliated, and hungry, were all words anyone could have accurately used to describe them as the hunters trudged along, with Sunny being propped up between Mick and Oscar. The scent from where her wrists had bled was reaching out, caressing Mick's awareness as her wrist dangled next to his head. It was driving him mad, enough so that he felt his now almost spent reserves of blood begging for replenishment.

He couldn't exactly say that he smelled her blood, because that would have implied he could pass oxygen through his nostrils, thus expanding his lungs. He could have done that once or twice and been overwhelmed by the scent of her blood. He had used the blood he feasted on to conjure such effects as to make his lungs function, but again, it expended a resource that was now in short supply within his frame.

The sight of her blood soaked gauze certainly set him on edge, but if he had to describe it, his awareness of her blood seemed to be more of a hyper, psychic awareness. As if his aura was reaching out, smelling things for him.

He snapped his eyes shut the second her bloody wrists came into his line of sight again. The gauze had by now been soaked through with the liquid medium of her life force. He could feel his tongue thrashing around inside of his mouth like an eel, and he bit down on it to quell its search. He felt the tips of his serrated teeth puncture his tongue, and it felt like biting into a slab of tasteless rubber. It did not have the intended effect he wanted however. He wanted something painful to redirect his focus. He realized that with his blood reserves so low, his senses were dulled to the point of feeling only the impact and friction of certain things against him. A barrage of bullets might hurt about as much as having skittles thrown at him, though he wasn't eager to find out.

They followed Rufus through the barren remains of the second story floor. The floor where the Collector's office was located. This floor looked much different from the first and third however. Whereas those floors were dilapidated and strewn with mounds of garbage, old crates, dormitories that weren't sanitary, flickering lights wherever the precious things could be found, this second floor was rather plain. Immaculately clean, but plain and otherwise holding no remarkable trait save for just the gray concrete floors, gray, faded walls and doors that looked newer than anything in the entire building.

Maybe since this is where his office is he wants it to be clean, Mick caught himself thinking. It seemed as good an explanation as any but in the long run was a trivial attempt to keep his mind off of the fact the friend between him and Oscar was a ready source of blood. Mick found himself wishing if only to suck the blood from the bandages around her wrists. He squeezed his eyes shut as he heaved her along. Sunny was able to walk, thankfully, but having Oscar and Mick prop her up helped relieve some of the stress on her already weakened body.

She's so weak...It would be so easy.

What the hell?! No! She's family!

"Hold on!" Rufus hissed as he held up a hand at the end of a hallway. The group froze as he craned his neck around a corner. Mick felt Sunny stiffen against him as she tried to steady herself from wobbling. He felt Oscar's hair bristle as if his hackles were rising in anticipation. After an agonizing period of a few seconds, Rufus sharply motioned with his hand and slipped around the corner.

As they did so, Mick saw the flickering lights of the ground floor below them, mounted on the sides of the walls and a few on the ceiling. They were approaching the balcony, overlooking the crude cage Hank had led him passed the night they learned what the Collector really was capable of. They approached quietly and cautiously, crouching down once they got close enough to the railing of the balcony to see most of the floor but still not reveal their position to any wondering eyes that may have been lurking down below. Oscar was already sniffing the air, his human face scrunching up into a silent snarl as his eyes flared white with Higher Sight. Rufus did the same. Sunny leaned her head against Mick's shoulder, small traces of Light coursing through her skin, trying to reach up into her face and take hold of her retinal nerves. Mick felt himself looking down out into the first floor, taking note of the bunk beds, the crudely constructed card tables.

"See anything?" Mick whispered. Rufus shook his head.

"It doesn't look like anyone is down there. But I'm seeing vague ripples just out of the corner of my eye, so something *is* down there."

"I smell it," Oscar huffed under his breath, "blood, and tar."

Suddenly, Mick's mind snapped back to several nights. He recalled the extermination/rescue job they all took part in at St. Andrews. The statue of Saint Michael, housing a creature within its marble shell. When the team used their Higher Sight in that building, each of them saw different things in regards to the body of the deceased custodian. Judah said that Father had been able to extinguish it for an extended period of time. The Collector had been able to stop it up inside their very veins, rendering them unable to change the properties of their weapons to have any lasting effect. Their enemies could manipulate it as well. Mick could no longer summon the Light. He was a creature of blood now. But that didn't mean he wasn't terrified for his friends who could summon it. Despite all the cool things it could do, helping them see spirits, energy fields, identify certain creatures on sight, and burn the hell out of the monsters, it could still be tricked.

"We keep going," Rufus said, "stay sharp. Mick, Oscar, you keep Sunny upright, close in tight around her."

"I think I can walk now," Sunny whispered. Mick imagined her voice was what a wilted flower might sound like. Rufus gave her a nod.

"Duly noted Chika, but you've lost a lot of blood. Don't be trying to prove anything to us. We don't need you collapsing."

Mick saw Sunny's expression become taut with annoyance as she tried to huff, but resigned acceptance of his words slowly took over. Rufus handed Sunny his machete, as he switched to the hatchet and gave Oscar the crowbar. Mick drew his machete out of his belt. Sunny walked between Oscar and him as they descended down the metal stairs, Mick keeping his hand on Sunny's shoulder to steady her.

The first floor sprawled out before them in all its cluttered, sad glory. Mick watched Oscar, his ears, though in human form for now, seemed to be standing erect as he stepped forward with a deliberate stride, nearly leaving Sunny and Mick behind. He heeled, and came back to protect her left side.

They were nearing the collection of bunks when Oscar's words burbled up in Mick's mind, *blood and tar.* Mick threw many a nervous glance over his shoulder, his eyes patrolling just as intently as everyone else's. They were escaping a building where vampires fed, so the smell of blood wouldn't be overly surprising. But tar?

"Hank?" Sunny's voice squeaked out. Rufus stopped, his stance calm yet ready if something jumped out.

"Chika, we don't have time!" Rufus hissed as he began moving forward again, his steps slow and full of ever mounting tension.

Mick suddenly saw what she saw, or rather, who she saw. It looked like Hank, from the back view anyway. The slope of the shoulders, the overall height, the long stringy white hair. Rufus stopped when he saw it too. Oscar was now growling defensively as his face was partially morphing to take on a more feral, lupine appearance, but not his full transformation.

The figure stood shaking, twitching, like its joints were on strings, being pulled by the hand of an unknown puppet master.

Blood, and tar…

Mick heard a droplet of something hit the floor. His eyes lingered on the figure. A droplet of black goop had landed next to their mud caked boot. His eyes traveled up the full length of the figure as it slowly turned to face them.

Oscar was expelling loud, threatening barks, and Mick thought he heard his bones start to stress and crack as his limbs began to elongate. Sunny's face was contorting into a mask of horrified shock. Rufus's face on the other hand, though tan since his Reclaiming, was now pallid and gaunt as if all blood had been drained from it.

"Ah! My estranged son and daughter, my rebellious pet…and my dirty laundry," a voice that was not Hank's said, the eyes landing on each of them with each noun spoken. The face was Hank's. But the way the mouth moved, the way the cheeks moved in an unnatural smile, made it seem as if the skin of Hank's face was being worn as a mask. The thing in front of them crossed its arms and leaned against one of the bunks, and the manner in which it did so made the limbs twitch and spasm slightly as it did. Black tar was dribbling out of the mouth, out of the nostrils.

Oscar tore passed them, his elongated limbs thrashing with the eager anticipation of a fresh kill. His body smacked into an unseen barrier, and he crumpled in an undignified, stunned heap.

"Down boy," the voice said, his tone almost amused.

"It's him," Sunny was breathing out, the words only audible to Mick as a collection of sharp gasps as he felt her nails digging into his shoulder.

"Yes my dear. Father has missed you. But I've kept up with you," he beamed, forcing a fake smile through Hank's face.

"Where is Hank and Trevor?!" She screamed, her tone instantly shifting from terrified to enraged. Still, her nails bit deeper into Mick's shoulder. He hardly felt it.

"I'm afraid your friend Hank was forced to depart. I liked him very much. It was the reason I chose his body as my next vessel after all."

Sunny's feet went out from under her, and Mick had to help her as she slide down onto her knees, gnashing her teeth, using energy she didn't have as tears of hot rage fell of their own volition.

Images of Mick's nightmare flashed through his mind's eye, and Father's eyes shot toward him, "I was so excited to show him off, I showed you first, Mr. Johnson. I wanted you to know I had moved on, and that there were no hard feelings on my end."

With a flick of a clawed hand, Mick felt pressure bearing down on his body, forcing him into the likes of a metal folding chair that skittered across the floor toward him. Rufus was fighting back against the increased gravity bearing down on him, his veins and eyes flickering impotently as a chair skirted across the floor and then, his bum became thoroughly rooted to the chair. Oscar and Sunny winced and screamed and howled with rage as the same force increased upon them. Sunny screamed until her face turned red, the Light not even so much as flaring up through her exhausted frame.

Father pulled up another metal folding chair, turned it backwards and sat with his front pressed against the backrest. The metal chair squeaked and creaked under the weight of the large vessel he now inhabited.

"I hear Valerie and Judah are expecting!" Father said.

Mick felt his own aura grow cold. If icicles could have manifested in the air around him, they would have. At his words, Rufus, Oscar and Sunny all fell silent. Mick could feel his heart, which had lay dormant moments before, speeding up like a jet engine the same way it had upon feeding, priming his body like a hair trigger. He could feel the blood rushing to massage his lungs, and he felt himself starting to breathe again, involuntarily as his mind reached out desperately for an answer.

Then he remembered, and as the blood coursed through his tissue, he felt that if he could have cried, he would have. To have gone back in time and warned them not to have been so careless for telling him in the presence of others who still carried the gray taint. His mind screamed back toward the night of St. Andrews, him waking up in the back of an ambulance, as gray skinned EMT's tended to him.

"You use those with the gray to spy on us," Mick said. Father's eyes twinkled as he drew Hank's cheeks up in a hideously contented smile. He brought a clawed finger up to the side of his new head and tapped on his ear.

"They really should be more careful with what they say. You never know who could be listening," Father said, and then lifted his eyes above, and all around. Mick's body, now sending blood to his extremities, was aware when the air began to ripple with the same cold energy he felt in his aura a moment ago. He looked up, trying to follow where Father's gaze went, and as he did, he thought he could feel the floor crumbling beneath him.

As if a curtain of camouflage had melted away from reality, he began to see various humanoid shapes beginning to solidify. Many of them walked toward the edge of the balcony, blurry, glitch shapes that bore more and more resemblance to the human frame as it went on. Others were walking out from between the bunks, crowding around the tables, filling in to surround them. When the optical special effects wore off, Mick, as well as the others could see the army of pallid white faces, mixed with the gray skinned, blood shot eyes of homeless, human Thralls filling in around them, on the balcony above, on the stairs, around the cage, walking between the makeshift tables, and filling in the spaces around the bunks. With the new flow of blood to his body, giving it a semblance of its former life, he again felt the claws of an old fear raking its nails around on the inside of his skull.

There's no way out! I can't breathe! I can't scream! I can't get out.......One hundred...Ninety nine...ninety eight...

THE TASTE OF A NAME

Mick felt his blood moving around his tissue as if it was nearly sentient. He could feel it chugging, slithering around inside of him, and he felt its intent more than anything else. He felt a chilling sense of reverence emitting from the stuff, the feeling rising to compete with his impending sense of suffocation. Then just when the feeling of being confined with no way out reached its climax, he saw a thick, roiling carpet of fog spreading out under everyone's feet, shrouding their ankles in churning white mist. An arm, slim and pale blue, shot out from the blanket of fog, coalescing into a solid form before Mick's eyes. Following the appendage was a lithe female figure, whose fountain of red hair flowed and billowed out from her head as if she were under water. Her beauteous face was young, appearing like that of a young woman in her twenties. Yet as Mick looked on, behind that delightfully, bewitching face seemed to lurk malevolence far older than his mind cared to inquire about.

Another form took shape next to Mick's chair and he jumped, turning his eyes abruptly as a stiff, rigid form began to shamble toward the woman who had just materialized. His limbs moved with an aching stiffness as he trudged toward her, seemingly with great effort. Sometimes the vampire managed to painfully shuffle one foot forward, and at other times, while holding an arm out for balance, he seemed to hop. The display would have almost been comical had Mick not seen his eyes. They were two foggy orbs with silver irises around a microscopic point of black for the pupils. His face was set with the intention of a primordial predator, being housed within a human façade, but seeming to stretch back farther than humanity itself.

The throng of vampires and ghouls began to systematically part as two more figures approached. One was the Collector himself. The other, a man much shorter than him, about as tall as Mick was if he had to guess, walked just slightly in front of him. More of a monument to time immemorial than a person, advancing with the patience of a mountain, he surveyed all present with a melancholic stoicism. His face looked to be the canvas of distant lives, philosophies and empires, all insignificant footnotes in the span of his unlife. Though he was much shorter physically than the Collector, he seemed to dwarf him just by his sheer presence, which made Mick feel even smaller by comparison.

Mick felt the Collector's eyes shoot over him in a scowl of contempt, and he felt the blood inside of him scream like a wounded rabbit at the invasive, overly personal scowl the Collector's eyes offered him.

Father caused Hank's body to stand, and he bowed his head. The reverent gesture was returned by the stiff vampire as much as he could muster. Father then removed Hank's fingerless gloves and shook the Collector's hand, the man who had accompanied him, and the hand of the fog woman.

"Elders," the Collector began, "I give gifts of old blood to you. Before you, is sample, purged of old taint."

"I will not debase myself by drinking from that dog!" the fog woman hissed out in an Irish accent, her eyes pointing toward Oscar's form being pinned down on the floor. Then her eyes landed on Rufus, and she smiled, "but *this* one appears to be quite nectarous!" She said as her fangs descended and her jaw unhinged. Mick watched as Rufus tensed in anticipation for the bite, his eyes and veins quickly flaring to a brilliant glow. Sunny and Oscar's eyes and veins lit up beneath their skin as well.

"Wait!" The Collector's voice boomed, causing several around to jump as if they had been goosed.

The Irish woman scowled at him, "Makari! Deal with your insolent spawn before I do!"

Makari, the one who had accompanied the Collector, stepped up to meet her gaze, "Elder Alana," he said, remembering formality, "Do not be so hasty. His blood pulses with a foreign power. Somehow I do not think it is the power Grigori mentioned." He said, his hand motioning toward the Collector.

So that's his real name, Mick thought as he tried to formulate a plan of sorts, his limbs still being held against his body by the gravitational force of Father, who was looking on with amusement. Ralph's words suddenly came screeching back to him, remembering how he said Mick's blood was useless now. How Mick had been an accident.

So as long as I keep quiet, he's not going to acknowledge me to these Elders, Mick thought.

"Hey Grigori!" Mick spat, and he watched as the Collector's body became taught, as if a jolt of electricity had shot through his spine.

"Why don't you tell your elders how you let another vampire be created! Here is your accident right here! Why don't you tell them that I used to have purged blood too before you let me be turned!" Mick said loudly, drawing the attention of the other vampires and ghouls that closed in behind him.

The Collector's body slowly turned toward Mick, as did the gazes of the three Elders. As the eyes of nearly every predator in the room drilled him, he could feel the blood inside of him reeling against his insides, trying to claw its way free from the dead flesh cocoon it dwelt in. He could feel its attempts at communicating with him. Bursts of intense emotional distress flooded him, urges to thrash against Father's binding and flee!

Instead of seeing an irritated Collector, he saw a smirking face that eyed him enthusiastically despite the contemptuous stares of the three Elders.

"It is true," Grigori admitted, turning his eyes casually to them, "he was accident, nothing more. There are remaining plenty more of purged blood where we are going."

"You know we do not create wantonly," Makari chided. To this, Father stepped up, clearly having seen enough.

"It was a mistake Grigori will not make again," he purred, and with a wave of his hand, Mick watched as the Light was snuffed out from Rufus, Oscar and Sunny. Alana's eyes darted hungrily toward Rufus, and she materialized toward him.

The stiff vampire smiled, slowly, painfully, made his way over toward Sunny. He withdrew a ceremonial looking dagger with a golden crafted handle that was sculpted in the form of a Chinese dragon, holding a jade stone in its mouth.

Mick watched helplessly, Father's grip around his body still absolute, as Alana sank her fangs into Rufus's forearm. Mick saw Rufus's jaw clench and his face flush with heat as he grunted loudly, refusing to scream.

Sunny screamed a curse and flailed under the weight of Father's invisible grip. A vampire and a thrall scooped her twitching body off the floor and held her steady so the Elder could sample from her. Her screams of rage were giving way to sobs of resignation as the vampire took her hand, held her palm facing upward, and drew the blade of his dagger across her palm. A long, slithery tongue unfurled from inside of the Elder's mouth, and the tiny black pupils in his eyes dilated to take over his entire eye, shrouding the silvery irises. Mick watched in horror as his limbs suddenly became less rigid, his shoulders cracking as he moved them like an athlete who just got done stretching.

Oscar thrashed as Makari walked over toward him and closed his mouthful of jagged fangs over the side of Oscar's neck. Oscar gasped, and a sharp howl involuntarily escaped his throat as he convulsed under Makari's grasp.

The Collector approached Mick, his smile broadening, as he bent down next to Mick's ear, "You seek to embarrassing me, little hunter…I make example of your comrades."

At his words, Mick began having flashbacks to the Collector's office.

Been shot before little hunter! Poisoned! Bludgeoned! Fed through hole in icy river!

Mick felt himself shaking uncontrollably now, shaking as the blood screamed inside like a cornered child. The Collector sauntered around to face Mick, his eyes burning with controlled rage. Suddenly, as Mick sat there looking up at the thing who's blood had brought him back in this state, images of the Collector flashed before his mind's eye. Not recent images from earlier, stored in the infinite bank of his memory, but images he had seen in *history books.*

"Ah," The Collector piped up, his tone more jovial, "You remembering who I am now?"

Mick said nothing, as he sat there trembling, the cries and howls of his friends mixing in his ears with the hungry hissing noises the other vampires were making. After a while, he managed to say something. Nothing that he thought would prove helpful to his friends, but it was something to keep him distracted.

"So, Grigori Rasputin…What brought you to the States?"

Grigori smiled and pointed to Hank's body, being animated by Father, "I owed someone favor for restoring my body," he said, flexing his fingers up by his face.

"You couldn't be killed, because you were already dead," Mick said, his teeth nearly chattering now. Grigori smiled and nodded.

"I thought, by sin, I could draw closer to God, thus repenting more fervently. Draw the taint out of blood. On night of failed attempt to kill me, I had been fasting from blood. Weakened, I could not much fighting back against attackers. It was Father, sent by God, who restored my body. And now, purged blood will draw us closer to God now." He paused for a long moment, invading Mick with his stare.

"You are not Devin Saint. Names, like blood, have taste. You are Mick Johnson," Grigori said, as he looked knowingly at Mick and winked.

Grigori turned toward the Elders as they finished sampling from his friends, their faces completely flush with new color, their eyes now glowing with red brilliance. Makari clasped Grigori's arm, whispered something in his ear as the others, and Father, gathered around them.

The Collector turned to address the swelling throng of his underlings, pulsing with desire and red hot hunger, "Escort guests back to their cells." He ordered, raising his voice so all could hear.

Mick suddenly felt the invisible grasp of Father slough off of him, as he made eye contact with the one who had deceived him three years ago. Father's eyes gleamed behind Hank's, as ice cold hands enclosed themselves all around Mick's shoulders, and the bodies of his friends. The Collector, Father, and the three Elders vanished as the crowd closed in over them, manhandling them to their feet and shoving them off in various directions. Separated. Defeated. Alone.

CROWD CONTROL

Mick felt the claws of the person or vampire behind him sinking deeper through his shirt. He tried desperately to search through the crowd for his friends. He heard and caught sight of Oscar, thrashing as a vampire was yanking him along with a tool that looked like a mediaeval version of a dog catcher's noose. He saw Oscar's muscles bulging and his face shifting, becoming more and more canine-like as the creature led him through the crowd.

Through the mob he managed to isolate and hear Rufus whispering something under his breath in Spanish. Something he had heard him whisper numerous times. If Mick remembered right, it was a prayer he would whisper while using his rosary.

He listened even harder, trying to hear something from Sunny, but to no avail. As he heard only the victorious taunts from those around him, he felt his undead heart twitch with regret, as if being staked all over again. He shook his head as the realization that his trying to humiliate the Collector hadn't gone as he had hoped, and Father just turned off the Light in their veins as easy as if he had flicked off a light switch.

Yeshua…If you're still around…If you still answer prayers from vampires… we're fucked.

Are you now? Yeshua's voice responded, and Mick flinched. He actually hadn't been expecting a reply, and one so quick at that.

The claws biting into his shoulder tightened, and then a mouth was leaning over Mick's shoulder, "Don't turn around," the voice instructed as something rubbery touched Mick's hand. The object bumped against his fingers forcefully a second time, and Mick looked down without moving his head. A gas mask was being held out to him.

"Get that to one of your friends. I've got masks for the others. You and I won't need them." the voice behind him said, and if Mick had had a living heart, he would have felt it speed up with a fresh adrenaline shot of hope.

Trevor had ahold of his shoulder, hood drawn up over his head, concealing his face deep in the shadows. Mick could already feel the stares of the other undead, slithering through the crowd, trying to pinpoint them.

"It's about to get foggy in here. When you see the smoke, move your ass and find your friends. Don't try to fight them all. Just hack your way through as many as you can and get the fuck out." Trevor instructed. Mick nodded, and then winced when a sharp, high-pitched whistle shot through the air next to his head.

The mob stopped, all heads turning in the direction of the whistle. Then a metallic, bouncing clatter was heard next, and with it, a gaseous hiss accompanied a billowing cloud of white gas. Mick looked upwards toward the balcony. Armored men with assault weapons were pouring down the stairs. For a second Mick was almost consumed with seething dread when he saw the armored uniforms, but the letters SWAT were clearly visible across the chests of the uniformed cavalry, and not the emblazoned logo of the CNHC.

Seconds later, all the homeless ghouls were choking, bent over as the teargas ravaged them. For a confused three seconds or so, the vampires looked on, like they were trying to process what was unfolding before them.

The sound of somebody's nose splattering on concrete seemed to jar them all toward action, Mick included. He clutched the gasmask in his hand and bolted as the rest of the crowd began to scatter, confused shrieks rising up from the mob. The crowd parted enough for him to see Rufus, slamming a ghoul's face into the concrete, disarm another ghoul of their firearm, and put a glowing round into the man's face just as the rolling cloud was about to engulf him.

"Rufus!" Mick yelled waving his arms and the gasmask out in front of him. Rufus spun at the sound of his name as Mick tossed the gasmask to him. Rufus gingerly plucked it out of the air and donned it as Mick hurried over to him. Neither of them said anything as Rufus brought his machete up to intercept the incoming clawed hand of a vampire to his right, Mick doing the same to a ghoul who lunged at him with a baseball bat. The machete bit through the man's neck, as the sound of automatic fire began to join in the chorus of madness.

Mick stole a glance upward. Vampires were tearing through SWAT in a shower of blood, guts and splintered bone, their bodies unaffected by the mundane rounds. Many of the undead did fall when a lucky couple of rounds exploded their heads.

The cloud was engulfing them as Rufus grabbed Mick by the shirt and hauled him forward, just in time for another pale body, or rather, half of one to sail past them. A hulking brute stalked out of the cloud to join them, muscles rippling beneath a fine coat of charcoal gray fur, wearing a gasmask.

"Where's Sunny?!" Rufus yelled, his voice muffled through the mask. Oscar's clawed hand pointed up toward the clearing in the direction of the exit where the fighting was beginning to thin out, and where the cloud's vapors hadn't yet engulfed. Sunny stood on shaky legs, wearing her gasmask and beating her glowing hatchet into the skull of a screaming vampire. A gloved, clawed hand was on her shoulder, urging her backward away from the carnage as Trevor fired into the crowd of advancing ghouls and undead with the pistol in his free hand. The three rushed toward Sunny, and her arm nearly came up to strike them before she realized who they were.

"Go go go!!!" Mick yelled, his hands pushing them all forward as Rufus and Oscar shielded her with their combined muscle. Mick turned, stealing one last look at the carnage before catching up to his friends. Trevor moved with deadly swiftness and grace unmatched by any who were living. The Reclaimed came close. He watched, transfixed as Trevor slashed the throat of one man, fire a bullet into the face of another vampire behind without looking, and stomped on another's knee, all seemingly at once. Mick heard the crunch and the muted gasps of agony that escaped the ghoul's throat before Trevor's maw clamped down over the carotid artery. He brought his face up and repeated the same process many times with different variations. If he could do such things, Mick was terrified to see what Hank could have accomplished.

"Mick come on!" He heard the muffled voice of Rufus yell his name down the hall and he turned, shooting down the hallway to join his fellow hunters. Mick and Rufus burst through the door to the side of the building. Mick's sensitive vision was nearly overwhelmed by the mini explosions of red and blue light covering the walls of the other surrounding buildings in the alleyway as officers in Kevlar vests, federal agents all trained their guns on them and instructed them to get on the ground.

Sunny and Oscar, now back in human form, had already complied and were having their gas masks removed by police, who stepped back and lowered their weapons when they confirmed their identities as the ones they had come to secure.

"Johnson!" Mick winced as he held his hands up and got down on his knees. That voice. That damned voice! Even as a dead guy, Pallacios's voice still felt like an icepick crammed down his ear. He heard her footsteps approaching on the concrete of the alley. He lowered his hands and looked up at her. The sight of her approaching made him grimace.

Definitely would never drink her blood, Mick thought.

Within minutes, Mick found himself being herded into the back of an ambulance with Oscar, and Sunny with Rufus, as they sped away from Whitehaven toward Rose Medical Center, leaving the authorities to face the horrors that continued to rage behind them.

PRIMAL SELF

Mick's eye lids sagged as he sat in the passenger seat of the vehicle they had taken up to Denver. When they were attacked at their hotel, the goons hadn't taken the time to vandalize their vehicle. A spare three hundred dollars in cash was still in its bank envelope, stashed under the driver's seat, as well as a few survival tools, a couple extra pistols and ammo, and a travel bag with hygiene products for everyone present.

Once thoroughly examined at Rose Medical Center, and answering a slew of repetitive questions by doctors and federal agents alike, they were finally released. The nurses and doctors who examined each of them were completely befuddled at how rapidly their injuries had healed, and alarmed when no one could detect Mick's heartbeat. Thankfully where Mick was concerned, it had been chalked up to faulty equipment. The physiological changes in his eyes, the pointed shapes of his ears and his restructured dental landscape he explained to the examiners as the result of torture. He said his teeth had been filed that way, the capillaries in his eyes had burst, and his ears shredded and surgically reconstructed. Sure, the teeth might be plausible, but the story he told about his eyes being the way they were, and his ears was laughable at best. He was trying to lie to medical professionals. Pallacios had shown up to the hospital at the height of the awkward examination, making an already uncomfortable situation unbearable.

"My God," she exclaimed, staring at Mick in utter revulsion, "You…Are you one of them now?!" She asked after the examiners had left them in privacy. Mick sat there, his eyes glued to the floor, not looking up.

"You blind?" he asked.

She didn't answer for a time. Instead Mick heard her pacing, saw her hands balled up at her sides for a second, then moved to fidget with the buckles of her shoulder holster.

"What happened in there Johnson?" she asked. Mick finally looked up, his eyes drilling her as his reply seethed out.

"I'll tell ya what happened! Your brilliant plan to have one of the Collector's guards as an inside man backfired on us! Nearly got my friends killed! It *did* get me killed!" He said, his voice rising with fury at the end of each sentence. He hopped off of the examination bench, hands clenched at his sides.

Agent Pallacios's gray face, froze in place as denial took root was replaced with sheer, animal panic as Mick approached. She backed away as he took another step closer.

"That's right Agent! I *died*. Now I'm one of *them* as you put it! I watched as more of them drank blood from my friends like they were juice boxes! You know what that's like?!" Mick nearly screamed, feeling the blood coiling around inside of him like a viper preparing to strike as Pallacios's face only widened further with terror.

He lost a few minutes after that. He didn't think vampires could black out. Didn't make any sense to him, but he remembered coming back to himself after what seemed like probably an hour, sitting in the passenger seat of the SUV with Trevor drilling him through the open door of the passenger seat.

"Your friends should be coming out here soon. You're welcome." He said.

Mick blinked, "What the hell happened?" he asked. Trevor folded his arms and looked down at him, his gaze akin to a hungry predator that was attempting to size up an inconvenience to its lair.

"You were about to let the blood get the better of you."

Mick's eyes widened, "Oh shit did I kill anybody?"

Trevor shook his head, "No, again, you're welcome. The Agent collapsed in a sobbing, incoherent mess. She'll probably be on leave for the next couple months. I worked some of my mojo on all the staff, they are releasing your friends right now as we speak."

Mick stared, wide eyed, words caught in his throat. He didn't know whether to laugh in joyous triumph over Pallacios's mental breakdown, or be horrified that he had accomplished such a feat without even trying.

"H-how did I—"

"The blood spoke to her primal self when you're were on your rant. You reminded her of why mankind never ventured far from their campfires and prayed to their gods for daylight to come." Trevor said.

"I did all that through eye contact?" Mick asked, stupefied.

"Yep. It's a handy trick to learn but in a crowded place like a hospital, it's a quick way to enter a blood rage. Not a good plan for our kind."

Mick considered that for a couple seconds, reliving the look of paralyzing hysteria that was growing on the agent's face, trying not to enjoy it. He tempered the mental images of a cowering Pallacios with the knowledge that Trevor had just pulled him back from the edge of a terribly high cliff.

"I almost lost control," Mick said softly, more to himself than to Trevor. He looked up, trying to meet Trevor's gaze, but feeling like an ant at the foot of a mountain.

"Thank you," Mick said. Neither of them said nothing for a long time. Only when Mick heard and smelled his friends approaching across the parking lot did Mick speak again.

"I'm sorry about your brother," he said. Trevor didn't say anything. When Mick looked up at him, Trevor had his eyes closed, nodding his head in acknowledgment.

"I'm sorry we didn't leave sooner." Trevor said.

Rufus had driven the team out of Denver and into Norton County, where they stopped for the night at a cheap, roach hotel. Given that it was almost six in the morning when they reached it, and with the sky beginning to lighten, Mick couldn't be too picky as he remembered Trevor's words about sunlight.

They paid the fee to stay for one night, which in this case really only meant during daylight hours, and then once the sun set and everyone had gotten a bite to eat, they checked out early and were back on the road, with Mick driving them the rest of the way into New Broken Edge. When they crossed over into Brigsworth County and passed the infamous Ironswrath Prison, Mick found himself accelerating, trying to put it behind him as quick as possible.

As they made their way down the staircase that plunged them deeper underground, into the bowels of Tom's Auto, Mick felt his chest tightening as he reached the bottom, put his hand on the door handle that would open up into the lair. He stopped, the others behind him.

"You alright Mick?" Rufus asked from behind him. Mick shook his head.

"Just nervous." Mick said, as he placed his head on the door for a couple more seconds.

He felt Sunny's delicate hand on his arm. She squeezed reassuringly.

"It'll be alright. They already know."

He turned to look at her, trying to keep his voice in check, "Knowing about it in advance and actually seeing it might not be the same."

He watched the comforting look in her eye fade, like a wounded duck being shot out of the air. Her eyes watered over as she took his hand.

"It'll be all right." She said firmly, looking him in the eyes.

He squeezed his eyes shut for a second, and pushed open the door. The smell of the place hit him in the face like colliding into a brick wall. He could smell the dirt from everyone's shoes on the concrete floor. He could smell the electrical currents running through the wiring that kept the lights on. The smell of gun oil, gasoline and the smell of Target's bed seemed ten times stronger than they were normally.

He felt himself tense as the shock of a canine's bark exploded in his ears, and the click-clack of a dog's claws on concrete began to get louder and louder. But there was something different in that bark, and as Target came into view from behind one of the couches, with his hackles raised and teeth flashing, Mick realized maybe he should have came in behind Oscar. Target, the dog Mick had basically saved the night that creature attacked him here in Tom's Auto, didn't recognize his scent. He now saw Mick as prey, something to be torn apart on sight.

"Target! Down!" Oscar roared, getting between Mick and the dog before it got too close. Target immediately halted in his tracks, paws somewhat skidding across the concrete before he managed to stop, and the dog sat obediently, looking toward Mick warily.

"It's just Mick, jeez," Oscar said as he held Target firmly by the snout. The dog kept trying to pull its face away and bark, until Oscar thumped him on the nose and he yelped.

"Great," Mick said, "Now the dog hates me too."

Mick tensed as he heard hurried footsteps approaching from farther off. He heard a voice. Someone talking into a phone. It was Valerie.

"Judah, tell Brandon to have Parish and Zach come back to the shop. They're back." She said. Mick felt himself trying to keep himself upright as she came into view.

Valerie stood there, hair bundled behind her head in a messy pony tail that hung down between her shoulder blades, her face sporting an urgency that Mick remembered seeing whenever she suited up with them to take down the abominations of the night. Mick found himself watching her hands, unsure of what he would do if he saw her reach for the pistol she had strapped to her hip. He was so busy trying to brace himself for the impact of a burning hot round to the forehead that he didn't see the expression in her face softening. He didn't see the tears swelling in her eyes as she bolted for all of them.

He tensed, and it almost didn't register when he felt her arms circling his neck, crushing him to her in a bear hug that would have hampered his windpipe when he was alive. Seconds later, her arms loosened, only to pull in Rufus, Oscar and Sunny as she kissed each of them on the cheek, tears streaming down her cheeks. Mick lost a few minutes here too. He let himself melt into the group hug, feeling the auras of everyone glowing warmer through the different spectrums in existence. He closed his eyes, realizing that it wasn't unlike what it had felt like when he was alive. He wasn't sure how long they all stood there hugging.

Mick eventually found himself being able to return the embrace, once he had room enough to move in the group squish fest. He felt his shoulder tensing as a series of shudders ran through him. His eyes blurred over with a red sheen, and he was blinking rapidly to try and clear it.

"It's okay Mick. It'll be okay. You're home now." Valerie whispered to him as her hands rubbed his ice cold back.

"I'm a monster now," he said.

"Do I have to give you the look?" She asked. Mick pulled away, feeling himself almost smile when she said that.

"I don't see a monster. I see my friend." She said.

"So...Damaged goods then?" He asked, trying to force a giggle. She slapped him. The crack of her palm against his cheek caused Target to start barking defensively again, to which Oscar stepped in and backed him down. Mick stood there, blinking rapidly and trying to figure out what the hell just happened.

"I'm just happy you're home, dumbass!" She said, smiling through her tears. Mick regarded her, taking in the warmth radiating from her. He became distracted by the sound of boots coming down the stairs behind him.

"Mick!" Parish called towards them as he came into view, removing a pair of heavy gloves and stuffing them into one of his many pockets. Judah, Brandon and Zach all piled in behind him, all of them drenched in the sweat of the night's activities.

"Welcome home!" Parish said as he threw his huge arms around Mick in his usual bear hug style. This was the one time Parish had ever bear hugged him, and Mick didn't feel the need to fight for breath. He would have almost laughed at that if the reasons why hadn't been that his lungs were no longer necessary.

"So," Parish said, pulling away to look at Mick, "I guess now you could kick my ass for all the times I threw you around on the mat huh?"

Mick smiled weakly, "Guess we'll have to find out."

He felt Judah's eyes on him, and he looked up sheepishly as everyone exchanged greetings.

"Hey," Mick said, barely above a whisper. Judah stepped forward, pulled him into a hug of his own, and said, "Welcome home brother."

Mick squeezed his eyes shut as the sheen of red he had been trying to clear from his eyes suddenly built up momentum behind it, trickling down out of the corners of his eyes.

"Thanks for coming back to us," Judah said.

"You don't wanna kill me?" Mick asked.

"You're still one of us. You're still Reclaimed."

TIME WILL TELL

Two weeks later,

"So what does it feel like?" Zach asked him. Mick heard his voice speaking to him from the edges of oblivion, and jerked his head up.

"What does what feel like?" He asked as he watched Valerie finish attaching the I.V. to Zach's arm.

"Well I've wanted to ask ever since you got home and I don't know how to ask delicately, so, how does it feel being a vampire?" Zach pressed as his crimson lifeblood began filling the I.V. tube. Mick stared blankly for a moment as memories of the old Mick's first encounter with Zach played through his mind. They had been in a small room, Zach seated at a table, with Mick asking him questions and getting frustrated. The rest of the details of that visit were lost to him, but his mind filled in the gaps with more recent information. Zach appeared to be as oblivious as a rock, with his nose stuck in a book or staring at a laptop screen as he did research into the lore of the monsters they faced. But actually talking to the guy showed he retained and remembered far more information that was said down the hall in a hushed conversation better than most other people in the group at times. He observed more than people realized. Even seemingly absorbed in another task, Zach could always surprise the group with a random bit of information others had forgotten.

"Well," he began after a thoughtful pause, "my sense of touch comes and goes at different levels. Sometimes I can feel pressure against my body when I bump into something, or like when I grab the edge of a table, but I can rarely feel texture. Like this table for instance," Mick said, grabbing hold of the white, plastic folding table next to him, "I can tell you that the surface is smooth just by looking at it, but if you blind folded me and had me touch it, I wouldn't be able to tell you what it felt like. Sometimes I can feel texture after drinking blood, but not always. It's weird not needing to pee, or eat people food, things like that."

The corner of Zach's mouth went up at the term "people food," and Mick gave himself a mental pat on the back for still being able to score a reaction from his cheesiness.

"All that being said, however," Mick resumed, "...I don't feel like myself. Even two weeks into this undead thing and I'm still not used to it."

Zach nodded, "well that would be a pretty big change."

"Right, but I guess I mean...like, I remember the person you guys call Mick. Every day I remember stuff about that person, and I try to act accordingly, but still something feels like its missing. I wonder sometimes...if I'm really Mick, or if something else woke up inside this body and is sifting through his memories, trying to act like him."

Mick watched Zach's face for any trace of fear squirming beneath the surface, any hint that his detached veneer was slipping as he realized he was in a room with something that could tear his throat out. To his surprise, Zach's expression only changed to one of fascination.

"So...You feel like you're just playing a part?" Zach asked, intrigue building in his tone instead of fear.

Mick nodded, "All the time. And it doesn't help that Target won't go near me except for to bark at me."

Zach nodded, "He might come around eventually man. Just give em time."

Silence stretched between them for a moment, only filled in by the whirring sounds of the equipment as it pumped Zach's lifeblood into a plastic pouch.

"Ya know," Zach started, "if you really aren't Mick, you made a grave error in confiding that to me right?"

Mick shook his head, "I know," he replied, watching the crimson race through the tube.

"But then again," Zach continued, "I think only Mick would be honest enough about his self-doubt once it had nowhere left to hide. So weather you are him or something else, time will tell. But I'm inclined to believe the Mick I know is still around in one form or another, holding whatever you are in check." He finished with a wink as his eyes lit up temporarily.

Mick nodded his head, feeling its weight increasing under the tension building inside of him. He stared at Zach's arm, strapped to the arm of the chair, the I.V. tube connecting to it like a straw he could sip from.

"I hope your right," Mick said, as he became keenly aware of how dry his mouth was. He didn't see Zach's other hand, but he heard the metallic ratcheting of a hammer being drawn back from somewhere.

"So do I man."

www.ingramcontent.com/pod-product-compliance
Lightning Source LLC
LaVergne TN
LVHW091126080826
845145LV00008B/2062

* 9 7 8 0 5 7 8 3 0 3 9 2 5 *